SON OF
GUN IN CHEEK

SON OF GUN IN CHEEK

BILL PRONZINI

THE MYSTERIOUS PRESS

New York • London

The Mysterious Press, 129 West 56th Street, New York, N.Y. 10019

Printed in the United States of America
First Printing: September 1987
10 9 8 7 6 5 4 3 2 1

Library of Congress Cataloging-in-Publication Data

Pronzini, Bill.
    Son of Gun in cheek.

    Companion vol. to: Gun in cheek. c1982.
    Bibliography: p.
    Includes index.
    1. Detective and mystery stories, American—History
and criticism. 2. Detective and mystery stories,
English—History and criticism. 3. Crime and criminals
in literature. I. Title.
PS374.D4P73 1987   813′.0872′09   87-7872
ISBN 0-89296-287-3

Acknowledgments

The author would like to thank the following individuals, whose help and encouragement were instrumental in making this book a reality: Otto Penzler, Sara Ann Freed, William Malloy, Marcia Muller, John Nieminski, Arthur H. Parson, Robert Sampson, William F. Deeck, Angelo Panagos, Ellen Nehr, Jeffrey M. Wallmann, Steve Stilwell, Julie Smith, Francis M. Nevins, Jr., Douglas Greene, Bill Crider, Jeffrey Meyerson.

Once again,
for all those who love a mystery.

Contents

Modus Operandi

A few years ago I wrote a book called *Gun in Cheek*. The original publisher's dust jacket blurb said that it was "an affectionate post-mortem of those unsung heroes and heroines of crime fiction." In various places throughout the text I referred to it as a "study of the 'alternative classics' of mysterydom." In fact, the book is a general history of (critically) inferior crime fiction published during this century, i.e., of bad writers and bad writing.

The purpose of *Gun in Cheek*, as I said in its prefatory chapter, was threefold:

> First, to rectify the neglect of these writers and their works, to give them the critical attention they deserve; second, to provide a different . . . perspective on crime fiction—its detectives, its subgenres, its publishers—and on the social attitudes it reflects (which are often more pronounced in the bad mystery than in the good one); and third, to add a few chuckles—perhaps even a guffaw or two—to the heretofore sobersided field of mystery criticism. It is all well and good to take the genre seriously . . . but it is not hallowed ground, as some would have us believe. Nor should it be so snooty in its newfound position as a "legitimate" literary art form to want to bury

1

its so-called black sheep or refuse to give itself an old-fashioned horse laugh now and then.

A corollary to this threefold purpose is implied in the title of the preface: "Without Malice, a Forethought." The fun I poked in *Gun in Cheek* was done with gentle and loving fingers. If it were not for "alternative" writers and the fruits of their labors, my world would be a much less sunny place than it is. I bear none of these lads and lasses any ill will; on the contrary, I respect them mightily for their accomplishments—fiction that stands well above the average and the mundane, that is every bit as pleasurable in its own skewed way as any perpetrated by those working at the opposite end of the mystery spectrum.

All of which—purposes and corollary—is true of this companion volume, and of those whose efforts are discussed herein.

I say companion volume rather than sequel because it does not follow the same structured format of its predecessor, in which each chapter examined, historically, a particular aspect or type of crime fiction: the amateur detective, the private eye, the spy story, the Gothic, and so forth. In truth, *Son of Gun in Cheek* follows no pattern at all. It contains (1) everything I couldn't fit into *Gun in Cheek* because of space limitations; and (2) everything of a classically alternative nature that has come to my attention since *GIC* was completed and packed off to its publisher in 1981. There are a couple of chapters of genre history (sex in mystery fiction, for one); others on alternative giants Michael Avallone and Harry Stephen Keeler; still others on such esoteric subjects as titles, publishers' dust jacket blurbs, and old crime films (the Charlie Chan series in particular). I've even included, in its entirety, an impressively awful short-short detective story from a 1930 pulp magazine. In a word, this book is a hodgepodge. In a phrase, it is a sort of whimsical hugger-mugger.

That being the case, some critics will no doubt claim that this is a technically inferior book. Undisciplined, they will say. Fragmentary. Totally lacking in cohesion and continuity.

Ah, but what *I* say is that this is a book about bad writing, and what is bad writing but that which is undisciplined, fragmentary, and totally lacking in (conventional) cohesion and continuity? Therefore, I submit that *Son of Gun in Cheek* is not imperfect; that in fact it is that *rara avis*: a book perfectly suited in every respect to its subject matter!

You can't argue with that sort of logic, folks—at least not with me, you can't. Don't even try. Just sit back, relax, and proceed. What follows may be hugger-mugger, but I think I can guarantee that it is *funny* hugger-mugger. And that is the whole point of the thing, after all.

To hell with discipline and continuity. To hell with technically perfect construction. I'll take chuckles and belly laughs every time, no matter what kind of bundle they come in.

Et tu?

Sonoma, California
August 1986

1

The Alternative Hall Of Fame, Part I; Or, "Justice Isn't Functioning Very Shipshape"

The air was surcharged with an invisible something which seemed to surround the house. Even that phlegmatic, nerve-proof group were not immune to the tuning in of the premonitory cross-currents.
—Florence M. Pettee,
The Palgrave Mummy, 1929

There was no activity about any of the dozen outbuildings which hovered at a respectful distance from the big house.
—Martin J. Freeman,
The Scarf on the Scarecrow, 1938

In crime fiction, as in all other areas of literature, there are great bad novels as well as great good novels. It may be the machinations (not to mention loose ends) of its plot that elevates a particular book to classic status. Or it may be the author's eloquence of style, the manner in which he or she turns a phrase (or stands one on its head), unleashes a runaway metaphor, or demonstrates an especially tinny ear for dialogue. Or it may be a combination of these and other elements. The important fact is that everything has come together— a perfect chemical balance—to produce a work of true genius.

Genius, as we all know, is a rare commodity in literature and therefore should not go unrecognized or unappreciated. That is why I have established an Alternative Hall of Fame for those novels whose brilliance, as one of their authors might say, shines like a balefire in the dark forest of mediocre mystery, dull deduction, and static suspense.

Early inductees into the Alternative Hall of Fame were discussed at some length in *Gun in Cheek*—such heroic efforts as Michael Morgan's *Decoy*, Eric Heath's *Murder of a Mystery Writer*, Milton M. Raison's *Murder in a Lighter Vein*, Sydney Horler's *Dark Danger*, James O'Hanlon's *Murder at Horsethief*, and Mary Roberts Rinehart's and Avery Hopwood's *The Bat*. A number of others have come to light since; those published between 1910 and 1940 will be inducted in this chapter, and those published between 1945 and 1985 will have their moment of glory in Chapter 12. Certain additional titles by Michael Avallone, Harry Stephen Keeler, and Anthony M. Rud, among others, will be inducted along the way.

The Mummy Moves, MARY GAUNT (1910)

The Mummy Moves is one of those rare published novels that reads as if it had been composed by (1) a functional illiterate; (2) a poorly programmed computer; or (3) a reasonably intelligent chimpanzee. Sentences do not make sense. Paragraphs do not make sense. Whole pages of narrative and dialogue do not make sense. The amazing thing is not that the book was written, but that it was published twice in the English language (originally in England by T. Werner Laurie, and here in 1925 by E. J. Clode) with no editorial guidance and no attempt to correct and/or make uniform such minor matters as grammar, syntax, and punctuation.

Mary Gaunt does appear to have been a human being, at least, and a British subject at that. Perhaps she was born somewhere other than in England or one of its colonies; that would explain why her prose reads as though English were a third or fourth language. The redoubtable Mrs. Gaunt (she had three names, the middle one being Bakewell, so one assumes she was married) published a minimum of one other novel, a nonmystery entitled *The Uncounted Cost*. If this novel is of the same chimplike virtuosity of *The Mummy Moves*, I would dearly love to read and attempt to decipher it.

Behold Mary Gaunt:

The girl's voice rose to a scream, and Langlands caught the detective's smile at feminine credulity, but bending forward he looked closely, and he saw that not only had the girl spoken the truth, the shrivelled bony talon-like hand of the mummy was covered with blood, but also inside the case was a handle as if the occupant were indeed living flesh and blood, and might perchance wish to let herself out, and this handle was stained and smeared with blood as if those fleshless hands had grasped it and left their impress there.

"[The room to let] isn't for us," said Dolson glibly. "A most respectable young man, a native of India, his father's in the fruit trade, and he's thinking of going for a waiter to learn languages, is coming to me, and I want to get him some place respectable, where he won't be too lonely, a poor lone man, you know, madam, is as bad as a poor lone woman, especially when he's but a boy."

Miss Morton was clutching the table cloth, the colour had gone from her face, and in spite of himself he wanted to help her, "but it was from West Africa that most of his specimens came," he said turning the conversation, and he saw with pleasure that she sighed a sigh of evident relief and a little colour crept back into her cheeks.

"Tut, tut, it is very trying, very trying indeed," he said looking up sympathetically. "You are over-wrought. I get my brain over-wrought sometimes labouring at a plot that will not evolve itself as it ought [the speaker is a writer], and I doubt not Mr. Langlands does often. There is nothing for but rest, perfect rest. I should advise you to go home and take some of nature's sweet restorer, though it is so early, balmy sleep."

The staring eyes were wide open, the jaw had fallen, and pillow sheets and pyjamas were soaked in blood, and at his throat, the two women and Fabian Eastman shrank back, and Langlands, bending over, felt impelled to do likewise, for the collar of the pyjama coat was unbuttoned and the manner of death was plain to see.

"Hold hard," said Eastman taking the dagger from Langlands; "why, that belongs to me. Now it's no good you're protesting," he turned on the Hindoo, who was doing nothing of the sort, "that knife is unique. It comes from West Africa. My uncle," he turned to Langlands, "told me there wasn't another to match it in the world."

"I positively assuring you most honourable gentlemen," said the Hindoo holding out his hand, "it is the capture of my bow and spear, it is the purchased of my shekels."

Christabel looked frightened. "It isn't canny," she said.

"Well, the party is slow no longer," said Virginia with a sigh of satisfaction.

"There's that beggar again, Emily. Sing, he can't sing for nuts, as my poor husband used to say. Here, take him out this penny, and tell him to go away at once."

"Kiss me strite on the brow and part," wailed the mournful wreck in the street, and Emily tossed her scornful head.

"Well, I call it encouragin' of thieves an' bad characters," said she, virtuously, "considerin' the things as have happened in the flat above, you ought to be special careful."

"Your ragged man isn't a professional thief as a rule," said her mistress, as if the argument had some weight.

"Dear me, Dodson," said Langlands . . . "what are you doing with newspaper cuttings? I thought you despised the modern in literature."

"Human nature's the same all through the ages. My idea is to translate some wise saws and modern instances into medieval setting. But sometimes the divine afflatus is not there, Phoebus' car won't go, the wheels are clogged."

"So I should think," said Langlands looking round.

Hidden behind (or among or underneath) all this gibberish, like a separate puzzle for the dedicated mystery reader to piece together, is a plot of sorts. It has to do with a murdered English curio collector, a female Egyptian mummy who may or may not be capable of ambulatory evil, a West African juju knife, some Australian bank shares, a "Hindoo" peddler, a mysterious beggar, fetishes, secret societies, blood sacrifices, and canary birds—among other things. The "hero" is a Scotland Yard detective named Dodson, who does not behave like *any* Scotland Yard detective in fact or fiction and who may therefore be an unmasked impostor. He is somewhat bumbling, somewhat cracked, and has the respect of none of the other characters, including his friend Langlands. He has literary pretensions—"frustrated snob" might be a good term for him—and insists on quoting inappropriate Latin phrases, complete with translations, at the drop of a winding-sheet (*"Homo solus aut deus aut demon*, which being translated means that a lonely man is either a god or a devil, where is this mummy?"*). He also insists on making all manner of cryptic statements, the most notable of which is: "Tut, tut, chaos is come again!"

It certainly is. *The Mummy Moves* is a monument to it.

The Palgrave Mummy, F. M. PETTEE (1929)

As its title suggests, this novel also deals with an allegedly ambulatory and wicked mummy. That is, however, the only similarity it bears in style and content to the Mary Gaunt novel. (Well, it does have a Hindoo in it; but since the Hindoo here is a microbe, not a person, that doesn't really count.) *The Palgrave Mummy* is written in a generally more intelligible version of English, has a simple plot (in more ways than one), and fairly bubbles with high melodrama. Which is no surprise, considering that F. M. (for Florence Mae) Pettee learned her "craft" in the pulp magazines of the teens and twenties, for which she created such series characters as the amazing Beau Quicksilver, criminologist Dr. Nancy Dayland, and "noted criminal investigator" Digby Gresham. Her pulp fiction seethes with silly situations, exotic murder methods, fractured prose, and any number of ridiculous pseudoscientific gimmicks—so much so that pulp historian Robert Sampson refers to her as "towering gigantically, an Everest of the inept." We'll take a close look at her pulp fiction in Chapter 5, where you'll have the rare and heady privilege of examining the complete text of one of her Digby Gresham short stories.

Florence Mae's alternative talents are abundantly in evidence in *The Palgrave Mummy*, her only full-length novel. It begins when Paris Palgrave, a Very Rich Person, pays a call on Digby Gresham and his properly fawning Watson, Detective Sergeant Allenby. Strange Things Are Happening on the island estate of the Palgrave family, most of them connected with the mummy of "a little brown princess, Amon-Ya, daughter of one of the Pharaohs." The mummy carries a curse that has already claimed the life of the man who found it and took it out of Egypt:

Living blood shall flow, without the hint of wound, without the seeming disturbance of flesh by the sharp stone of priest or vandal. Blood shall flow—ghost-blood— from dead and from living flesh alike, without a sign, a symbol, or a scratch to explain the bursting of its veins, quick or dead. Blood shall burst its bonds— avenging blood as a sign that doom has fallen on desecrating hands. Beware the *ko*-blood of a Pharaoh's daughter.

But *is* the curse responsible for the Strange Things and the archeologist's death? Could it be that some ancient and clever poison was secreted on the mummy or in its wrappings? Palgrave is determined to find out, which is why he has asked several experts in various fields to come to his island estate—a medical doctor, a toxicologist, an Egyptologist, and now a detective.

Digby is only too happy to oblige. Along with Sergeant Allenby, he ventures to the island, where he meets the other experts, Palgrave's wife and daughter, and a woman mystery writer who gave the world "that ripsnorting, odd thing, *The Shrunken Arm*." No sooner do Gresham and Allenby arrive than More Strange Things Happen. An escaped convict from a nearby prison is on the loose and perhaps has made his way to the island. The Palgrave Diamond is stolen. Amon-Ya's mummy case is likewise purloined. Murder most foul is committed in the mummy room, and an investigation of the mummy reveals that it is "bleeding." It looks as though the terrible curse has claimed another victim.

Ah, but what is the significance of the freshly baked biscuit? Why does Digby Gresham mutter "Holy kettlefish!" to himself while skulking around the grounds that night? Why does Allenby exclaim, "Holy catfish! Wouldn't that rattle your wisdom teeth?"? Is something fishy going on? And can it be that part of the answer is the Hindoo microbe, the one that produces a red fluid that looks so exactly like blood you can't tell the difference except under a microscope?

There is more to the plot, much more, but these are the highlights. What also towers gigantically throughout are the lofty peaks and crags of Florence Mae's prose. Unlike Mary Gaunt, she possessed a ready command of the English language—a *too* ready command, in fact. Her problem can be traced to the obvious facts that she did not own nor had she ever studied a grammar textbook, and that she did own and was forever consulting both a dictionary and a *Roget's Thesaurus*. Unfortunately for her, she never quite grasped the proper usage of either Webster's or Roget's. Shades and nuances of meaning escaped her. Exact definitions of words seemed to befuddle her. She seemed to believe that *all* the words listed under a particular entry in Roget's were exact synonyms, to be used interchangeably with that entry. She also seemed to believe that substituting big words for little words, and/or colorfully offbeat words for common ones, was the key to Good Writing.

Consider, first of all, her blithe experimentation with verbs, nouns, and adjectives:

For Digby Gresham's diggings were salted away in a side street where traffic didn't boil over much, especially on climatically indisposed evenings.

The guard squinted at each in turn. Then his gaze volleyed to the locked rear deck of the roadster.

"Justice isn't functioning very shipshape."

Olive's hands went to her head. She held the coppery locks tight as if either to stem the dull ache or to force her ideas back to their original jumping-off place. . . .

Tragedy is seldom to be seen all labeled and carefully pigeonholed. It's a matter of atmosphere, requiring a barometric nature to divine it.

Nowhere else, in those dainty rooms, was there a sign of any lurking, impish face, spying on the antics she had been maneuvering.

Instinctively Allenby's eager, boyish glance romped to the girl's left wrist.

From the percolator in the recessed window, the house-keeper turned out another steaming cup, which she tempered deftly.

Out of the unknown, the hinterland of the inexplicable, he divined the potency of what he had seen.

Similes and metaphors were one of Florence Mae's specialties:

Gresham's steel-gray glance crossed Allenby's like swords suddenly freed of their scabbards.

Again he blew pale amulets of [cigarette] smoke quite soberly.

[The letter] drooped from his fingers like a limp chewed cigarette butt.

[The wide piazza] was smothered in a riot of climbing roses, a pale patch of white, pink, and blood red, like the varied corpuscles in human veins.

The siren was broadcasting, with all the strength of its metal lungs, the news that a man had escaped, a living link from the chain of human beings bound together in durance by the law. The siren started again, bellowing discordant yelps, signally out of tune on that peaceful, purple landscape.

The two faced each other in that house of subtle double deaths. The soundlessness of the place was funereal, pent-up to the bursting point. It crashed about them in the utter absence of all movement.

Her descriptions of people and places were another of her long suits:

His face was brown, almost leathery tinted.

His hands were extraordinarily delicate, out of proportion to his big, burly frame. The strength of his body seemed to have petered out also in his head.

Delilah's soft knock tapped on the door. It was like the woman's cattish tread; like, too, the low swish of her gray uniform, which clung to her gaunt figure like a bit of fabric as bleached and flabby as if drained of all vitality.

They ran along through tiny, tucked-in villages clinging to the rock-bound coast like barnacles, intershot with neatly tufted evergreens. A thousand-thousand Christmas trees reared emerald pompoms on the landscape.

A half-dozen guards sprang up here and there on the rocks. The purple of twilight glazed the sea; a patch of contorted seaweed, matted and clumped like some aboriginal seine, bobbed between the accidental catamaran made by a couple of logs lashed together with driftstuff.

The guards began a systematic peppering of weeds, logs, and all suspicious flotsam.

Fog swathed the sea in thick bandages, coffin-cloth windings from out of the dusk. The house stood out, a patch of black, rent by placques of light. The fog sloughed away, like amorphous flesh, from the sloped sides of the bungalow.

Florence Mae was no slouch when it came to dialogue, either, especially when either slang (Allenby) or pontification (Gresham) was involved:

"Now," appealed Allenby, with a long sigh that freedom of speech was his again, "what kind of a nut would light out with a mummy-case and go to such pains to snitch it? What under the cartouche of Amon-Ya would a guy want with such a thing? Unless he was a 'cuckoo' on ancient Egyptian stuff, bitten by a scientific bug or some great idea that he had lamped out something to startle the world with."

"So he's a dealer in dope! And that's why he's so flush on the kalos. This stuff [money] looks like a young bank."

"Why, that's worse than yellow! It's canary—it's cuckoo! Man alive, if you should whisper that to the yellowest journal afloat, they'd quash the tale as something born out of hash-hish or loco-weed. And yet—I know you. . . . There's something very dark in Denmark or in the House of Palgrave."

"If the murderer himself is penned against his will to the unpleasant scene of crime, along with other nerve-wracking occurrences, his conscience will begin to peck at his vitals and his security. He'll begin to conjure up bogies about something he imagines he has overlooked or overdone. Penning a murderer in close confinement, not only to the place of his crime, but to the victim, is strong, annihilating, nerve-wracking medicine. It's the most powerful third-degree in my experience. For the really to-be-depended-upon inquisition is dealt out by human conscience, no matter how petrified it may be with the winding-sheet of many crimes."

"You've the wrong idea, Palgrave, that crime breeds only in filth, in poverty and in ignorance. . . . The crime of today is a high-powered, educated caste of monster which a terribly efficient twentieth century has developed to pernicious precosity."

And finally, Florence Mae was a mistress of the anticlimactic statement. She might as well have been summing up *The Palgrave Mummy* itself when she had one of her other characters say with a perfectly straight face:

"It beats the devil. It's diabolical. It's fiendish. It's just not right."

The Merrivale Mystery, JAMES CORBETT (1929)

When this alternative tour-de-force was first hatched in England in the late twenties, Dorothy L. Sayers and S. S. Van Dine were among the leading exponents of the formal detective story. Little wonder, then, that young James Corbett should have wanted, in his very first mystery novel, to capitalize on the popularity of the likes of Lord Peter Wimsey and Philo Vance by creating a cultured, snooty, somewhat effete super-sleuth of his own—one with ratiocinative powers far exceeding those of mere mortals in the detecting racket. Thus we have Victor Serge (evidently pronounced "surge," not "sir-gay"), "a man with a distinctive personality, and nothing was more impressive than his two brilliant dark eyes. They took in everything in a flash, yet they remained eternally smiling and self-possessed." Serge occupies a London flat, "sumptuously furnished, with every sign of luxury and comfort," which boasts of "two of the finest oil paintings in Europe, and the piano was the most expensive of its kind. Serge could play that instrument exquisitely, and as for the bookshelves, they were lined with a rare collection of treasures."

This "sleuth hound's" philosophy of detection centers on something he calls "an occult pointer." As he says early on to Ralph Moreton, his novelist friend and nominal Watson, "Just when a clue is remote, Moreton, when everything seems dead against you, and all the papers cry out about your lack of intelligence, Fate steps in with an occult pointer." And just what *is* an occult pointer? Neither Serge nor Corbett ever explains, although Serge does offer this cryptic comment when Moreton ingenuously asks how long a clue has eluded him: "Two years. That happened in the Plymouth murder after the Armistice, and the Yard was baffled over that business. I had to confess failure for a long time, but I kept in touch with it, and in two years I got an anonymous post card and arrested my man."

According to Corbett and Serge, Scotland Yard is populated by dunces who blunder about obliterating evidence and who couldn't solve a murder if the murderer sent *them* a postcard with his name on it. Nothing will do but to call on Serge at the drop of a corpse, any corpse, as long as it's a member of the upper class. Which the Yard does when Sir Philip Merrivale is bumped off at Merrivale Hall, "a great lump of mystery" some two hours outside London. Will Serge take the case? Well, of course—but not until he and Moreton have discussed crime and criminals for a dozen pages, with special attention to the perfect crime. (Serge modestly says that if anybody could commit one, he's the chap.) Serge also makes a number of other impressive statements during this interlude, among them: "The passion crime looks easy of detection, but after the passionate act is committed, and when the brain has cooled, a man often resorts to subtle stratagem to hide his guilt. A woman is different. A woman is at the mercy of primitive elements." Not to mention occult pointers and male chauvinists.

So Serge, with Moreton in tow, hies himself off to Merrivale Hall to dazzle us with his investigative prowess. Moreton is able to go along in the guise of Serge's secretary because, we are told, "he had been studying for the Bar, but his pen brought him to a London publishing house, and his work secured him independence. Apart from that, he was the son of a wealthy stockbroker."

Upon arrival at the lump of mystery, Serge is immediately shown into the library, where "the dead body . . . remained on the floor as it had fallen [the night before], and the relatives, presumably acting on a hint from [Scotland Yard detective] Bancroft, made no effort to remove it." Corbett, you see, had a blithe disregard not only for police procedure but for the laws of human decency. While Philip Merrivale's corpse is allowed to lie undisturbed on the library floor overnight, a later victim of foul play is permitted to remain untouched for *two days* because an inquest into the death was postponed. None of the whacko inhabitants of Merrivale Hall seem particularly perturbed by this cavalier attitude toward the recently extinct; neither do Serge, Moreton, or any of the Scotland Yard cops. But then, these are not ordinary crime-solvers. Do they look for fingerprints or other clues? Or course not; Bancroft simply announces that there are none, and that's that. Do they call in a police surgeon to examine any of the corpses littering the place? No way; they permit a relative of the victims to do the examining, without even bothering to check his credentials.

What does Serge *do*, then, by way of master-detecting? Well, first of all, he whips out a cache of "wonderful instruments" that he proceeds to "pass over" the corpses—wonderful instruments that include a "magnetic lens and gleaming microscope." (How he manages to find out anything by passing a gleaming microscope over a dead man is never explained. Secrets of the sleuth-hound trade, you know.) Serge also conducts interminable interviews with everybody in the household, most of whom are Merrivales and all of whom hate and keep trying to incriminate each other. And of course he runs around on all sorts of mysterious errands and in the interim makes cryptic remarks to let us know that he is ratiocinating furiously inside his wonderful brain.

What he ratiocinates (after three murders by gunshot and an attempted poisoning) is a devilish scheme involving strange pacts, weird disguises, identical twins, a butler named Proust, and a sliding panel behind a revolving bookcase that leads to a secret passage. The motive behind all this mayhem doesn't make much sense; neither does the rest of the plot. And neither does some of Corbett's prose. While much of it is about as stimulating as watching grass grow, every now and then he makes you sit up and take notice with an alternative sparkler.

[The Yard men] worshipped Serge as a super-intelligence, an admiration they did not extend to Frank Bancroft, who they felt was too conscious of his superiority, and although they respected him as a brilliant colleague, they had an instinctive sense that he was mediocre.

The look on Stephen's face was distinctly unpleasant. It contained all the malignity of hate, all the malevolence of evil, and even at a normal moment the features were not prepossessing.

[George Merrivale] was a remarkable man in many respects. His dome-shaped head suggested the thinker and philosopher, and . . . he could change his expression without effort [which] signified great mobility of thought and temperament. Serge saw at a glance that he was dealing with an intellectual.

"You don't mean you will eat anything in that house?" [Moreton asked].

"It depends on the courtesy of the inhabitants. Frankly, I am not thinking of the intestinal glands at present."

"Stephen is selfish and pig-headed to the bone. I never liked him, and never will. Has he offered you anything to eat? That's what I'd like to know!"

"We are putting up at the Talbot Hotel, Dunseaton," Serge explained, with a little air of independence, "and we are not in the mood for gastronomy at present."

"Proust," said Serge sternly, "who taught you to walk in that fashion? Your steps are feline and cat-like."

Had Tabitha's words impressed Serge with real significance, and despite his protest at their incredulity had he given reality to the statement?

"It seems that Cecil is killing himself with the accursed
stuff, and the other two half-brothers are developing into
congenital idiots."

The [police] men saluted in the darkness and stole away
with furtive tread. They knew the anticlimax was at hand,
and their satisfaction was unbounded.

Such an auspicious debut did not go unrecognized in this country;
The Merrivale Mystery was published here in 1931 by Mystery
League, an outfit whose editorial staff had a keen eye for the
alternative masterwork. Others that they gave us in the lamentably
brief three years of their existence include Sydney Horler's *The
Curse of Doone* and Gwen Bristow's and Bruce Manning's *The
Invisible Host*, about which see *Gun In Cheek*.

Corbett went on to publish another forty-one novels in England,
but it is not known by yours truly whether such early titles as *The
Winterton Hotel Mystery*, *The White Angel*, and *Murder at Red
Grange* (which presumably has nothing to do with the All-American
football player of that era) also feature the deductive talents of
Victor Serge. Sad to relate, only one of those other Corbett novels
saw print here—and that one in 1957, half a dozen years after his
last book appeared in the United Kingdom. This fact should not
serve as a pat on the back for American publishers, however, or as
an indictment of British publishers. Or vice versa.

Hell in Harness, JOSEPH AUSLANDER (1929)

1929 was a very good year for Hall of Fame classics, if not for
stockbrokers and their clientele. What we have in *Hell in Harness*,
though, is a most unusual inductee. On the one hand it is one of
those Prohibition gangster sagas in which a tough kid from New
York's "Hell's Sink" rises, falls, and winds up in the electric chair
at Sing Sing. The kid's name is the Kid; some of his hoodlum pals
have monickers like Lefty Louie, Gyp the Blood, and Panther
Roop; the Sing Sing chaplain is Father Caffery. . . . Well, you get
the idea.

On the other hand, all of this is written in *verse*.
Yes indeed. Thirty-five pages of rhyming verse, giving *Hell in Harness* the distinction of being the genre's only epic mystery poem (the only one published by a major house, anyway). And such verse! Such alternative rhyming genius!
Here are just a few examples:

This story will not stop or stray;
The Kid will put it his own way
Straight from the shoulder as the Kid
Always did the things he did.
The Kid will carry it to that night
At the Crescent Club when he pulled the fight
Out of the trap; and I will tell
Round by round, bell by bell,
Every blow as it fell.
Then the Kid picks up the thread
With Spike and the bullet in Spike's head.
He drops it there; I step in there,
Tell how they burned him in the Chair.
Then it is over; there is no more:
Someone opens and shuts a door.

And:

You couldn't have paid me to go to school—
I wasn't built for the brand of drool
They dished out; so I hookeyed instead
and racked the cues for Sullivan Red
Whose pool joint was the hang-out for
Every pimp who had a whore
Hustling for him: Hell's Sink, all right,
And no mistake, where day was night
And night was the gunmen's get-together;
Talk about your birds of a feather—
Well, these were the birds and the cat's meow.

I used to sling their hash—that's how
I got wise to the sonofaguns
Who'd bump a guy off for a couple of buns.

And:

There wasn't a job pulled off I missed.
And I've seen a yap with a yen for some twist
Gum the works because the yap
Got needled and blew off his trap;
And the fall guy did a stretch in stir
All on account of him and her.
When he stepped out of the cooler, Gawd,
What didn't he do to him and his broad!
Hell, how can an egg expect a skirt
To be on the up-and-up; they're dirt,
Give 'em sugar and a nifty spiel,
Load 'em with ice; just let 'em feel
The old hoop on that finger, Christ
They're yours and crying to be spliced.

And:

I lamped Spike's mug; his glims were wide,
He had a pound of hop inside.
Crazy with coke he swayed there grinning,
It damed well looked like the snowbird's inning—
And all of a sudden his rod went spinning,
And down he crumped [sic] like a hunk of wood
Slithering into the Panther's blood.

And:

The Kid is smoking a cigarette.
"Lord, have mercy . . . !" (Your hands are wet.)
"Christ, have mercy . . . !" The Kid is smoking.
The Father's voice is thick. You're choking.

The Kid takes the cigarette out of his mouth:
"Don't weaken, Father . . . I'm heading south.
We all got to croak. And I'd rather sit stiff
In a chair than be coughing in bed. What's the diff?"
He paces the twenty feet to the Chair,
Puffing his cigarette, sniffing the air
Greedily like a young horse. The beat
of the priest's voice quickens. "Well, here's the hot seat!"

This amazing little book, complete with several dubious illustrations by somebody named Ervine Metzl, is dedicated to Ogden Nash. It is not known whether Nash ever read it; or if he did, whether he took any sort of legal or physical action against Joseph Auslander.

The Scarf on the Scarecrow, MARTIN J. FREEMAN (1938)

This novel's chief claim to alternative fame is that its opening two pages are told from the point of view of a buzzard.

> Twenty-five miles southeast of Chicago a gaunt buzzard spiralled nervously above the twelve hundred acres of the Wendover Dule estate, his hunger-sharpened brain vexed by three fears and one desire.
> His nostrils scented and his keen wings felt the coming Autumn storm, forecast by purple clouds aswirl beyond the Dule woods to the northeast, like larger and unwelcome birds swept forward by the wind to join him. He also feared the night, upon whose darker wings the storm was riding. . . . If the storm came, if night came, before the buzzard got what he wanted, he would return dinnerless to his wretched nest of dragged-together sticks.
> His third fear, and the one that made him angriest, because without it, night and the coming storm would not have troubled him, stood in the deserted garden six

hundred feet beneath, gesticulating in the wind with gloved yet boneless hands.

This was a scarecrow, and harmless, although the buzzard did not know that. . . . Men erect, the buzzard knew, were always dangerous; men supine or prone less often so. The buzzard preferred them motionless, sprawled on their backs.

The rest of the book, unfortunately, does not live up to the promise of this masterful and innovative opening ploy—although the ploy itself is enough to elevate *The Scarf on the Scarecrow* to Hall of Fame status. Humans take over, in particular a criminologist named Jerry Todd and his lady friend, Molly Clerkenwell, and the action and story line become all too prosaic and familiar. A horny female cat named Ethelberta makes an appearance, but not for long; and we are not made privy to her thoughts.

The buzzard, annoyingly enough, does not reappear. And the mystery of what happened to *him* is far more intriguing than the one surrounding the murder of Wendover Dule. I mean, did he or did he not keep returning dinnerless to his wretched nest of dragged-together sticks?

The Bat Woman, CROMWELL GIBBONS (1938)

No, this is not a novel about a female Caped Crusader. It is a novel about a female vampire. It is also a novel about a *lot* of other things, among them (in the appoximate order of their appearance):

• A man who runs into his dead wife at the opera.
• South American headhunters and shrunken mummified heads and bodies.
• Piratical soldiers of fortune hunting platinum in a remote region of the Amazon.
• Hairy jungle beasts who wrestle giant crocodiles.
• Children born with vestigial tails.

- A bilious-looking, emaciated Chinese with a walruslike mustache who speaks in aphorisms reminiscent of Charlie Chan.
- The scar-faced, rum-soaked captain of a tramp freighter who issues such curious orders as "All hands on deck and the cook!"
- A typhoon and a sort of mutiny on the Java Sea.
- Ten mysterious oaken chests perforated with small holes, from which emanate weird muffled squealings and rustlings.
- The live burial of an Indian yogi.
- A respected mortician who has an underground reputation as a corpse snatcher.
- A Long Island lighthouse called Execution Light because a "jolly-boat of rebel malefactors" was hanged there during the Revolutionary War.
- A captured female gorilla named Miss Congo.
- A Russian vampire who "pinched his wife most cruelly."
- A nocturnal visit to a cemetery to "snatch a moll what's croaked" and not incidentally to have a dentist examine her teeth.
- A case of South African sleeping sickness.
- A trip to the New York City morgue and some dialogue with a misanthropic attendant named Pedro who once "got drunk and mixed up all the stiffs."
- Two corpses whose bodies have been drained of blood by an alleged "voodoo fiend."
- A cat that "coyly cocks her head and begs for sugar."
- A mad scientist's laboratory lighted by a mysterious purple glow.
- "A chubby little beetle [that] flashes a red light at both ends of its body, and green lights along its sides [and as a result] almost meets a maritime regulation."
- A hypodermic needle filled with "a glandular secretion—a duckless [sic] gland . . . prepared from a living person" (the "duckless gland" being "the seat of the human soul," as if you didn't know).
- A gaggle of *Desmodus rufus* or bloodsucking bats from the tropics which "rear up on their hind legs and walk" and "guzzle blood with their long tongues like a cat lapping a bowl of milk."
- The severed brain of a beautiful blond woman kept alive in a jar.

- An electric needle or "heart-starter" which can shock dead people back to life.
- A shipwrecked sailor turned cannibal who prefers to eat people "who did not smoke, as the flesh of the chronic tobacco-user was bitter and not to his epicurean taste."
- The wee-hours kidnapping of a half-naked young woman with a "firm, slow-curving breast."
- And last but by no means least, a rousing climax in a brownstone fortress in the heart of Manhattan in which a dead young woman dies a second death as an old hag, the gaggle of vampire bats is unleashed on a raiding party of New York's Finest, and the shell of a human nut is perforated by a tommy gun that "belches a chattering burst."

The detective who tries (and fails) to make sense out of this mind-boggling potpourri is a criminologist named Rex Huxford, who is also the "hero" of Cromwell Gibbons's only other mystery novel, *Murder in Hollywood* (1936). Huxford, who has dubious credentials at best (one of his pals works for the Gestapo in Nazi Germany), is little more than a cipher who stands ever-ready to spout all sorts of esoteric information, some of which may even be accurate. Not much more memorable are his trio of "assistants"— two ex-Prohibition plug-uglies named Spike Salieno and Plugger Martin, and a Stepin Fetchit black called Zipp. They appear in only one chapter, so we are treated just that once to such stirring dialogue as, "Say, nigger, shove me yuh mit," and "Yessir, yessir. Yessir, Mr. Spike."

Far and away the most interesting character is the villain of the piece, Dr. Eric von Schalkenbach. We first meet him early on, in a flashback to an incident in the Amazonian jungle, as narrated by a member of the Explorer's Club:

> "We were even more astonished to see grappling with this giant crocodile a powerful beast, more powerful than anything I had ever dared to imagine—a hairy thing like a gorilla. . . . Yet the monstrous thing looked even more like a rugged primitive man—perhaps, a descendant of

some prehistoric race like the Neanderthal, a brute species of giant man from the lost world. What was it . . . this creature, hideous beyond belief, that at any moment might spot us and annihilate our puny group?

"I raised my gun and fired a shot high over the beast's bushy head. It bounded around in startled surprise. Its shaggy hair fell away from its face, its eyes flashed with savage rage, and its enormous lips curled into a menacing snarl.

"'*Pass auf! Pass auf!* Don't shoot, I'm a white man!' the thing bellowed, sticking its chunky hands up.

"We were stupefied. I lowered my gun but kept my finger on the trigger. On he came, in a shuffling, awkward gait, weaving [sic] his massive arms fearsomely, the jungle growth giving way before his beastlike bulk.

"'I'm Dr. Eric von Schalkenbach,' the brute announced, towering above us and extending his hand in greeting. 'I apologize if I have caused you alarm. You must forgive my unkempt appearance.'"

Von Schalkenbach, you see, is a freak of nature, "an extraordinary throwback, with the inherited characteristics of the powerful cave man of the Stone Age . . . a giant man with prodigious intelligence and superknowledge." He is an expert on the shrinking and mummifying of heads, a hypnotist, a biologist, a "dexterous field surgeon," a plastic surgeon, an accomplished ship's helmsman and navigator, a devotee of the opera, a brilliant organist, a platinum prospector, *and* a "finite creature who defies the Infinite" by monkeying around (pun intended) with experiments into the nature of "things Man was not meant to know." He went off to live in the jungle like an Amazonian Tarzan, Gibbons tells us, because he got tired of people making fun of his hideous physiognomy. He came out of the jungle, Gibbons further tells us, because he finally discovered the secret of how to turn beautiful young women into slavering vampires (that secret being the "duckless gland," of course) and because, being a virgin, he figured it was the only way he would ever get laid. What woman would willingly go to bed, after all, with a guy whose "thick lips bulge ungainly in his evening dress and stuffed shirt"?

Unfortunately for Eric, though, he never does succeed in losing his virginity before the good guys blow him away. The best planned lays and all that. Moral: Freaks of nature, no matter how much superknowledge they might possess, never get to have any fun.

Crime Hound, MARY SEMPLE SCOTT (1940)

It would be unfair to say that *Crime Hound* is a real dog—a pedigreed alternative purebred, as it were. It does, however, have sufficient kennel credentials to lift it out of the mongrel class and justify its inclusion here. Immediate proof of this is its howl of an opening paragraph:

> The first mournful notes of the noon whistle startled Herbert Crosby's unaccustomed ears. He looked through the agent's second-story window as if expecting reactions in the heavens from such a blast of sound. But the calm bright blue of the sky showed no sign of agitation as the crescendo pulsed against it before dropping down scale to the final moan. The powder-puff clouds were not hastened in their lazy course. The pointed tops of the tall pines on the lake front beyond the main street did not bend.

The "crime hound" of the title, and the novel's protagonist, is this fellow Herbert Crosby, who purports to be "Fourth Assistant" to the District Attorney of St. Louis. He has enough money, however, the source of which is never explained, to rent a fancy summer cottage on a secluded lake and to "laze through a long vacation under the ministrations of mother and sister who would follow," the St. Louis D.A. having allegedly given him as much time off as he needs to recuperate from solving "a grueling crime investigation." Hmmm. He doesn't even seem to know just what it is a D.A. *does*. When an attractive (but obviously not very bright) young woman asks him, "What is a *District* Attorney?" he says

glibly, "One who catches the bad boys and sends them to jail."
Double hmmm.

While in Brantford, a lakeside town in an unnamed Midwestern
state (presumably Wisconsin, since it has a town called Sheboygan
in it), Crosby runs afoul of some local intrigue and finds himself
mixed up in the murder of a sleazy real estate agent named Jediah
Cook, whose avocation was defiling young women. Being an avid
crime-hound, Crosby sniffs around and "hops with great agility," as
the dust jacket blurb puts it, mixing its animal (and other) metaphors
nicely, "from a series of frying pans into corresponding conflagra-
tions until at the climax of the book he, with the evidence of the
murder in his grasp, [is] handcuffed and chucked into jail." Along
the way he meets a fascinating array of characters, among them:

- An Indian trapper named (Honest Injun!) Chief Rain-in-the-Face,
  a.k.a. "Rain," one of whose many children was born blond and
  blue-eyed.
- Dr. Gaius Giddens, a G.P. who doubles as coroner and who
  possesses a magnificent storehouse of medical knowledge, such as
  is demonstrated when he runs his fingers down the back of a
  corpse's head and then announces, "There's another welt here,
  just above the medulla."
- Countess Ozorsky, the wife of a dead Russian prince, who was
  born in Oklahoma and who knows more than she's telling about a
  leaky canoe.
- And Tender Teddie, a former bootlegger who "got into trouble
  during prohibition days and was senteneced to a long term in the
  pen," but who is now paroled for three months every summer so
  he can run a fashionable underground supper club for "young
  dissipators."

Triple hmmm. . . .
Another bark in the *Crime Hound's* favor is Mary Semple Scott's
exemplary style—a sort of shaggy *je ne sais quoi* as epitomized in
its opening paragraph. A few other examples:

> The nerves that had temporarily calmed began to shrug his
> shoulders, to flare his nostrils.

[The man was] tall, straight, with intelligent eyes and a smile that imperilled the cigarette that stuck to his lower lip.

He saw them go off with the girl he'd been talking to, who—wonder of wonders, was wearing a skirt. It was the only skirt he'd seen on girls of her age that morning. But he knew there was something more than a skirt to give her distinction—something deeper and less easily defined.

[The Crime Hound, in a brilliant deductive observation to the local sheriff]: "Cook must have been crazy, drunk, or dead when he negotiated that road [in his car]."

This is Mary Semple Scott's only published novel. Dammit.

2

Of Talking Skeletons, Noseless Monsters, And Boomalacka Browne

"After all, Jigger," [the medical examiner] suggested familiarly, "why don't you let it go at that? Andrews knows his business pretty well. Chances are he's right. This isn't like that Corlaes affair, where murder was plain right from the start, and corpses were falling around us like pulpy persimmons from the tree. Men *can* get up on their hind legs, and die under their own power, you know!"
—Anthony M. Rud,
The Stuffed Men, 1935

In the good old days of publishing, when paper was cheap, readers were plentiful, and network television was just a gleam in the Devil's eye, certain houses could be counted on to consistently produce certain types of books. Down on the alternative level, there were the lending library publishers of the thirties and forties— houses such as Phoenix Press (to which an entire chapter of *Gun in Cheek* is devoted), Arcadia, Gateway, Godwin, Hillman-Curl, and Dodge, among others that provided a steady stream of mystery, Western, and light-romance novels. But these houses did not have a lock on the mediocre-to-bad genre fiction market, not by any means; nor were they the first to specialize in this kind of "hardcover pulp." As far back as the teens, there were enterprising purveyors of popular schlock between cloth covers.

One such early publisher was Chelsea House, whose "Popular Copyrights" line of mystery, Western, adventure, and love novels vied, from 1924 to 1933, for shelf space in bookshops with inexpensively produced reprint titles from such houses as Grosset & Dunlap and A. L. Burt. Chelsea's claim that "this line represents a distinct innovation in book publishing [for] the books are not what are known as 'reprints,' but are original stories that have never appeared in any other edition" was essentially true, although a great many *did* appear first in pulp magazines. Among Chelsea's more notable authors were Johnston McCulley, the creator of Zorro and of such forgettable detective heroes as the Thunderbolt, the Avenging Twins, and the Crimson Clown; and Carroll John Daly, whose collaborative first novel (with C. H. Waddell), *Two-Gun Gerta*, was published by Chelsea in 1926 as "A Western Story," although it is actually a mystery/adventure novel set in Mexico. It features a movie actor and stuntman, one Red Conners, who sounds (and acts) suspiciously like Race Williams:

> The pay was bound to be big. Any American is the kitten's patent leathers in greaserland; and for an all-around, high-class guy like myself—well, they'd have to bid some if they wanted my services. As for any incidental gun play, I can twirl a fairly mean gat myself.

Chelsea House, at least, made no real attempt to hide the fact that it was a schlock peddler. Other publishers of the period did. G. H. Watt was one; Penn Publishing Company, out of Philadelphia, was another. But the very first, and certainly the greatest, of the schlock houses—the publisher whose line of general trade books in the twenties and early thirties was to alternative publishing what Phoenix Press's lending-library line was from the late thirties to the early fifties—was the "pride" of 381 Fourth Avenue, New York City: The Macaulay Company.

Macaulay appears to have gotten its start sometime prior to World War I; but it was not until the Roaring Twenties that it hit its alternative stride. One of its specialties was "novels of dangerous love," a.k.a. "novels that make striking revelations," a.k.a. "novels with a modern tempo," a.k.a. "novels of life's passionate affairs"—euphemisms for what passed for sex novels in the flapper era. These carried such provocative titles as *Passion Lighting the World*, *Lovers Should Marry*, *Glorious Flames*, and *The Mighty Thing*. Another of their specialties was the "exposé," i.e., nonfiction books about sex. One example is *Coquetry for Men*, by Horace Coon, which contains such chapters as "How To Select a Lady," "The Platonic Affair," "The Brief Affair," "The Selection of a Mistress," "How To Keep Her," "How To Get Rid of Her," "The Selection of a Wife," "The Affair During Marriage," and "The Divorce."

But what Macaulay *really* specialized in was what it called "weird mysteries" and "supersleuth mysteries."

In its early years, Macaulay was strictly a reprint publisher; in the criminous category, it gave American readers the works of such French and English writers as Gaston Leroux, Maurice LeBlanc, and William Le Queux. It was not until the late twenties that it began to ease into the original market, while at the same time offering a steady flow of second-rate British imports; this was the primary Macaulay fare until the house's demise in 1937.

Almost all of its mystery originals were by American writers, among them such major exponents of the detective story as Herbert Crooker, Charles Reed Jones, S. Fowler Wright, Frederick Eberhard, H. L. Gates, J. Breckenridge Ellis, R. Francis Foster, Oscar Gray, Anthony M. Rud, Samuel Spewack, Frank R. Adams, Frank Shay, and Mrs. Wilson Woodrow. (At the same time its stable of illustrious British authors included E.C.R. Lorac, T.C.H. Jacobs, Gregory Baxter, Spencer Simpson, T. Arthur Plummer, Gerald Verner, and Andrew Soutar.) Macaulay *did* publish a couple of Arthur B. Reeve's later Craig Kennedy novels and two mysteries by Frederick Faust (Max Brand) under his Walter C. Butler pseudonym—but if you feel as I do about Reeve and Faust, that fact may also be entered as evidence for the prosecution.

Are there alternative bigwigs among this splendid array of puzzle-making talent? There are indeed. Take, for instance, H. L. Gates, whose métier (other than sex novels) was the tale of "Oriental mystery." Chinese, Malays, Siamese, Egyptians, Hindus, and Cambodians, among other nationalities, are featured performers—most often in villainous roles, naturally—in such criminous sagas as *Murder in the Fog*, *The Laughing Peril*, and *The Scarlet Fan*. But the most interesting thing about Gates's work is not his plots, or his settings, or his characters, or even his prose style; no, it is his strange delusions, repeated in one form or another throughout his books, regarding both the human anatomy and the human (especially the Oriental) physiognomy.

> Stanley chafed her pulses. They were beating slowly, faintly. (*The Scarlet Fan*)

> Stafford's fingers found the man's pulse and his ear sought a sign of life in the heart under the gleaming evening linen. When he raised his head he let the inert pulse drop and whispered aloud a single, terrified word: "Dead!" (*Death Counts Five*)

> In expressive answer Walker's both hands went to his own throat, the tips of their fingers touching his throat chords [sic] gingerly. (*The Scarlet Fan*)

> Only with his eyes Meng Fu seemed to grin. His face was blank. (*The Laughing Peril*)

> [She was] lovely beyond words and strictly modern in every detail. In the loveliness, however, he surprised [sic] a quality far deeper than the surface audacities of pert modernity. (*The Laughing Peril*

> He was conscious of beige legs that descended rhythmically to tiny pumps. (*The Laughing Peril*)

> It came to Stafford that the man would be a Hindu, of one of the southern Indian states where the races are sun-baked to a dark green. (*Death Counts Five*)

Then we have Frederick G. Eberhard, who was a practicing physican as well as a scribbler and who, according to his publishers, "won fame for his scientific mystery stories." There is plenty of scientific stuff in his books, to be sure—much of it rather obsessively (and dubiously) involving chemical ways to dispose of corpses. ("'Potassium dichromate dissolved in concentrated sulphuric acid will dissolve a body, leaving paltry residue of calcium sulphate, carbon, and calcium phosphate. That's just the common cleaning fluid used in all chemical laboratories. Remove the gold and platinum from their mouths, take off their rings, and all you have to do is pour 'em down the sink.'") His publishers' claim notwithstanding, Eberhard's fame clearly does *not* rest on his scientific expertise. Rather, it rests on two other factors: his plots, which are nothing if not ingenious; and his dialogue, which is nothing if not moronic.

One of his more outrageous plots is that of *Super-Gangster* (1932). The supreme villain of this title is in fact a lunatic with a Napoleon complex who calls himself the Emperor (his moll's name is Josephine, what else?) and who, early on in the narrative, undergoes plastic surgery to transform himself from a handsome dude to an ugly one. Reason: So he can walk into the Big House and bust out a couple of his pals (Creepers Clarke and the Rambler, who are awaiting execution in the hot squat) and at the same time knock off a couple of his old enemies (Sleepy Withers and the Hoot Owl). How is he able to walk into prison unchallenged? you may well ask. Why, his new ugly puss is an exact duplicate of Warden Hunt's (the warden's ugliness being the result of an old war wound), and he, the Emperor, has kidnapped the real Hunt so as to be able to take his place.

Two other of *Super-Gangster's* dizzy plot components are worth mentioning. One is "an unexpected spinal operation" that leaves the Emperor paralyzed below the waist, causing him to lose interest in Josephine but allowing him, as the dust jacket blurb says, "to fully appreciate a gift copy of *Lady Chatterly's Lover*." The other is a castle hideout on the Hudson River, known as "The Castle Home for Feeble Minded," which is outfitted with a surgical chamber of horrors, dozens of thugs and mugs, and machine-gun nests in the turrets. It is at the Castle Home for Feeble Minded that the Emperor, fittingly enough, meets his Waterloo.

As alternatively dazzling as *Super-Gangster* is, it is not Eberhard's masterwork; that honor belongs to *The Skeleton Talks*, published the following year. This one is a full-fledged detective story, featuring the exploits of "supersleuth" and "investigator

extraordinary" Bradley Holmes. Holmes is "one of those strange
mortals who exist on loss of sleep," so courageous that he thinks
nothing of taking "a copious drink from his decanter in spite of the
thought that it might contain a poison," and given in his less exalted
moments to such exclamations of amazement as "Jumping Jee-
whiziz!" A man to be reckoned with, you will agree.

In *The Skeleton Talks*, Holmes is on the trail of a mysterious
"super crook" (Eberhard's heroes and villains are always "super")
known as the Hawk, who "sets murderous traps and kills his
victims in devious and obscure manners." One of these devious and
obscure manners is an innocent-looking paper bag, sealed at the top
and stuffed into the victim's desk drawer—an infernal device of
diabolical cunning. To wit:

> "The bag, as you know, was loaded with concentrated
> hydrocyanic acid gas," Holmes explained. "You saw the
> [sharp knife fastened to a set spring] before the bag was
> split. The spring was released by a very sensitive
> thermostat which was fastened to the electric light bulb."
>
> "Clever and utterly hellish," said Martin as he ex-
> amined the thermostat.
>
> "The murderer may be mad but he is also a satanic
> genius. Why, he even removed the incandescent bulb
> from the lamp and substituted an old carbon light—one
> that would generate more heat. The heat expanded the
> thermostat, it in turn released the spring and the knife
> sprang upward to slit the bag and release the gas."
>
> "You are right, Holmes. The man is an intellectual."

Indeed he is. And he leads the "detective extraordinary" a merry
chase through a publishing office (one of the Hawk's victims is a
mystery writer named Braxton Hicks), a curio room full of
skeletons, an undertaking parlor, a mausoleum replete with secret
passages, a series of catacombs "in the bowels of a cemetery," the
cemetery itself, and numerous other locations. Along the way we
find out the answers to such puzzling questions as : Why has the
Hawk stolen the manuscript of Hicks's latest mystery novel, *The*

Skeleton Talks? Why has the Hawk machine-gunned a carload of cops? Why has the Hawk scragged Scruggs, the wise-cracking mortician? And why would this "underworld demon" want to keep moving a dozen skeletons from one place to another—unless it is to prevent one of them from "talking" and revealing his true identity?

We are also, along the way, treated to a great deal of Eberhard's inimitable dialogue. Here is a conversation between a cop and Medical Examiner Martin:

> "Looks like a post mortem in this case," said Martin after his examination [of a corpse]. "It's either poison or death from a natural cause."
>
> "Could he have passed out from fright?" suggested O'Grady.
>
> "Possibly," returned Martin. "However, I never went in much for that solution of a death. Shoot him to the morgue. I'll slice him up and see what happens."
>
> O'Grady turned [to one of his men]. "Shoot both stiffs to the slab house." Turning to Martin he asked, "It's all right to give the Sawbones [i.e. the dead man] formalin?"
>
> "The undertaker can pickle him," Martin replied. "He's been murdered. But don't let Hicks pass on to the coffin sellers until I whittle him."

And here is Holmes introducing himself to Dr. Martin:

> "Dr. Martin, my name is Holmes, Bradley Holmes," said Holmes by way of introducing himself.

And here is some telephone conversation between Holmes and a police sergeant:

> "Is O'Grady there?"
>
> "No he isn't. What's more, he isn't likely to be here."
>
> "Sure he will be," replied Holmes. "He just left me a while ago. He's probably run into something. . . ."
>
> "Yeah, he ran into something all right. Someone turned

a chopper on him at 10th and Armitage. His whole squad
was knocked off.''
    "What?" yelled Holmes.
    "Somebody bumped them off.''
    "Who?"
    "How in hell would I know. It wasn't the Boy Scouts."
    "You're kidding me, Sergeant."
    "If I'm kidding you my grandmother was a virgin."

And here is the venal Hawk, soliloquizing in his lair:

    "Gone!" he exclaimed, and as evil a looking expression
as ever characterized madness came over his countenance. "Damn her! No wonder she didn't bring the junk.
She's taken the money instead and is probably telling the
police about me anonymously. Once rid of me she intends
to enjoy my riches. Well, I'll get her before they get me—
the lousy hussy! Doomed! Duped! Me, the Hawk! And by
a woman! I should have known better. Why did I ever
allow her to come here? Kipling was right, a woman's a
woman and a good cigar's a smoke."

And finally here is an extremely telling passage of dialogue
between Holmes and a publishing house editor, proving that
Eberhard may have been an alternative giant but he was not without
his pithily accurate insights:

    "These authors are cranks. They imagine things. They
wouldn't be authors if they didn't. . . ."
    "I can readily imagine that a mystery story writer might
go haywire."
    "Not only they," said the editor as he threw up both
hands. "The highbrow scribblers, the sex mongers and
the birds grinding out westerns! They're all temperamen-
tal—goofy—haywire or whatever you choose to call
them."

As marvelous as Gates and Eberhard were, neither could match the sheer inventive acuity of the premier Macaulay author, Anthony M. Rud. Rud's three novels published in 1934 and 1935 might have been used by the firm's editors as models to which their other writers should aspire. Two of these, *House of the Damned* and *The Stuffed Men*, are alternative works of considerable stature.

Rud, a Chicago native who turned to fictioneering not long after his graduation from Dartmouth in 1914, was first and foremost a pulp writer. Of his eight novels published between 1923 and 1941, at least three were first written as pulp serials. In the twenties and thirties he contributed numerous jungle adventure, humorous cowboy, criminous, science fantasy, and macabre stories to such magazines as *Argosy*, *The Lariat*, *Thrilling Wonder*, *Detective Fiction Weekly*, *Weird Tales* (where his best-known story, "Ooze," was first published in 1923, in the debut issue), and even *Black Mask* in its infancy. He understood better than most that pulp readers craved the unusual above all else (an understanding that allowed him to find work as a pulp editor on both *Adventure* and *Detective Story* to supplement his free-lancing income). In those days it didn't matter if stories remained within the boundaries of probability, or if they even made much sense at all; what mattered was that they be fast-paced, exciting, and imaginative. Rud gave readers what they wanted in abundance and with appropriate pyrotechnics. His imagination was nothing if not fertile. At their most unfettered his flights of fancy are every bit as wild and wonderful as those of Harry Stephen Keeler, Tom Roan, and Sydney Horler.

Rud specialized in eccentric (and eccentrically named) characters, many of whom are either blessed or cursed with strange powers, maladies, and/or thought processes, and in eerie and *very* improbable plot situations, often constructed to include fantastic schemes and large casts of characters. In his detective fiction—all three of his Macaulay novels are, among other things, detective stories—he likewise specialized in sinister private estates and architectural monstrosities full of trap doors, secret passages, and any number of weird gadgets, and in bizarre "impossible" murders, usually perpetrated with the aid of pseudoscientific gimmickry. Corpses litter the fictional landscapes of *The Rose Bath Riddle*,

House of the Damned, and *The Stuffed Men*—not as many as
Hammett provided in *Red Harvest* and "The Gutting of Couffig-
nal," perhaps, but more than enough to satisfy the most bloodthirsty
of readers.

The protagonist of all three of Rud's Macaulay novels (and of a
series of novelettes in *Detective Fiction Weekly*) is J.C.K. "Jigger"
Masters, a former "whistling caddy" (golf, not tea) turned Long
Island "crime analyst." Masters first came into the public eye, Rud
tells us, at the tender age of eleven, "back in the days when golf
sticks had names instead of numbers." While caddying on the
Burning Bush Club Course No. 3, Locust Valley, Long Island, "he
had discovered a corpse with an iron club, a jigger, crammed down
his throat. Weeks after police had given up the case as an unsolved
mystery, he appeared at the station with a complete case against a
man who had not been suspected. And the iron jigger, a peculiar
club designed to combine loft and distance as well, had been the
arch key of his evidence." Some eleven-year-old kid!

Now, at the age of thirty, there is "nothing of the dilettante-in-
crime, or the brilliant amateur, about Masters." No, sir. He is now a
full-fledged, card-carrying supersleuth. He *has* had one "failure,"
though, since becoming a detective of Holmesian skills: he hasn't
been able to find a suitable Watson, "some kind of dependable
companion . . . who could keep level eyes on the horizon, and
feet on the ground." Instead he has "developed an organization of
subordinates who did excellently well in following his directions in
the routine work. Not one of them, though, was any more of a
friend or a companion than was his inconspicuous Studebaker
coupe, or his .32-20 S&W revolver." These subordinates include
Mitsui, his "Jap servant" (who sounds suspiciously Chinese in his
speech patterns); Tom Gildersleeve, a meerschaum-smoking ex-
automobile mechanic whose favorite expression is "For the luvva
some Dago woman"; and Marshall Vandervoort, a young man-
about-town who helps Jigger over the protestations of his socialite
wife, and who also has a favorite expression—a Robin-the-Boy-
Wonderish "Holy Helen of Troy!" (Not to be outdone, Jigger
likewise owns a favorite exclamation: "Now what in the name of all
the seven sacred sea lions . . .") Lieutenant Conner of the Essex

County Police is staunchly in Jigger's corner, as are all other Long Island police agencies: they seem willing and eager to turn complete control of an investigaton over to him at the drop of a corpse. Even the governor stands in awe of the former whistling caddy's deductive talents.

Lest you think Masters is purely a cerebral sleuth—all brains and no iron jigger, as it were—it should be pointed out that he can fight and shoot with the best of the hard-boiled dicks. He also comes prepared for any emergency, any contingency. Not only does he carry his trusty .32-20 S&W revolver in "an armpit sling," he also carries a fascinating array of other lethal—and nonlethal—articles which he uses for offensive or defensive purposes, depending on the situation. He doesn't just secrete these items in his (doubtless) capacious clothing, either. No, Jigger is too clever for that. He uses his head in more ways than one:

> Near the roots of his wiry black hair at the crown of his head, the detective had a . . . small phial hidden. This contained exactly ten drops of the same liquid once carried by the women of Russia's famous Battalion of Death, when going forth to do battle against bestial male enemies. But Jigger kept it hidden there as a last-ditch offensive weapon, ordinarily. Only once in his career had he been compelled to use it. That time he killed a degenerate who otherwise would have added another horror to his roster of sex crimes.

Jigger's first full-length case, *The Rose Bath Riddle*, was published by Macaulay in 1934, and is somewhat disappointing from an alternative point of view. It starts promisingly with the murder of Simon Corlaes, a nationally known "chemical magician" and amateur satyr, in his private bath: he is literally frozen to death in the midst of a scalding hot shower, while trying to wash off some body dye he put on himself as part of a practical joke on his guests. But Rud explains this "impossible" all too quickly: in Corlaes's adjacent laboratory, the murderer hooked up a tank of liquid oxygen to the water pipe supplying the shower bath. From then on the narrative degenerates into a lot of uninspired twaddle: more homicide-by-chemistry, familial intrigue, and double-dealing, much dithering around on and off the Corlaes estate, a secret passage behind a bookcase, and a lawyer named Jellybean Binney, who looks "something like a spinning top, with his small head, seeming lack of neck, and corpulent body tapering down to very tiny feet." Minor stuff, compared to what Rud accomplished in his next two Jigger Masters adventures.

The *House of the Damned* is Fernycroft Towers,

> situated on the highest knoll for miles around, and built of gray stone which shone like silver in the sunshine after a rain. Its architecture resembled slightly the bastard Gothic to be found in many a German *schloss* of the fourteenth and fifteenth centuries. But there was a freakish motif, more ancient and more sinister. Viewing it for the first time, an observer felt oppressed. Some young people who came to stare commented that it looked to them like a bit of scenery out of a film—"The Cabinet of Dr. Caligari," or "The Golem."

The owner (though not the builder) of this monstrosity is C. A. Braithwaite, a wealthy widower and architect who "was credited with never refusing shelter and food to a genuine scientist threatened with starvation in the years of world depression, or unable to hold his usual post through a breakdown in health." Very noble, to be sure. The only problem is, Braithwaite seems unable to tell the difference between a "genuine scientist" and a crackpot of the first magnitude. Witness the three "scientists" presently residing under his roof:

Peter Unger, a deformed neotroglodyte who believes "that ancient lie . . . that the whole of Long Island lies over a big river flowing down from Connecticut, under the Sound" and that "some day the shell of the island would cave in"; consequently he spends most of his time in a shaft deep underground, listening to subterranean vibrations by means of a "large, rubber-rimmed horn" and muttering things like "Domus Damnatus!" to himself. He is also a member of a secret society called the Royal Chancellors, a "murder fraternity" founded in medieval times that has helped infamous people (Cagliostro, Lord Bacon, Aaron Burr) disappear by faking their deaths through an elaborate substitution process.

Dr. Leo Spinelli, an Italian alleged by one of Braithwaite's servants to be conducting terrible experiments involving vivisection and cannibalism, but who is actually a religious fanatic engaged in transcribing the entire Bible on a one-inch square of glass.

And Stonewall J. "Boomalacka" Browne, a former musician and former expert radio sound man, who now professes to be blind (ah, but *is* he?) and who delights in performing all sorts of outlandish practical jokes with sound effects. Such as imitating the death throes of a man being executed in the gas chamber of a Nevada prison—a truly amazing feat considering that Nevada has never used that means of capital punishment.

Rud provides no explanation as to why Stonewall J. is called Boomalacka. It may just be that Rud had an inordinate fondness for the word, both as a name and as a descriptive adjective. In his last novel, the 1941 Western, *Black Creek Buckaroo*, published under the pseudonym Anson Piper, he has one of the characters say, "Hell's bells an' boomalacka bunions!" As to what "boomalacka bunions" might be, your guess is as good as mine.

This is what Boomalacka Browne looks like:

> [He] looked seven feet in height, framed for an instant there in the door. He was clothed all in black, in what looked like a priest's robe, coming all the way to his feet. The cowl was turned back; and out of it projected a stalk-like neck with protuberant Adam's apple. The neck was dead white, and so long it looked as if it might snap, like a curved, crisp leaf of endive. The staring face above it was white, too, and the irregularly dome-shaped skull was yellowish white and repulsively scaly. There was not a hair on the man's head, not even an eyelash or eyebrow.
> . . . He walked with a multitude of mincing, shuffling steps. And he kept both hands and wrists buried in the sleeves of his robe, like a Chinaman!

But these are not the only loonies connected with the House of the Damned. Another is the brash young man calling himself Nathan Ertz, who applies for the job of Braithwaite's personal secretary by presenting him with a card on which is written, "I have decided to accept you as my employer." (Nathan Ertz. N. Ertz. Get it?) And then there's Braithwaite, who is not too well wrapped himself. He is engaged in designing a fantastic new style of skyscraper—"the tower of mirrors," the model of which he intends to enter in a $100,000 contest sponsored by a New York newspaper. He believes (and Jigger agrees with him) that this skyscraper will revolutionize the building of tall buildings.

> In the tower all space required for interior lighting, beauty and strength had been given to windows and wall partitions, of course. The outside spaces between the windows, however, differed from such spaces on any other skyscraper ever imagined. They were covered neatly and completely by convex mirrors, arranged so the beams from their diffusing surfaces were directed *downward*!
>
> "This will make it glitter in the sun, as though shingled in newly burnished silver!" said Braithwaite, showing his old clay model to Ertz. "But more than that, it will light some of the streets below, ending canyon darkness in cities! If future builders follow the plan, the time may come when *every* street in downtown New York has its full amount of sunlight!"

But all is not well (obviously) among this bevy of banana-heads. Braithwaites's original secretary, a nondescript young woman, is hideously—and "impossibly"—stabbed to death while walking alone across otherwise unmarked snow. Since there seems to be no motive for this heinous crime, Braithwaite calls in Jigger. Owing to the fact that he is giving testimony in another case, Masters can't look into the matter personally; he assigns one of his helpers, a fellow named Barnes, to take up residence at Fernycroft Towers as Braithwaite's new secretary and see what he can find out. Which isn't much. Almost immediately Barnes is blown up by a gallon jug of nitro dumped into the radiator of Braithwaite's Chrysler—an explosion that creates havoc "comparable only to the sudden opening of a new volcanic crater."

Is some madman bent on murdering private secretaries? Is *that* what is going on at the House of the Damned? It seems so when N. Ertz, Braithwaite's *third* secretary, turns up missing and is presumed murdered. But no motive so prosaic is behind these fiendish deeds, and those which follow: Peter Unger attacks Jigger, on leave from his trial testimony, and whittles him up with a jackknife. While Masters is recuperating in the hospital, Unger is murdered in his jail cell by means of a poisoned note he is instructed to eat after reading. Then Boomalacka Browne is stabbed to death in his room at Fernycroft Towers, and in the search that follows, a diabolical "murder machine" (one even more diabolical, in fact, than Frederick Eberhard's loaded paper bag) is found under Dr. Spinelli's bed. It is the very same murder machine, we subsequently learn, that was used to knock off Braithwaite's female secretary in the field of unmarked snow.

> The weapon was most evidently home-made, but none the less dangerous. It resembled a crossbow in principle, with an extremely powerful coil spring taking the place of the bow.
>
> The missile lay on the floor beside the gun. It was a slender, hiltless stiletto with a diamond-shaped blade, and a purple stone set in the end of the handle.
>
> ". . . But how does it work? That fish reel thing on top of the gun?"
>
> "That ought to explain a whole lot," answered the detective. "There is a loop—right here—at the end of the fish-line on that reel. Do you get it? That loop fits around the butt of the handle of this little stiletto. When the spring was set, the stiletto was placed in the groove—here." He pointed. "Then the gun was aimed, and the trigger released. The stiletto leapt out swifter than any hand could wield it in striking. Because of its slender blade, it

penetrated plenty far—going right through Sally Holworth's neck, as you'll recall. . . .

"Recall the path, lined with silver cedars? The murderer . . . lay in wait somewhere at a little distance, where she would not see him. Then he shot the stiletto into her neck, seized the fish line, and yanked back the weapon. That was what made the tiny smudge of blood you discovered on the cedar. The search for footprints was made immediately around the body. No doubt by the time any one circled wide enough to find where the killer actually lurked, there were scores of lines of footprints made by the searchers themselves. At first glance it doesn't look possible for a girl to be stabbed, when no living soul is within five yards of her!"

Well, the cops arrest Dr. Spinelli (a.k.a. "the Wop") for the murders, over Jigger's protests that the Eyetalian is innocent. And of course Masters is right: Spinelli himself becomes the next victim, when he is dispatched in *his* jail cell, in this case by a silenced revolver fired through the bars of the window. Now confusion reigns. Is there a lunatic killer on the loose, bent on exterminating bunches of private secretaries *and* weirdo scientists? Braithwaite and the press and the general populace, understandably enough, are up in arms and demand positive action. But the cops don't know what to do. As one of them says defensively, referring to Braithwaite's scorn, "These darned rich people think us detectives mere ringworms on the rump of crime!"

The cops may be baffled, but Jigger isn't. And the killer knows it, which is why he tries to murder Masters (and Tom Gildersleeve) with a hydrofluoric acid gas bomb. When this ploy fails, his doom is sealed. Relentlessly, implacably, Jigger tracks him down and exposes him and his devilish plot.

It seems that N. Ertz wasn't really murdered after all; his true name is Louis LeNarre, he's the megalomaniacal secretary to an explosives manufacturer, and his elaborate plot was conceived to murder Braithwaite and take over his identity because they look enough alike to be twins! So he joined the Royal Chancellors murder fraternity, bumped off Braithwaite's other two secretaries so he could become the new secretary and thus study the architect's habits and life style from within, bumped off the scientists for various (and not very plausible) reasons, and finally offed Braithwaite by "liquefying" him in quicklime and nitric acid and flushing him down the drain. After which he assumed Braithwaite's identity and somehow managed to fool even those who knew the architect intimately—everyone, in fact, except Jigger Masters.

As for the ingenious manner in which Ertz/LeNarre murdered Boomalacka Browne, the master crime analyst explains it thusly:

> "That slaying of Boomalacka Browne was crudely staged, yet clever. There were only two possible killers— Dr. Spinelli and the man then accepted as Braithwaite. And the latter was naked and in a shower bath. There was only one possible way by which Braithwaite could have done the deed. That was to climb over the roof—naked, and at a temperature of twenty-five degrees above zero Fahrenheit, mind you!—enter Browne's room to wait behind the screen, and knife him. Then, still naked, to slip along the ledge to Spinelli's room, leave the accusing evidence [the murder machine] under the latter's bed, and dash back over the roof to his bathroom!"

Jigger's third case for Macaulay, *The Stuffed Men*, is much different in substance, if not in alternative pizzazz. This one is a "Yellow Peril" novel. For those of you with no outraged sense of literary history, Yellow Peril novels are flights of fancy in which the villains are evil Orientals bent on taking over the world, enslaving the white races, and turning them into laundrymen, servants, and coolie labor. Usually these wicked Orientals are Chinese, although the Japanese have been victimized often enough, particularly between 1936 and 1945. If there are any Yellow Peril novels in which the villainous Oriental hordes are Korean, Laotian, Cambodian, or Vietnamese, I'm not aware of them. Those folks have been getting short shrift *everywhere* this century, it seems.

Yellow Peril novels are all racist, of course. But then so were a lot

of people in England and the United States between the two world
wars, when Fu Manchu and his ilk were at their most appealing. All
bogeymen in those days had either yellow or black skin; and yellow
was preferable because of the much-publicized (and specious)
"inscrutability" of the Oriental races. Sax Rohmer's first adventure
about the mad "devil doctor" with the long fingernails, *The
Insidious Doctor Fu Manchu* (1913), met with instant success on
both sides of the Atlantic; subsequent adventures made him a best-
selling author. And where best-sellers lurk, imitators and exploiters
flock in droves in the hope that a smidgen or two of success—not to
mention success's filthy lucre—will rub off on them. Scores of
writers tried their hands at the Yellow Peril novel in the twenties and
thirties, including such alternative impressarios as Tom Roan and
A. E. Apple (see *Gun in Cheek*). Anthony Rud, among other
Macauley authors, likewise decided to cut himself a slice of the
Oriental-villain pie.

This is the slice he cut:

In the middle of the night a couple of mysterious intruders enter
the home of Ralph Marriott, a wealthy collector of Ming porcelains,
throw a cloth bag "smelling musty and fetid" over his head, tie him
up, set a small charge of dynamite with an "instantaneous fuse"
that blows up his entire collection, and then fade away into the
night. Enraged by what he perceives as police indifference to this
outrage, Marriott tells Lieutenant Connor that he'll hire a private
dick to investigate and "show you up like a—a Fourth of July
pinwheel trying to be an autogyro!" The private dick he hires,
naturally, is Jigger Masters.

While Masters pokes around Marriott's house, looking for clues,
the wealthy collector's health rapidly deteriorates: he struggles to
breathe, his face becomes "congested and cyanosed," and finally
he dies gasping. As a post-mortem is about to be conducted by the
medical examiner, Dr. Cortelyou, "something unnatural and hideous" happens to the corpse, causing it to turn bright yellow and to
bulge monstrously as if something were growing inside it. And
indeed something *is* growing inside—strange bacteriophages, or
"ciliated zoospores," that have literally stuffed Marriott with a
rampant yellow fluff. "In some places," Cortelyou tells Jigger,

"like the abdominal cavity, it's grown so luxuriantly that it looks like fungus in a tropical jungle."

What is this horrible saffron substance? Why was Marriott killed with it and his Ming collection blown to smithereens? Jigger's investigation subsequently determines that the dastards responsible are members of the Tao Tong, a Chinese secret society also known as the Illustrious Society of Executioners and the Society of Fictile Artisans. ("Fictile," in case you didn't know, means "molding plastic materials, precious stuff like those Ming porcelains.") But their motives remain shrouded in mystery.

After an attempt on Masters's life—the Tao Tong puts a cobra wearing a collar imprinted with its seal in his bed—he finds out that a couple of other men have been stuffed with "natatory vegetables," notably a Japanese collector of porcelains named Ichiara Kagodi, who frequented a Manhattan art gallery owned by Devereaux Yancey (who also turns up murdered, though not stuffed). And another of Yancey's customers, it develops, is an old codger named Seth Bryson, a recluse who owns and lives in a freak Essex County house known as the Brick Wart.

So Jigger and his assistants hie themselves off to the Wart, which is "a monstrosity, impure and sinister," standing in the midst of a "milky yard of solid brick, where stood a white stag of solid iron, and a coterie of little, bearded gnomes play[ing] bowls like the men of Henrik Hudson." The house itself looks "like a bubble, puffed up out of boiling syrup. There was not an angle, not a straight line to the exterior. Instead of rising sheer on a vertical basement, like any sensible dwelling, the brick floor of the yard slanted up more and more sharply, not reaching vertical until the ceiling line of the first floor was attained."

Inside this architectural gargoyle, Jigger finds Seth Bryson's granddaughter, Lois Ingalls, held captive in a weird room on the second floor. He also finds a bunch of Tao Tong villains who have "hideous noseless faces" and hands that "glint brassily like the paws of an iguana lizard, clutching for its prey." Masters attempts to rescue Lois, only to find himself trapped in the room along with her. Then the fiends spray him with a gas that knocks him out . . . and when he wakes up, he is tied to a table and vis-à-vis with the head of the Society of Fictile Artisans, the vicelord Wun Wey.

Now Wun Wey is a *very* evil Chinese, one with an "ice-cold brain." He orders two of his henchmen to rip off Jigger's shirt and then to place an inverted silver bowl on the detective's abdomen. Then he himself pours two or three ounces of "a pungent, colorless liquid into the recessed top of the bowl," strikes a match, and sets the liquid on fire. *Then* he opens a cage which he happens to have handy for just such torture sessions, hauls out a rat, and slips the rat under the fiery silver bowl on Masters' naked flesh. "In a moment or two," he says with great relish, "the creature will begin to feel the uncomfortable heat. Then he will try harder to escape his small and stifling prison. He has long, sharp teeth, of course. And the only way he could hope to chew a way to freedom, would be downward."

Well, you or I would no doubt feel terror in a similar situation. Even the fearless Jigger grimaces with momentary apprehension. "Was that peculiar rubbing sensation," he thinks, "the first bite of the hot rat?"

But no, it wasn't. In fact, the rat never does bite our hero. When the rodent fails to perform as intended, the impatient Wun Wey whisks away the bowl to reveal a round, circular spot on Masters's abdomen that "glows dull red from the heat," and in the middle of the spot, the body of the dead rat. What killed the creature? Jigger's ingenuity, that's what. Seems that Masters, foreseeing the possibility he might be captured and tortured by the noseless monsters, had earlier applied collodion laced with prussic acid to his abdomen; the collodion had dried into a sheet "like a mustard plaster," and the hot rat had croaked when he gnawed on it.

What Wun Wey and his crowd are after are a pair of ancient Chinese manuals containing directions for "a certain process" written in ideographs on watered silk, which Seth Bryson bribed a minor priest to sell him when he was in China. Realizing torture won't help him, primarily because Jigger doesn't *know* where the manuals are, Wun Wey decides to go a different way after all: he orders Masters to find the manuals and bring them to him: "Let us know you have them by wearing a yellow tie and walking around the block on which this house is located." Otherwise, he says evilly, Miss Ingalls will suffer the Death of a Thousand Slices. And Jigger wouldn't want *that*, would he?

No, Jigger would not. By this time he's fallen in love with Lois and stands willing and ready to do anything necessary to "save the white, satiny breast of Miss Ingalls from the caress of those delicate, beautiful knives with the sharp lips."

So Masters is released, via a "secret elevator"—and the first thing he does is to mobilize all the police agencies on Long Island into a hunt for the missing manuals, and also into a minute search of the Brick Wart to determine the whereabouts of the hidden lair where Lois Ingalls is (or was) being held captive. They are momentarily thwarted in both searches, even though the Wart "astonished them continually during this investigation, revealing itself as a thoroughly modern castle in which every contrivance of spy holes, secret passages and the like to be found in any old German *schloss* was added to and improved by the most up-to-date electrical signals, locks and chain-gearing." But what they *do* find in the basement of the Wart is a giant hogshead, which turns out to be full of the saffron death; and what they also find, in the garage next door, is an escape tunnel that apparently leads to and from Bryson's laboratory inside the Wart.

The tunnel is booby-trapped, however, as Jigger and Tom Gildersleeve and Marshall Vandervoort discover when they try to enter it: another instantaneous fuse ignites and races toward a charge of dynamite. There's no time to run; they're trapped, seemingly doomed. . . . But no! Jigger to the rescue again! Whipping out his jackknife, he drops to his knees, cuts part of the fuse—no time to cut all of it—and then "bends his head to the spot he had cut, chewing, soaking the tough fuse with saliva," and thereby quenching the fire just in the nick of time.

Whew!

From this point, *The Stuffed Men* races to its climax on, if you will, an instantaneous fuse of even more frantic excitement. During another intense search of the Wart, Jigger finally finds the two missing manuals hidden inside Bryson's big, expensive camera. He arranges with the Tong to trade these for Lois Ingalls; but when the trade takes place, Masters is double-crossed and held at gunpoint by one of the noseless monsters. That's not the worst of it, though. Another noseless monster, brandishing "what looked like a miniature bellows," squirts a thick cloud of dust into Jigger's face, dust that contains the "zoospores of the yellow fungus, the eggs of the deadly vegetable that swims in human bloodstreams!" And subsequent examination of Lois Ingalls's unconscious body (Masters managed to wrench her from the clutches of the noseless Celestials as he was being sprayed) reveals that she, too, has inhaled the ciliated demons of the saffron horror!

Lois is rushed to the hospital; Jigger valiantly hangs on to lead a savage assault on the Wart and the ensuing gun battle between police officers and the hell-spawned minions of the Illustrious Society of Executioners. And what a battle it is: dozens die before it ends, including Wun Wey by his own hand. But not before the vicelord has destroyed the watered silk manuals, not to mention taken time out to smoke one last pipeful of Chinese tobacco.

Masters is by then in a state of near-collapse. He is hustled off to the hospital, where he and Lois undergo an experimental treatment frantically developed by Dr. Cortelyou and involving "paroxysms of high fever." The fever, induced by means of "an oscillator," kill the parasitic zoospores, and Jigger and his lady love are saved.

Explanations follow this tension-relieving deliverance. It seems that the Tao Tong enslaved a number of fictile artisans way back when and forced them to devote their talents to the manufacture of fake Ming antiques, using the secret process outlined on the now-destroyed manuals. That process was the "lost art of crackle-glazing" (whatever *that* is), which has never been duplicated and which makes the fake porcelains impossible to tell from the genuine. But then Seth Bryson bought the manuals from the minor priest and started to turn out Ming porcelain of his own, which caused the Tong to have "a spasm of rage" and to set out to smash every piece made and sold by Bryson. That was why Marriott and the Japanese collector were knocked off and their collections destroyed.

As for the fungus . . . well, it was an integral part of the process for making the phony Mings (remember the vat in the basement of the Wart?). And why did the dastardly Chinese use it to kill off everybody? Two reasons: "A sort of bitter humor peculiar to Chinamen"; and "it was probably a much less expensive means [than using] one of their yellow silk strangling ropes."

The noseless monsters? Oh, well, they weren't really noseless, *or* monsters, and they didn't really have iguana claws for hands. See, the Society's members had to wear gas masks in order to keep from breathing the sinister fungus-laden gas, and they had to wear gloves in order to keep from leaving fingerprints—"yellow gloves finished with scales and claws to look like talons of a fabled dragon."

Anthony M. Rud did not publish another mystery novel after *The Stuffed Men*. Nor, to the best of my knowledge, did he write any more stories about Jigger Masters, whom he married off to Lois Ingalls at the end of this Yellow Peril classic. And that is as it should be. Once a person achieves perfection in a particular art form, there's just no incentive in struggling to duplicate it.

After all, did Michelangelo paint any more ceilings after he finished the Sistine Chapel?

3

Gold Is
Where You Find It

"If we knew the Captain's claim upon my father, we could take counter-measures," said Ann, sagely. "I know the very thing. You must screw the secret out of the Captain."

"I?" I stammered, for the suggestion was so novel.

—A. Salusbury MacNalty,
The Mystery of Captain Burnaby, 1934

"Gold is where you find it" is an old prospector's phrase, used by old prospectors in the old days when folks asked them where to go looking for paydirt. Meaning it might be anywhere; you just have to keep looking, keep prospecting in likely areas. The same is true of alternative fictional gold. There's plenty of it just waiting to be unearthed from the mountains of crime fiction published here and in England. Look long enough and hard enough, and there it is—right where you've found it.

Sometimes—all too infrequently—what you'll stumble on is a rich vein, an alternative bonanza such as those assayed in the previous chapters. More often you'll find a nugget or two buried in otherwise perfectly ordinary surroundings. These nuggets may be large, which is to say paragraphs or whole passages of description or dialogue. Or they may be small—one or two sentences that glitter and shine with alternative radiance.

One or two or even a handful of nuggets, large or small, do not a bonanza make. You can't get rich mining them; it takes a hell of a lot of nuggets to make a book like this one. On the other hand, you can—if you persevere—mine enough of them to make a *chapter* in a book like this one (short chapter though it may be). I have persevered, and that is what this chapter contains: nuggets large and small, painstakingly gathered here and there, round and about, hither and yon.

Gold is where you find it.

Alternative nuggets come in different types as well as different sizes. For starters we have the category of Fractured Similes and Metaphors:

> His words spluttered like a hose nozzle being adjusted, the stream of his conversation turned into a flood of apology. (Lois Eby and John C. Fleming, *Death Begs the Question*)

> Her voice had a unique deep resonance, like a cannon fired in a cathedral. (Tedd Thomey, *I Want Out*)

> Words came out of Pedersen's mouth like clay pigeons shot from a blind. (Arthur M. Chase, *Peril at the Spy Nest*)

> I felt as gay as a bedbug in a flophouse as I meandered down the rows of figures and marked the plump, pettable totals at the bottom. (Joseph Shallit, *Lady, Don't Die on My Doorstep*)

> Long years of experience had taught him to sniff at coincidence like an Englishman in a foreign restaurant. (Van Wyck Mason, *The Rio Casino Intrigue*)

> Maitland colored like a schoolboy, blurted, "I'm sure glad you admire her, Major. You see—I—I . . . well, I expect to marry her very soon."
> *Marry!* Had the floor opened and permitted Hugh North to drop five floors, he could not have been more taken aback. (Van Wyck Mason, *The Rio Casino Intrigue*)

The category of Anatomical Oddities:

He nodded once, mostly with his eyes. (Richard Burke, *Barbary Freight*)

My scalp tried to crawl away from my startled ears. (Jeremy Lane, *Death to Drumbeat*)

I could feel my adrenal glands start to vibrate cheerfully. (Tedd Thomey, *I Want Out*)

My brain was doing athletic flip-flops, which I hoped didn't show. (Tedd Thomey, *I Want Out*)

Freddie's tongue shot out between his lips like the fangs of a poisonous snake. (J. C. Lenehan, *The Tunnel Mystery*)

He looked up, his eyes snarling viciously. (Rufus Gillmore, *The Ebony Bed Murder*)

Lloyd felt a little piece of his heart work its way loose. (James Ellroy, *Blood on the Moon*)

A muscle in her jaw did a nervous do-se-do. (Milton K. Ozaki, *Dressed To Kill*)

The blonde strolled to the cabin and unlocked the door. She went in, leaving the door invitingly open. I looked at it and my red corpuscles began to get redder. (Milton K. Ozaki, *Dressed To Kill*)

Mr. Purdy . . . set forth for the nearest restaurant, cafeteria or drugstore with a lunch counter. He needed coffee at least. With a stomach as hollow as his the grit, the guts that he must rely on, would not function. (Arthur M. Chase, *Peril at the Spy Nest*)

My head bumped the rough pavement and pain flared behind my eyes, sending echoes skyrocketing through my aching body. I sat up fast, biting back the groans, and worked myself to my feet. I leaned against a building, feeling dizzy and sick, and my stomach went up on its toes and began to jog into a danse macabre. (Robert O. Saber, *Sucker Bait*)

Tonight she was lovely in white, which did something for her smooth honey-blonde head. And, where dinner dresses usually have a deep V in front, for allure and ventilation, Francine's had a Y. (Jeremy Lane, *Death to Drumbeat*)

The category of Magical Feats, Language Division:

"Thank you." The interrupting click of her instrument cut the last word in half. (James Benet, *The Knife Behind You*)

The category of Sudden Revelations:

I . . . finished the sake and put my arms around Harukoma. Now frankly, I'm strictly a bosom man, and believe me I was ready. The last thing I remember was reaching inside of Harukoma's kimono. The fact that she was flatter than a flounder didn't surprise me nearly as much as the realization that I had been drugged. (Earl Norman, *Kill Me in Tokyo*)

As he bent down he let his hands wander slowly down her body. He made two discoveries at almost the exact same moment. She wasn't a girl and something heavy had hit him in the back of the head. (G. P. Kennealy, *Nobody Wins*)

The category of Brilliant Deductive Reasoning:

I could hardly wait to begin the investigation. Somehow, I firmly believed that (at last!) we were following a course that would clearly reveal—*something*! (W. Shepard Pleasants, *The Stingaree Murders*)

"Of course it is possible that one of them has got entangled with the real murderer, but highly improbable. The cook is a respectable widow and the maid has a sweetheart in Devon." (George Goodchild, *Jack O'Lantern*)

I acknowledged the brilliant timing of Mr. Roberts' murder; the selection of an hour or two at midday on Saturday when the chance of a complete alibi for every moment is unlikely for anyone who chances to be alone. (Sarah Rider, *The Misplaced Corpse*)

I . . . stared at the purse again. A thought was nibbling at my mind.

Usually a girl and her purse are inseparable. Its contents are highly personal. Most girls hug them under their arms, hold them in their laps, clutch them by a strap, keep them handy to their hands, even carry them to the bathroom with them. It was possible that Betty Brandt had come in, changed her clothes, and decided that a switch of purses would make her outfit more harmonious—but obviously this wasn't a purse which had been discarded. The wallet was an evidence of that; also, people simply don't leave charge-plates lying around, not if they have any sense at all. The purse, then, strongly suggested that its owner was still in the immediate vicinity. Involuntarily, I stiffened and looked around. *Perhaps she was still in the apartment.* (Italics Saber's) (Robert O. Saber, *Too Young To Die*)

The category of Corpse-Frisking, Contents-of-Pockets Division:

"Rod, what did you find in his pockets?"

"The usual stuff," answered Rod. "A couple of bucks, a red address book filled with hookers and bookies, a ringful of keys, a couple of bills and love-letters from a babe named Imogene." (Milton M. Raison, *The Gay Mortician*)

Opening the envelope, I dumped Felix Pia's effects out onto the desk. It was the usual miscellany of a man's pockets—sixty-five cents in change, a ring of keys, a pencil stub, a newspaper recipe for Lobster Cantonese. (Tedd Thomey, *I Want Out*)

The category of Male Chauvinist Piggery:

> Like all women in a crisis, she said something foolish.
> (Henry C. Beck, *Death by Clue*)

> "Are women much use as detectives?" one of us
> asked.
> "Rather!" said Carrington; "for certain things, and
> within their limits, they are first-rate. . . . Women don't
> generalize as well as men, but then very few men have the
> habit of observing small things as well developed as most
> women. Also, their boldness at jumping to conclusions
> often takes them straight to the bull's-eye, where the more
> logical male would regard the connection of ideas as too
> fanciful to be treated seriously. On the other hand, they
> constantly jump to the wrong conclusions, where a bit of
> stern reasoning would have kept them straight." (J. Storer
> Clouston, "The Haunted House," in *Carrington's Cases*)

> "He'd tried to rape me that night, and I'd completely
> forgotten about it." (Charles Runyon, *The Prettiest Girl I
> Ever Killed*)

The category of Purple Prose:

> Eager editors played Ellen's trial to a fare-thee-well, while
> an equally avid public welcomed the concupiscent and
> caitiff affair as an antidote for estival doldrums. (James A.
> Brussell, *Just Murder, Darling*)

The category of Geographical Oddities:

> But how was I to know the state of Michigan dwindled off
> into wilderness after the railroad said the equivalent of no
> soap? (Sue MacVeigh, *The Corpse and the Three Ex-
> Husbands*)

> Almost the four corners of the U.S.A. are represented:
> Massachusetts, Wisconsin, Kansas, New Jersey. (Stanton
> Forbes, *The Will and Last Testament of Constance
> Cobble*)

The category of Narrative Hooks, First-Sentence-of-a-Novel Division:

> When the gentleman who had been waiting for me walked into my office, it was evident by the look of fear in his eyes that he was frightened. (Thomas K. Makagon, *All Killers Aren't Ugly*)

The category of Startling Transformations of Nouns into Verbs:

> "What the hell is this all about?" Hara demanded. "Damnit, I thought I made it clear that you weren't to do any private dicking!" (Milton K. Ozaki, *Maid for Murder*)

The category of Odd Achilles' Heels:

> [Private detective Napoleon B. Smith] has one passion in life, and one only; he will walk a mile on aching feet for ice cream, never less than three dishes, often a half-dozen, with the odd banana split sandwiched in for relief from the white expanses of frozen delight. No matter how his doctor rails against this practice, Napoleon B. continues to eat ice cream. He always says it's insurance; the Devil will never be able to thaw him out. I firmly believe that the nearest he came to letting a criminal slip through his fingers was when that clever Doctor Arnheim tried to bribe him with strawberry flavor. (Leslie Allen, *Murder in the Rough*)

The category of Novel Murder Methods:

> "I believe Mrs. Leonard was murdered with a vacuum cleaner," Stephen said. . . . "We know that death was caused by an extreme deflation of the lungs. There are no marks on the body to show other means of suffocation or strangulation. The nozzle of a cleaner, not the old-

fashioned type vacuum, but the new compact kind, is the logical explanation for the absence of bruises and accounts for the arc-like scratch on the deceased's nose. . . .

"The way I re-enact the crime is this," [he] went on excitedly. "The murderer managed to come here while Harriet was asleep. If there is no vacuum in the house, then probably he brought it with him. . . . He simply plugged in the cord, affixed this chromium tube to the front of the cleaner and pressed the nozzle against the sleeping woman's nose and mouth. . . . He held it there until he had drawn every drop of air from her body."

"My God!" the constable murmured, aghast. "Robbed of the very air she breathed!" (Sidney A. Porcelain, *The Crimson Cat Murders*)

The category of Life's Most Embarrassing Moments, Tough Private Eye Division:

I moved past her quickly, kicked open the door and stepped inside. Something brushed my forehead. I darted sideways, jamming down on a wall switch and on the .32's trigger simultaneously. Powee! The room swelled with sound and light. . . . A pair of black lace panties went fluttering through the air from the impact of my bullet which had torn them off a wire hanger.

"Hey!" The red-headed doll came running in angrily. "You shot a hole in my underpants!" (G. G. Fickling, *Naughty but Dead*)

The category of Whacky Word Choices:

It was a whirlwind courtship that ended in marriage at St. Malachy's three years later. (Frank Kane, *The Living End*)

Almost before the Intelligence officer was aware of it, the police car stood panting before the Copacabana Palace. (Van Wyck Mason, *The Rio Casino Intrigue*)

My car hesitated on the curving drive. Chipmunks stood inverted on the mighty tree trunks and watched me brightly. (Jeremy Lane, *Death to Drumbeat*)

He sat on the edge of the bed, slid his hat back on his head and grinned at Eric tersely. (Lois Eby and John C. Fleming, *Death Begs the Question*)

To return the money to the Israeli treasury would mean so much. Hospitals, roads, schools for all those whose lives were lost. (Anne Reed Rooth and James P. White, *The Ninth Car*)

He started deeper into the blackness, heard two voices speaking excitedly in German, and flopped on the floor of the concealed hall. Bullets chattered above him. (Dan Streib, *Hawk #6: The Seeds of Evil*)

When the coffee had arrived and Senor Alverez's cigar was in full blast, he continued the narrative, to which I listened most attentively. (A. Salusbury MacNalty, *The Mystery of Captain Burnaby*)

Carr stopped his nervous hair pummeling. (Lois Eby and John C. Fleming, *Death Begs the Question*)

The category of Inarguable Logic:

You could have cut off an arm or a leg and I wouldn't have been able to lift so much as a finger in protest. (Amber Dean, *Chanticleer's Muffled Crow*)

"I'm not crazy about risking my life. Not for free, anyway. Let's not forget, in the midst of all this fun, that whoever killed the guy is a killer." (Shelley Singer, *Free Draw*)

The category of Unintentional Puns:

Alden said, "I'll never forget the day I married Mae—she was wearing a bustle and it busted. Say, if Ruth wants her bustle pumped up, I'm just the man—"
    That went uncomfortably flat. (George Worthing Yates, *If a Body*)

". . . You know, there's a hell of a lot of screwballs around. They come in to report all sorts of stuff to the cops. People with persecution complexes are the worst. For awhile . . . the desk sergeant used to sick some of the choice ones onto me." (Dale Clark, *Focus on Murder*)

". . . Somehow, I am terribly afraid out here [swimming] to-night—more afraid even than I was back there on the schooner."

"You needn't be!" Ronald cried out buoyantly. (Frank L. Packard, *The Gold Skull Murders*)

"Enough to poison you for it?" His tone was skeptical. "You'd never get me to swallow that." (Helen Traubel, *The Metropolitan Opera Murders*)

"It's tough for her to fall like that," said Monk, "for the woman isn't made who can get a rise out of Doc Savage." (Kenneth Robeson, *Quest of the Spider*)

The category of Portentous Statements:

That was my first look at Merriwether Manor, where Murder had rented a room ahead of me. (Jeremy Lane, *Death to Drumbeat*)

The category of *Reductio ad Absurdum*:

On the other side a man in a uniform clanged the door shut behind me. Now I knew how Jimmy Cagney felt in *The Big House*. (Dorothy and Sidney Rosen, *Death and Blintzes*)

The . . . paper and suit would be gone over by a magnifying glass, a fine tooth comb, or any other simile you could think of for thoroughness. (Amber Dean, *August Incident*)

On the street outside, a MUNI bus blurted out a few exhaust remarks.

The frosted glass [door] showed the gray silhouette of a figure. A woman. And something tightened across Carver's chest. Hunch time in the old coconut. (Kenn Davis, *Melting Point*)

The category of the Ill-Advised Said Substitute:

"Then it *is* Piper?" she horsed [sic]. (Lawrence Lariar, *He Died Laughing*)

"You're getting off easy," farewelled Comfrey. (Dale Clark, *Mambo to Murder*)

"Fool!" he apostrophized himself bitterly. (Gwyn Evans, *Mr. Hercules*)

"Keep telling it," I shoved at Vivette. (Dale Clark, *Mambo to Murder*)

"Oh, pardon me, honey," Sue gargled, voice dripping crocodile apologies. (Rick Wayne, *Play Rough!*)

"He's going to get a doctor for her?" nasaled Doyle. (Dale Clark, *A Run for the Money*)

"A man can be wrong once," he twinkled. (George Joseph, *Leave It to Me*)

The category of Missing Sibilants (or "The Snake *Doesn't* Have All the Lines"):

"You animal!" she hissed. (James Ellroy, *Blood on the Moon*)

"What would I naturally be doing?" he hissed. (Isabel Briggs Meyers, *Murder Yet to Come*)

And finally, the category of "Huh?":

The wretched bird dog that looked like a hatrack lay full-length in the middle of the floor. (Sue MacVeigh, *The Corpse with the Three Ex-Husbands*)

The anticlimax was terrific, it was catastrophic. (Arthur M. Chase, *Peril at the Spy Nest*

He looks like a basilisk [Jean thought]. She wasn't quite sure about it—what a basilisk was, much less what one looked like—but its sound had the *feeling* of his face. (Rufus King, *Valcour Meets Murder*)

". . . and I was in New York [and] my God, you wouldn't believe what they've got . . . alligators and crocodiles and beavers and rats and who the hell knows what else lives in the sewers. (Thomas Gifford, *The Cavanaugh Quest*)

Until he had thoroughly satisfied himself that none of these four had had a hand in the killing, it would be foolish to go off on wildgoose chases in other directions, no matter how promising or inviting they might seem. (Joseph Bowen, *The Man Without a Head*)

Thereupon North released a small mental spring which tilted gallows of cold caution over this young woman's rising appeal. (Van Wyck Mason, *The Cairo Garter Murders*)

Thoughtfully he dropped his eyes down at the glass in his hands. A strong highball, whose strength was already beginning to gain an affection over his brink. (George Fredrics, *Consider Yourself Dead*)

Promises lurked in her voice. Though square rigged, she was a luscious parcel, and gift wrapped. Carmody had to quit denying that he had a nagging urge to unwrap Velma. The shirred blouse, reaching to the collarbone, gave no glimpses of curves worth a fortune in TV, but by way of compensation, it did a more striking job than any sweater could have done. . . . There was a tantalizing suggestion of pliability which belied the expression around the eyes and mouth. All the earlier antagonism was being submerged by friendliness. . . .

Fully dressed the woman was a strip-tease. She radiated magnetism; and what little there was left of her subtle air of defying the world now served only to stir up an urge to make her totally sweet, wholly clinging, entirely submissive.

Her voice, and that double-breasted perfume made him too woman-conscious for clear-thinking. . . . Once more, the thought that her solidity was concentrated where it would do the most good disturbed him. (Hamlin Daly, *Case of the Cancelled Redhead!*)

4

The Amazing Adventures Of The Kracked King Of Keelerland

The man who came in . . . was about 35, and exceedingly dark of skin, though by no manner of means a Negro; indeed, his blue-black hair was as straight as hair could be; his jet eyes were a cold black, and there was a scar on one cheek. Dressed in green-striped trousers of almost dandified cut, he was in his shirtsleeves, which, patterned with pink stripes and interlocked green flowers, were the final touch that proclaimed plainly his Sicilian blood.
—**Harry Stephen Keeler**,
The Case of the 16 Beans, 1944

He turned back in the direction he had come, and walking rapidly eastward soon passed under the same viaduct from which he had descended a short while before, and Chinatown now lay in his rear.
—**Harry Stephen Keeler**,
The Green Jade Hand, 1930

One of his publishers said of him: "This master-mysteryman writes baffling, fast-moving yarns [whose] odd plots relate some of the strangest things that ever happened to man."

The San Francisco *Chronicle* challenged readers to "just try to worry about your own trials and tribulations when you're working on [one of his] conundrum[s], slinking down dark alleys, trailing Oriental and Occidental villains, examining curious lethal devices employed by the Portuguese, the Armenians and the Greeks to say nothing of the Chinese!"

The Baltimore *Evening-Sun* offered one of many dissenting opinions: "He writes in a strange jargon which eschews the distinctions between the parts of speech, and employs such a system of punctuation as no other writer save perhaps Gertrude Stein ever dared."

The New York *Times* put it even more succinctly: "All [his] novels are written in Choctaw."

Critic Art Scott opined that his "preposterous tales might best be described as the sort of story you might expect to get had W. C. Fields ever managed to spin out to full length the tales he was always beginning: 'Yas, my dear, I remember once when I was 2,000 miles up the Umbobo river, armed only with an assegai . . .'"

He himself, in a letter to a fan, cheerfully admitted that "some people have claimed (librarians) that the author is certainly insane."

And Francis M. Nevins, Jr., perhaps the most passionate of his champions, eulogized him thus: "When they made [him] the mold self-destructed. For close to half a century he stomped through the staid precincts of the mystery story like King Kong crossing a country churchyard. His . . . novels form a self-contained world of monstrously complicated intrigues, half farce and half Grand Guignol, half radical social criticism and half a labyrinth in which he hid himself. . . . He was the true original of Kesey's R. P. MacMurphy and Vonnegut's Kilgore Trout, the sublime nutty genius of the mystery genre."

The subject of all these comments is, of course, Harry Stephen Keeler. And a nutty genius he indeed was. More to the point of this narrative, he was also the first great alternative writer—and one of the three or four greatest of all time.

Some Keeler devotees might take exception to the last statement. He was *sui generis*, they might say; he transcended any labeling of bad or good; he and his work stand aloof. Ah, but you can say the same about Michael Avallone, Michael Morgan, Florence M. Pettee, Anthony M. Rud, or any of the other alternative behemoths. Indeed, you can also say the same about Doyle, Hammett, Christie, Carr, Spillane, and others at the opposite end of the criminous spectrum. Fact is, we live in a world of labels and categories;

everybody got to fit *someplace*. I say Harry Stephen fits here better than anywhere else, so at least for the duration of this chapter I lay claim to him and his fifty-odd (very odd) novels published in the English language.

Dissenters may skip to Chapter 5. The rest of us will proceed.

Harry Stephen Keeler was a Chicago native, born in 1890. He spent most of his life in the Windy City, where he worked as an electrician, in a steel mill, as a pulp magazine editor (*10-Story Book*, one of the lesser pulps, from 1919 until the magazine's demise in 1940), and of course as a freelance writer. He wrote his first short story in 1910, made his first professional sale in 1913, and published his first criminous story in 1914: "Victim Number Five," in *Young's Magazine* (reprinted thirty-eight years later in the 1952 Mystery Writers of America anthology, *Maiden Murders*). In 1919, the same year he began working for *10-Story Book*, he married Hazel Goodwin, also a pulp writer, who specialized in light fantasy and love stories of the forgettable variety. It seems to have been a perfect union, in that Goodwin not only encouraged Harry Stephen's literary endeavors but collaborated with him on numerous manuscripts and evidently inspired more than one of his screwball plots. Three years after Goodwin's death in 1960, Keeler married a second time, to his long-time secretary, Thelma Tertza Rinaldo, who also collaborated on his novels. This second marriage ended with Keeler's death in February of 1967.

His first novel, *The Voice of the Seven Sparrows*, was in fact one of many magazine serials he penned between 1919 and 1924; it was first published in book form by Hutchinson in England in 1924, and didn't see print here until four years later (E. P. Dutton). His third book, *The Spectacles of Mr. Cagliostro*, seems to have been his own personal favorite among his early work; he once said in a letter that it was "scornfully rejected by nearly every publisher in the U.S.A., none even vouchsafing me a letter on it, and then issued by a firm [Dutton] which turned it down (as optional book) and did mighty damned well." Two other early titles, *Sing Sing Nights* and *The Amazing Web*, were also well received in both England and this country. In *Blood in Their Ink*, British mystery writer and critic Sutherland Scott said of *The Amazing Web*: "It would be quite impossible to attempt to analyse the plot, which darts hither and yon with quite indescribable abandon. Yet it remains a truly great mystery story." On the other hand, Francis Nevins, in an article for *The Armchair Detective*, called it "the worst legal mystery in the world."

All in all, Keeler published some forty-nine novels in the English language between 1924 and 1953. Numerous other novels appeared only in Spanish and/or Portuguese throughout the 1950s and into the 1960s; still others exist only as unpublished (and mostly unpublishable) manuscripts. Keeler's particular brand of lunacy, reasonably popular in an era (the twenties and thirties) that embraced the likes of Doc Savage, the Shadow, and entire magazines devoted to stories about zeppelins, was not met with favor by the serious-minded folk of the post–World War II years. Keeler's last novel to appear in the United States was *The Case of the Transposed Legs* (in collaboration with Hazel Goodwin) in 1948. And its publisher—in fact, the publisher of the last nine of his novels to appear here, from 1943 to 1948—was that colossus among alternative houses, Phoenix Press.

Just what *is* a Keeler novel? those of you who have never read one might be asking at this point. The answer to that question is by no means an easy one. "A Keeler novel," Art Scott says, "is a stupefyingly complex skein of multiple interlocking plots and subplots, the whole mass structured according to a scheme of Keeler's own devising." Harry Stephen labeled this complex skein a "web-work plot" and early in his career wrote a treatise on the subject: "Mechanics and Kinematics of Web-Work Plot Construction," which was published serially in *The Author & Journalist* between April and November of 1928. Here is Francis Nevins's explanation of the web-work plot novel, from a four-part article on Keeler and his work in *The Journal of Popular Culture*:

> The web-work novel may be defined as a book of pure plot which bears not the slightest resemblance to real life but which is so meticulously constructed that regardless of the book's length—and Keeler's lengthiest run over 1500 pages—every absurd complication turns out to make blissfully perfect sense within the author's zany terms of

reference. Keeler intensifies the deliberate and gleeful artificiality of his novels by using certain devices much as wild cards function in poker; among these devices are lunatic laws, nutty religious tenets, wacky wills and crackpot contracts, but his most famous and most characteristic ploy is the system of interlocked back-breaking coincidences.

Keeler's other favorite "wild cards" include rare books of one type or another, most of which have elaborate titles and histories of his own devising; oddball curios such as human skulls and ancient pieces of Chinese jade; cryptograms and puzzles; quasi-science-fictional devices and situations; and a seemingly inexhaustible storehouse of esoteric information on such topics as literary incunabula, politics, safes and safecracking, clocks, electricity and neon signs, steel mills, mathematics, horse racing, Chinese history and philosophy, lunatic asylums, lighthouses, circuses, embryonic television, and Nicaragua. He owned a "private morgue" of thousands of newspaper clippings which he kept in a series of little drawers in a huge filing cabinet, each marked after the fashion of an encyclopedia. When he was ready to embark on a new novel, according to bibliophile and fellow mystery writer Vincent Starrett (who knew him well), Keeler "would grab a hatful of [these clippings], stir them together, and select anywhere from six to a dozen at random; and these became the basis of his story. However disparate in time or place or circumstances, he welded them into a continuous narrative and forced them to 'click.' "

Another of Keeler's favorite ploys was to recycle his own and Hazel Goodwin's magazine fiction, using it whole or in part, revised or unrevised, expanded or compressed, as the foundations of some novels and as web-work plot elements in many others—making him the champion self-plagiarist of this century. In some cases he included complete stories, word for word and with their original magazine titles, plunking them into the narrative anywhere from near the beginning to near the end; these stories always have some integral plot function, although that function may not be clear to the reader at first. In *The Face of the Man From Saturn*, for instance, an enthusiastic paean to socialism (one of Keeler's pet causes, along with such others as political corruption and the evils of capital punishment), there is a long science fiction story called "How Socialism Finally Arrived in the World," set in the year A.D. 3235 and featuring a professor of history at the University of Terra. A pulp gangster story, "The Search," concerning a pickpocket known as the Eel, can be found in *The Man with the Magic Eardrums*. The *Vanishing Gold Truck* contains what Keeler, in the novel's dedication, calls a "beautiful little circus story" ("silly" and "unreadable" are more appropriate descriptive adjectives) by Hazel Goodwin entitled "Spangles," which first appeared in *Best Love Stories Magazine*; Keeler so admired it that he used it's central characters, the circus folk of MacWhorter's Mammoth Motorized Shows, in this and five subsequent novels. Two other Goodwin stories, "Slim Decides" and "20 Minutes," appear verbatim in *The Case of the Mysterious Moll* and *The Case of the Barking Clock*, respectively. And an unintentionally hilarious Keeler "Chinese fable" called "The Murder of Chung Po: The First Detective Story: The Fable of the Murdered Hermit, the Assortment of Variegated Eggs, the 3 Superficially-Thinking Wisemen, and the Cogitating Magistrate" graces the pages of one of Harry Stephen's alternative masterpieces, *The Case of the 16 Beans*.

Still another of his stocks-in-trade was a positive Dickensian flare for endowing his characters with unusual names—so unusual in some instances that they are downright chucklesome. Here are just a few of his more inspired *noms-d' absurdité*:

> Rudolph "Blue-Bow" Ballmeier (lawyer)
> Nyland "Golden-Tongue" Finfrock (lawyer)
> Mulchrone KixMiller (writer)
> Mingleberry Hepp (writer)
> Charley Squat-in-Thunderstorm (Indian)
> Ebenezer Sitting-Down-Bear (Negro Indian)
> "Poke-Nose" Hohoff (reporter)
> Judge Fishkins Dollarhide
> Count Ritzenditzendorfer
> Pfaff Hufnagel

SON OF GUN IN CHEEK

Bucyrus Duckstone
Hutchcock McDolphus
Isdale Archdeacon
Bogardus Sandsteel
Ochiltree Jark
Balhatchet Barkstone
Jeronymo Ashpital
MacAngus MacWhiffle
Abner Hopfear
Oswald Sweetboy
Joe Czeszcziczki
Maltby Lawhead
Scientifico Greenlimb

As for his characters, they are like no other in fiction. Their speech, relationships, and behavior are so bizarre that they might exist on another planet only approximating Earth—a planet where freaks and screwball ethnic minorities abound, mostly for the amusement of the "normal" white majority. Keeler thought nothing of introducing a major character one hundred pages or more into a novel, or of totally abandoning a major protagonist two-thirds of the way through one. He also thought nothing of using an *object* rather than a person as a novel's main character. A mythical rare book of Chinese aphorisms entitled *The Way Out*—a book, we are told, that contains "all the collated wisdom of the Chinese race"—gets people into and out of hot water in five novels published between 1941 and 1944: *The Peacock Fan*, *The Sharkskin Book*, *The Book with the Orange Leaves*, *The Case of the Two Strange Ladies*, and *The Case of the 16 Beans* (the "Chinese fable" mentioned above is supposedly from *The Way Out*). About his "Way Out" stories, Keeler once said that he "had a hell of a damned time trying to slant each to a bit of Chinese wisdom and then write the bit of wisdom to fit the story. I had to be brief, pungent, Chinese in flavor and where possible, with a bit of humor. And I nearly busted my cerebellum making them up." Those who read the "Way Out" stories, in particular *The Case of the 16 Beans*, may be inclined to believe that Keeler did indeed bust his cerebellum in making them up.

Gangsters run rampant in his novels—toughs with such names as Al "Three-Gun" Mulhearn, Two-Gun "Polack" Eddy, Louis Rocco, Scarface Scalisi, and Driller O'Hare. Most of the nonethnic ones speak in a strange, slangy patois that would have had Dutch Schultz and the boys, had they ever read any of it, out of their chairs and convulsed on the floor. For instance:

> "2 and 2's [statistics] collected by this lone hustler through casing the court convictions over 20 years shows that in 81 percent of acquittals there's always one hustler that's well heeled with scratch, and conversely 76½ percent of convictions shows a mob without a cent of coin back of anybody. And why am I handing you this fakealoo? Because, Kid, always work in a mob where there's one geezer handsome-heeled; in catching the best mouthpiece money can buy he has 81 percent chance of a kiss-off from the jury. Then you'll catch his kiss-off at the same time, 2 and 2's, boy, are never a shill." (*The Green Jade Hand*)

> "Okay! Ask 'em, then—one question each—and one only—and in a low voice—because any minute now he'll be up on this level [of the building]. And I don't want nobody's bazooing to drown out his approach. For I want him safe in here—beyond all three doors and beyond yonder bolt—so's I can be putting that rod on his spine and letting him know it's a snatch." (*The Case of the 16 Beans*)

Ethnic characters, gangsters and otherwise, also run rampant in Keelerland. As Nevins says, "Everyone in a Keeler novel, including the hero and the heroine and even Keeler himself in the third-person narrative portions, is a blatant racist; every conceivable race and nationality is systematically and uproariously libelled over and over again." But in spite of this, Nevins contends, Keeler was not in fact a racist: "[He] knew he lived in a racist society, knew that he couldn't do a thing to change it, hated rascism deeply, but refused to be solemn about the subject and insisted on his right to express

himself in a way that could be misinterpreted." Nevins bases his
defense of his hero on a handful of scenes, characters, and plot
elements in the Keeler canon; but the overwhelming volume—and
not-occasional viciousness—of racial slurs, jokes, and stereotyping
also to be found in the canon would seem to make that defense
insupportable. Harry Stephen may not have been a card-carrying
white supremicist, but neither was he an advocate of the NAACP or
the Italian Anti-Defamation League. At best his racial attitudes
might have been ambivalent.

Not only did he and his WASP characters regularly refer to
ethnics as "niggers," "wops," "Hunkies," "Heines," "Chinks,"
and so forth, but anyone and everyone with an ethnic surname was
made to speak in some of the most shamelessly awful dialect ever
committed to paper. In such novels as *The Vanishing Gold Truck* and
The Case of the 16 Beans, dialect of one kind and another takes over
the narrative and goes on for page after page after page, until the
deciphering of all the elided, bastardized, and phonetically mis-
spelled words becomes a mind-numbing chore to tax the patience of
the most dedicated cryptographer. Any reader who attempts to
pursue either of these titles (and a few others) would do well to lay
in a supply of Excedrin-Plus before beginning.

Here are a few illustrations of Keeler's brand of ethnic dialect, all
from *The Case of the 16 Beans*:

> Black: "An' he say, kinda jokin' lak, 'Soun' to me lak
> dey's a Shylock Home aroun' dis place—on'y he is a punk
> Shylock Home, 'kaze he don't obsarve nothin'. Now
> huccombe, Shylock Home, Ah could go 'way downtown
> to Six' Ab'noo yistidday, wid you traipsin' all obah
> Alb'ny? Somebody hatter tek keah dis house, an' get de
> th'ee 'potent tel'phone calls I 'uz 'spectic', an' dat
> somebody wuz me! W'y, Ah lak to have die wid bo'dom.'
> Den ob co'se Ah say, stubbo'n lak—'kaze I 'uz puzzle
> 'bout dem 16 seeds—'Well, 'twuz day befo' yistidday,
> den, dat you wuz dere.' An' he grunt an' say: 'Seem lak
> Ah cain't call my own doin's mah own in dis town! An' he
> add: Yassuh, Shylock Home, '*twuz* day befo' yistidday,

an' Ah picked up a crooked pin on Broadway an' buyed mahse'f a malted milk on Fo'th Ab'noo—now you know ebberting 'bout my movements. Is you satisfied? If not, whut else mebbe you lak know?'"

Chinese: "Gleetings, Mistel Palladine. I makee big mistook las' ni'te, w'en I sellee you sholt shoestlings, 'stead of long shoestlings like you wan'. But I no likee bothel you this molnin' fo' to le' me extsange—you plob'ly lots busy in molnin's, yes, no?—but allee lite!—come I now, aftel you' lunch, to makee extsange."

German: "Bod afder dot, Roggo, vy nod we boomp him off ride avay? Unt schnake his potty oud-d-d-d tonide bevore—?"

Sicilian: "Bot wance we catch thoz' ransome monee, Loo-ee—you no mebbe gonna try order us for to mak' beeg scatter—weeth heem knowin' 'oo we are."

Keeler's narrative prose is often enough in the same headache-inducing category. Art Scott says that his style is "florid, gramatically knock-kneed"; and so it is. It may also be described as a savory goulash of Edwardian verbosity mixed with the color purple, spiced with slangy words and phrases both generic and Keelerian, and leavened by jawbreaking sentences and confounding paragraphs of such awesome composition as

Not only had the safe quite evidently been cast in days before the modern combination dial had been thought of, but it had moreover been through a fierce fire at some far-gone day, for its door was warped as though the most intense of flames had played over the entire mass of metal, and it could be seen that the door no longer fitted snugly into the framework machined for it. Indeed, it was evident that the very lock itself must have melted in those flames, and that the original owner had had to chisel away both lock and site to operate the single sliding bolt and gain access to the charred remains of his papers and, perhaps, Civil War currency, for a square of powerful steel containing a single milled slot—literally a section of armor plate a half-inch thick—had been riveted by four rivets over the site of the old lockwork; and that newer, and no doubt more thief-proof, mechanism had been installed in the open orifice back of this steel plate was indicated by the long-stemmed but powerful key which Jech at last succeeded in extracting through his shirt-bosom to the extent that the long leather thong holding it around his neck permitted, for the key's complicated notches and prongs suggested from the extreme intricacy of their pattern that if the safe and lock makers of several decades back could not construct an impregnable strong-box, they could at least create an unpickable lock. (*The Green Jade Hand*)

Ironically he gazed at himself—gay, yet penniless, bird of plummage as he was—with his striking driver's costume of short-sleeved green flannel shirt, belted into black trousers with red stripes on edges, the legs of the latter buckled into shin-high thong-laced yellow cowhide boots, his short bullwhip—mere symbol, no more, of old circus-wagon days—swinging, by a snap-catch, from his side; then tilting back on his head the flat broad-brimmed Australian-like grey hat, with brim rolled up on one side, that was part and parcel of the costume, he swung his troubled gaze in a great arc across the desolate country-side region where the wagon stood—a region of unculti-vable knolls, becoming apparently bigger and bigger toward the south, or left of him, with here and there, in all directions, patches of malignant-looking weeds, and here and there, too, clusters of scrub oak—and more patches, like actual woods of the same, in the distance, left, right, and forward—and no fences anywhere, because of appar-ently nothing that had to be kept in *or* out; after which troubled surveyal, he dourly regarded the lonely store that stood off from his wagon. (*The Vanishing Gold Truck*)

Glumly he gazed out of the broad window next to the capacious chair in which he sat, which looked down on the morning traffic pouring, this sunny June morning, past 47th and Broadway, far far below, then, withdrawing his gaze, he contemplated himself glumly, across the thickly green carpeted and mahogany-furnished office, in the cheval mirror fastened to the closet door in the opposite wall, seeing only, however, just a young man of 28 or so, with steel grey eyes, who, not so terribly long ago, as it seemed to him, had been wearing a blue naval coast patrol uniform, but who today, now that the war was over and gone, was dressed in a brisk pepper-and-salt suit, and four-in-hand tie with a colorful plaid of just such a degree as the modern New Yorker might safely wear. (*The Case of the 16 Beans*)

Harry Stephen's fine hand with ethnic dialogue has already been demonstrated. Here is an example of how he handled more conventional dialogue between two supposedly intelligent WASP characters—and of his unique method of dispensing pertinent facts to the reader through colloquy.

"What on earth do you mean, Boyce? About knowing 'smart-alecky wisecracks'—and handing them out free gratis? Just because you've run your grandfather's poky, stodgy little real-estate business for 6 years, there at the 242nd Street station of the Broadway Subway—or 6 years minus your year-and-a-quarter time out while serving on that Navy coast patrol vessel—doesn't mean you can't speak—as a young man might—any longer. Real-estate men aren't supposed to be old fogies, are they? And besides, the matter has nothing whatsoever to do with your grandfather's will, so far as I see it."

"Oh, no?" was Boyce Barkstone's sepulchral rejoinder, the while he gazed oddly, in turn, at the other. "Well, listen to this little incident then. . . . The last time I saw Grandfather alive—which, according to the date on this will, was the morning of the day he drew the will—I said, inadvertently, and not knowing I was addressing him—it was a beastly comedy of errors, understand—a ghastly mistake—a case of—of two other men, as you might put it—anyway, I said to him—inadvertently and unwittingly: 'Nuts to you, you old fool!' " (*The Case of the 16 Beans*)

But it is not in his prose that Keeler's real genius lies; it is in his plots. Most of them defy synopsizing at any but great length. Some defy synopsizing at *any* length, among them such massive single-volume works as *The Box from Japan* (1932, 765 pages) and *Finger, Finger!* (1938, 536 pages). At 360,000 words, *The Box from Japan* is the longest single-volume mystery novel in the English language—a book which Keeler himself, with puckish humor, described as "perfectly adapted to jack up a truck with."

What I *can* do to give you an idea of the nature of his web-work plots is to list the essential characters and plot ingredients in some of the more memorable ones. Keep in mind that these are the essential, not the *only* ones, and that they interrelate and interlock by means of manipulation, massive coincidence, and all manner of literary pyrotechnics.

The Green Jade Hand (1930)

A stolen book of exquisite rarity and value, the "De Devinis Institutionalibus Adversum Gentes" a.k.a. the "Vindelinus de Spira," which likewise bears the weighty title of *Lucius Caecilius Firmianus Lactantius* and which was published and bound by Wendelin of Speier in 1472; a couple of unscrupulous Chicago bibliophiles; a venal—and deaf—curio shop owner named Casimer Jech; an excon cracksman whose entire savings of over three hundred dollars (earned by working extra hours in the machine shop at Joliet) is stolen on the day he is released from prison; a panhandling hobo who finds a tiny, carved, six-fingered green jade hand in a bowl of chop suey; two "colored women safeblowers" who turn out to be former circus acrobats and "strong-arm women" once known as the Indian Sisters from Rangoon; a conniving Cleveland rooming-house owner called Sadie Hippolyte; "the biggee king of Chinatown," Wah Hung Fung; the only male descendant of a master jade-carver of the Ming dynasty, who happens to be an embezzler of bank bills and unregistered American Liberty Bonds; *another* Chinese thief, this one a coolie with a cork leg; a pair of young Caucasian lovers named Dirk and Iolanthe, Dirk being the inventor of the Mattox Noiseless Platen for typewriters; Iolanthe's long-lost black-sheep brother; a feeble-minded police-station janitor, Simon Grundt, who fancies himself a great detective; a foppish, eccentric "scientific investigator," Oliver Oliver (a.k.a. "old Double-O"), who is fond of "exposing his super-brilliant private detective badge" to cab drivers, among others; a bejeweled bracelet in the form of a golden snake with its tail in its mouth; a thousand-year-old Chinese book entitled *The Sayings of Tu Fu* (a forerunner of *The Way Out*); a weird reward offered by the Bohemian Society of Chicago and matched by the Archeological Museum of Evanston, Illinois, involving the determination of a person's sex; a scheme to raise funds for a plainclothes policemen's ball at the Fireman's Hall (?) by selling tickets to a bogus investigation conducted by a half-wit inside a murdered man's shop; a "diabolical burglar trap"; some crackpot policework, based on all sorts of illogical and erroneous assumptions; and the most outrage-ous, vaudevillean (literally) unmasking-of-a-"murderer" scene in all of crime fiction.

The Man with the Magic Eardrums (1939)

A rich Minneapolis racetrack bookie, Mortimer Q. King, a.k.a. "Square-Shooter" King, a.k.a. "Camera-Shy" King, who is ostensibly married to a well-to-do ex-Southern belle but who is actually married to "the world's most notorious Negress" as the result of a "noxious lost chapter" in his life; the degenerate Negress, Jemimah Cobb, owner and operator of a London whore-house populated by freaks (a woman with seven fingers on each hand, a female Quasimodo), who is presently awaiting the hangman's noose in Pentonville Prison, London, for murdering her rich Chinese lover, Mock Lu, and who has vowed to reveal, as soon as she steps onto the gallows, the identity of the white American to whom she is legally married "as a revenge against the entire white race"; the baffling "Mulkovitch Riddle," in which a bearded Russian was known definitely to walk into Jemimah's dive but never to have walked out again, with no trace of him having turned up when the police shortly afterward searched the place; King's present wife, Laurel, who is on a three-day "novena" in sackcloth and ashes, praying for her dead father, Catholic prayer-book publisher Ignatius van Utley, in the Convent of St. Etheldreda in Milwaukee; a burglar named Peter Givney, whom King catches trying to break and enter his home and who wears a pair of artificial eardrums called the Cromely Micro-acoustic Sound-Focusing Auricles; a freak in the manufacture of these hearing aids which provides Givney with supersensitive hearing that enables him to open burglar-proof safes, not to mention "hear a lady fly sighing after her gent fly has kissed her [and] a dago eating spaghetti in Naples"; a telephone call and eventual visit from a Buffalo lawyer who offers to buy a human skull King uses as a good-luck talisman; a "Senatorial Investigation Toward Abolishment by Federal Statute of All Race-Track Booking in America, by Machine, Oral and All Other Recording Devices or Systems"; a lawsuit brought by a Chinese laundryman against the Buffalo Trust and Savings Bank, claiming he owns the land under their skyscraper; a Polish doctor, Stefan Sciecinskiwicz, who has been dating King's maid and who is the brother of a "notorious mankiller" called Two-Gun "Polack" Eddy; the human skull (Mr. Skull, King calls it), which was given to Mortimer by a Wisconsin farmer who dug it up in one of his fields and which he (King) has loaned out to a friend for a pre-Halloween party; some other gangsters, one of whom is a one-eyed gigolo named Blinky who is beheaded by his pals; some dazzling legalistics and some even more dazzling misinformation about the effects of marijuana cigarettes (e.g. "If you smoke one, atop any kind of alcohol—let alone absinthe—you'll just tell your whole family history"); a limping, simple-minded Negro windowwasher; a short story written by still another gangster, this one known as "Big Shoes," who is trying to crack the New York fiction markets; a train called "the famous Minneapolis-Chicago Non-Stop Perishable Through Freight"; a seven-foot traffic cop; one hundred thousand dollars in diamonds; a racehorse named Who-Was-Greta-Garbo; a British Negro odds-figurer known variously as "Horses," "Milkwagon," and "The Clock"; an old gentlemen who secretly collects emeralds; a disgruntled exnewspaperman who broke into the Multi Connection Room of the new Minneapolis Telephone Exchange, threw a switch ringing at least half a million Minneapolis telephone bells, and then delivered a speech stating that each subscriber was to be named Jemimah Cobb's white American husband; an explanation of the Mulkovitch Riddle that involves transvestitism and a bearded lady; and a perfect deus ex machina resolution of Mortimer King's problems with Jemimah and her vow to expose him. *All* of this takes place over the course of a single night, inside King's Minneapolis home, and is told primarily through dialogue.

The Case of the 16 Beans (1944)

A wacky will in which sixteen beans of various types and colors comprise the entire bequest from a rich eccentric, Balhatchet Barkstone, to his young nephew Boyce; a cryptic accompanying note written by Balhatchet urging Boyce to "find a good spot—the right soil, in short!—to plant all his beans in, where, growing simultaneously, they may grow him a valuable crop"; a crazy misunderstanding; a lecture at the Philosopher's Club entitled "Continuation of Proclivities and Talent the Only True Basis for Calculating Legal Family Descendancy"; a copy of *The Way Out*, the book of Chinese aphorisms; another rich eccentric, Gilbert Parradine, owner of (among other things) the Parradine Moderne Motion Picture Theatre and the Parradine Tower; "the most diabolical and policeproof kidnap plot ever invented by gangsters"; a film starring a British comic named Broom Sherwood; a secondhand book-dealer, one Ochiltree Jark; a deceased upstate New York farmer who had such an anti-Chinese complex that he bought up dozens of Manhattan chop suey restaurants and canceled their owners' leases, with the idea that the poor devils would then "go off and blow their brains out, or something"; an intellectual Chinese exlawyer who lost his legs in a train wreck, turned to selling shoestrings on the streets of Chicago, travels by means of a platform cart outfitted with "strange water-encased paddle-blades," and is known as "Half-a-Chink, King of the Roller-Skating Rink"; a micro-brained, book-collecting dealer in animal hides called Hutchcock McDolphus; a European opera singer with a voice of "cool, molten gold"; a scientific specialist in beans, i.e., a "beanology professor"; the aforementioned Chinese fable entitled "The Murder of Chung Po: The First Detective Story"; the working out of what may well be the weirdest cryptogram ever invented in or out of fiction; a miraculous rescue utilizing the marquee of the Parradine Moderne Motion Picture Theater; and the revelation of a demented "family history" in which generations of Barkstone patriarchs bequeathed their male heirs increasingly more elaborate puzzles and cryptograms that the heirs must solve in order to "earn" the family fortunes.

The Marceau Case (1936), *X. Jones of Scotland Yard* (1936), *The Wonderful Scheme of Mr. Christopher Thorne* (1937)

This is the first of several multivolume Keeler "meganovels"—a tour-de-force that runs more than 1400 pages in its three volumes and that Nevins says is "beyond the slightest sliver of a doubt one of the great goofy masterpieces of world literature." He'll get no argument from me on that score.

All three books are based on a single "impossible" murder case, in which yet another rich eccentric, this one living in England and named Andre Marceau, is found strangled by an acid-soaked wire garrote in the middle of his newly rolled croquet lawn. His dying words were "The Babe from Hell!" which leads to the case being called the "Aeronautic Strangler-Baby Case." Other salient facts: A stolen autogiro apparently piloted by a child was seen to hover over the Marceau house at the time of the murder (Marceau, who was an airplane enthusiast, had placed a fifteen-foot, red-neon-lighted arrow on his roof, pointing toward London); a set of tiny footprints leads up to and away from the body, but doesn't reach the edge of the lawn; Marceau's ascot had been removed and stuffed into his pocket, and smells oddly of fish; and many years before, Marceau had written a letter to the London *Times* advocating the extermination of all Lilliputians, i.e., dwarfs and midgets, because their genetic defect, "nanism," would eventually cause the entire human race to shrink in size and thus all of mankind would be devoured by voracious insects.

The All-American Press Service, in the person of American detective and dissolute womanizer Alec Snide, embarks on a race against Scotland Yard sleuth Xenius Jones to solve the case. Snide wins out (sort of) in *The Marceau Case* by using his wits and by concocting an elaborate ruse to befuddle his opponent; Jones triumphs (sort of) in *X. Jones of Scotland Yard* by means of a fourth-dimensional method of detection he calls "Reconstruction of the Complete Invisible Stress-Pattern in a Medium Lying in a 4-Dimensional Continuum, by Analysis of the Surrounding Rimples." Keeler spends a dozen pages explaining this theory, but most of the explanations seem to make little or no sense, and in fact appear to be written in a language only approximating English. Choctaw, perhaps, as the New York *Times* suggested?

These first two books in the trilogy/meganovel are comprised of literally hundreds of letters, telegrams, newspaper columns, photographs (one of a bare-breasted woman, another of Keeler himself), advertisements, cartoons, courtroom transcripts, and humorous booklets called "Chinaboy Chuckles." The third entry, *The Wonderful Scheme of Mr. Christopher Thorne*, is done in "straight" narrative form and not only offers yet another explanation of the Marceau murder but also stops every so often, as Nevins says, "to interpolate a disquisition on Oriental philosophy, or a brain-teaser riddle on how to get oil, water and gas pipes into three adjacent houses while drilling no more than 18 holes and having no pipe cross over or under any other pipe."

Among the solutions to the Aeronautic Strangler-Baby Case offered in the three novels are ones involving a cabal of enraged midgets plotting revenge against Marceau for his attack on Lilliputians, and the theory that Marceau was not murdered after all, but that he died of a rare hereditary disease called tetanoid epilepsy, imagined as he was expiring that an evil baby was flying the autogiro above his croquet lawn, and earlier placed the acid-dipped wire around his own neck as a home remedy to prevent a skin rash from spreading upward to his face. Among the strange characters who appear and disappear in astonishing ways are a religious cult of astro-extentionists (folks who believe you must never throw away anything left in a house by a previous owner or tenant), and a midget circus performer known variously as Little Lucas, Guy Ezekiah, Yogo Yakamura, The Juggling Jesus, and the Six-Toed Polish Dwarf.

So there you have Harry Stephen Keeler—or as much of him as I can give you in a single chapter in a single book. If you'd like to take a trip to Keelerland on your own, his books, though long out of print, can be found with a little diligence. But I warn you, just as Nevins and the eminent critic Will Cuppy warned me and others before me—a warning whose validity I can personally attest to.

Once you've spent a couple of hours with the Kracked King of Keelerland, you'll never be quite the same again.

5

The Shame Of
Black Mask,
And Other Pulp Paydirt

The house was set far back from the road and heavily ambushed in shrubs and trees which formed the scheme of landscape decoration.

—Florence M. Pettee,
"The Clue from the Tempest," 1921

Her eyes were kicking off sparks like the flint of an automatic lighter. . . . Her jaw line began to flex and I admired the firm, strong chin which she wore below the softness of her face. She had the sort of chin which goes with plenty of giblets.

—Michael Morgan,
"Charity Begins at Homicide," 1950

During the period between the two world wars, and throughout the forties, pulp magazines ruled the popular fiction roost in this country. At the height of their popularity in the late thirties, there were more than two hundred different titles on the market—titles featuring action stories of mystery, detection, adventure, war on land and sea and in the air, life in the Old West, modern-day romance, sports, science fiction, fantasy, horror, and such esoteric interests as zeppelins, pirates, the Civil War, and railroading.

Pulp fiction, by its nature, was hastily produced by good writers and hacks alike in order to satisfy the annual demand for millions upon millions of words during the boom years. Some of it managed to be surprisingly good in spite of this. Most of it was either blandly mediocre or undistinguishedly bad. If you mine enough of it, though, you're bound to find not only alternative nuggets but full-fledged (if miniature) alternative bonanzas. And as is the case with novels, you're liable to find them in the damnedest places.

Black Mask, for instance.

Now *Black Mask*, as any pulp aficionado will tell you, was the *crème de la crème* of the detective pulps. In addition to providing some of the best criminous short fiction by Dashiell Hammett, Raymond Chandler, Norbert Davis, Frederick Nebel, Horace McCoy, and a host of others, it was also—under the ten-year editorial reign of Joseph T. "Cap" Shaw—a pioneer publication in the development of the American school of realistic crime fiction. In his introduction to *The Hard-Boiled Omnibus* (1946), Shaw described this new style as "hard, brittle . . . a full employment of the function of dialogue, and authenticity in characterization and action. To this may be added a very fast tempo, attained in part by typical economy of expression."

Those who believe that *Black Mask* was always a showcase for tough-guy writing are sadly mistaken, however. The magazine was founded in 1920 by, of all people, *litterateurs* H. L. Mencken and George Jean Nathan—primarily because they were co-owners and coeditors of *The Smart Set*, a glossy Jazz Age "magazine of cleverness" that was in constant financial straits. Mencken thought that by establishing "a new cheap magazine" he and Nathan could bail themselves out of debt. As it turned out, he was right. The first issue (April 1920) met with immediate favor from readers and led Mencken to comment a short while later, "Our new louse, *The Black Mask*, seems to be a success. The thing has burdened both Nathan and me with disagreeable work." Still later he stated that *Black Mask* was "a lousy magazine—all detective stories. I heard Woodrow [Wilson] reads it."

From 1920 to 1926, its contents pages featured an oddball combination of pallid drawing-room detective fiction, Western yarns, and adventure stories with exotic settings. Hammett's first story ("The Road Home," as by Peter Collinson) didn't appear until December 1922; Carroll John Daly's first hard-boiled Race Williams adventure, "Knights of the Open Palm," wasn't published until

June 1923, four months before Hammett introduced the Continental
Op. In June of 1921 what you had were stories by the likes of
Hubert Roussel, Harold Ward, Vincent Starrett, John Baer, Gaius
Drew, George Allen England, and Frederick Ames Coates—stories
with such titles as "The Story-Book Clue," "The Eyes in the
Alley," and "A Double-Barrelled Joke."

What you also had was an alternative classic: "The Clue from the
Tempest," by Florence M. Pettee, the issue's lead novelette.

Florence Mae, as we've already seen in Chapter 1, was a mistress
of melodrama whose forte was silly situations, exotic pseudoscientific gimmicks, and a passionate misunderstanding of the proper
usage of *Webster's Unabridged Dictionary* and *Roget's Thesaurus*.
Her pulp fiction is even more redolent of these alternative essences
than her lone novel, *The Palgrave Mummy*. One wonders, in fact,
how she managed to convince any pulp editor of reasonable literacy
to purchase one of her deformed little brainchildren. And yet she
did, and with astounding regularity in the twenties and very early
thirties. She was a frequent contributor to such magazines as
Flynn's, Detective Story, and *Argosy All-Story Weekly* and also
appeared in numerous others. "The Clue from the Tempest" is the
first of two of her stories to stain the pages of *Black Mask* in consecutive 1921 issues.

The editor who bought these two Pettee marvels was not, of
course, Cap Shaw; she could not have sold Cap Shaw a story if she
owned the magazine. Rather, it was one F. M. Osborne, who did not
last long at the editorial helm for reasons which will become
obvious. He was succeeded by George W. Sutton, who was in turn
succeeded by Shaw in 1926.

Like *The Palgrave Mummy*, "The Clue from the Tempest"
features Digby Gresham, "the master mind for the unentanglement
of knotty mysteries," also known as "a superman in seven-leagued
boots." But it is the narrator, a fellow named Brandon, who first
stumbles on murder most foul at Clapham House, the estate of
wealthy industrialist Robert Clapham; he immediately convinces
everyone involved to call in Gresham ahead of the police. Our hero
arrives, pokes around the corpse of beautiful young Avis Clapham
with Sherlockian avidity, commandeers the kitchen for some
scientific experiments, and essays such brilliant—and brilliantly

skewed—deductions as: "Some one plunged [a] bloodstained knife several times into the earth to clean it. Some one stabbed that tell-tale blade five times into the soil in a furious desire to blot out any incriminating clue. *And the last time the blade was plunged in, every trace of blood had been scoured off!"* (Italics Florence Mae's). How Digby is able to deduce, through scientific experimentation, that every trace of blood had been scoured off the knife when he doesn't have the knife in his possession, nor has he ever laid eyes on the knife, is a feat of legerdemain even Houdini couldn't have duplicated.

After this there is much pointless questioning, some pointless running around, a violent storm (or "tempest," as Florence Mae prefers to call it), the discovery of the missing knife, which had been hidden inside a storm drain and was washed out by the storm ("the clue from the tempest"), and the revelation that the death of Avis Clapham was actually a suicide that her father tried to cover up for the good of the family name. It seems that the girl, like her mother before her, suffered from a mysterious *petit mal* that wasn't so *petit* after all, and stuck herself when a "sudden attack of her mental trouble seized her" while she was outside looking at an "uncannily full" moon. A canny twist on the old werewolf theme, you will agree.

But as always with Florence Mae's work, it is her off-the-wall prose that provides the most memorable moments in "The Clue from the Tempest." First of all, some of the more interesting results of her constant and ill-advised communion with Webster's and Roget's:

> Her eyes were as wide and basilisk as though she were a somnambulist, stunned to time and place.

> Suddenly the [flashlight's] powerful white circle with its livid eye swung in concentric circles away from the inert figure.

> His fingers opened and closed spasmodically, and the whipcords stood out on his forehead.

> The ground was damp and sodden.

> Avis' mental trouble was very erratic in its appearance.

Although inventive said substitutes were not generally one of her alternative virtues, she did have a fondness for a particular one:

> "What?" I monosyllabled.

Unusual similes and metaphors *were* one of her virtues. She could also mix a mean metaphor when she set her mind to it.

> Like a well-trained marionette he bowed somewhat jerkily and hurried toward the house.

> A great livid eye of lightning seemed to sear the room.

> As though dramatically staged for [Gresham's] express help a livid sheet of flame seemed to envelop the entire room in its fiery blanket.

> "If there is a scintilla of evidence to verify this extraordinary hunch of mine—well, I shall be at one end of a thread which has begun to disentangle itself from the whole maze."

Digby Gresham was not the only mastermind for the unentanglement of knotty mysteries birthed by Florence Mae. Another was Beau Quicksilver, "that damned dude dick" as he was known to the underworld. Beau starred in seven stories for *Argosy All-Story Weekly* in 1923—seven consecutive issues from February 24 through April 7, each published under the umbrella title "Exploits of Beau Quicksilver"—and then vanished, never to detect again. Pity, for he was "an enigmatical crime chaser—a mercurial mystery master. Like a chimerical will-o'-the-wisp, he lunged to the answer in each cryptic case. No wonder they dubbed him Quicksilver. He ran through a fellow's fingers just like mercury." He was also "finical," as Florence Mae puts it, "an obtuse riddle" who "wouldn't touch a case with the tip of his nobbiest cane if the thing didn't interest him." Sound familiar? Beau and Philo Vance may well have been cousins—and Beau was there first! He even talks like Philo, in "a cool, domineering, petulant voice," saying such things to visiting police dignitaries as: "Go back and shut that door again! Make it soft—pianissimo. *Pronto!* Where do you think you are? In a blacksmith's shop? Well, you can cut out the anvil chorus here."

Beau's most impressive case is his first, subtitled "A Tooth for a Tooth." And tooths is what it's about—or, more exactly, toothmarks. In a piece of cheese. Roquefort cheese. Seems another wealthy industrialist, this one named Cyrus Whitney, has been "laid low by the Czar of Violent Death." The cops are totally helpless, so they call on Beau, who deigns to take the case. He finds a piece of toothmarked cheese in the murder room, but the toothmarks, he deduces, don't belong to the victim even though Whitney was "a nut on cheese." Do they belong to the murderer, then? Well, that's what the villains want everyone to think; what they've done is left a set of incriminating toothmarks belonging to an old enemy of Whitney's, utilizing a "superb set of false teeth" supplied by the enemy's dentist. Nevertheless, Beau also deduces that some of Whitney's food *was* devoured by the murderer, and "there is only one criminal who is glutton and ghoul enough to gorge himself over the body of the man he has just slain . . . Peter Scarlet." So Beau, knowing that both Scarlet and his partner-in-crime, the Falcon, are superstitious louts, sets a trap at their hideout to work insidiously on their guilty consciences and thus force a confession— a trap that consists of nocturnal sounds of chewing and gnawing, as if from some "devil ghost" feasting on Roquefort cheese.

Now if that isn't an alternative plot you can sink your teeth into, I don't know what is.

Florence Mae'e prose, of course, is down to its usual standards throughout the Beau Quicksilver series. As in the following bright examples from "A Tooth for a Tooth":

[The chief] flung himself into his car waiting at the curb. He stepped on the gas until the motor shot ahead like an enraged comet. It reminded him of Beau Quicksilver on the chase—playing a hunch with every nerve strung to capacity speed and acuteness.

The chief leaned forward purposively. He breathed of leonine strength.

The peevish irritability of a moment before had vanished. It was as though dark and rumbling clouds had suddenly been blown away by a whiff of quickening ozone. Again the air was surcharged with mystery. It quickened him like some dose of super-strychnine.

The hush of death was upon [the room]. The air breathed of the untoward. It smelled of crime.

His shoulder breadth would have made him an admirable model of Atlas. Its girth was splendid. It suggested the far spaces and twelve-cylinder lungs.
    "Were you in the house last night?" instantly lunged Beau Quicksilver.

And now, the Florence Mae Pettee *pièce de résistance*: one of her Digby Gresham stories, "Death Laughs at Walls," a locked-room short-short that would have left John Dickson Carr gasping, reprinted for your delectation in its entirety. This lump of alternative gold first appeared in the January 1930 issue of a Fiction House pulp called (appropriately enough, though not for the reason its publishers intended) *Detective Classics*. It represents Florence Mae in all her glory and magnificence; and I think I can guarantee that after you've read it, you'll never again feel quite the same about either the mystery short story or the English language.

DEATH LAUGHS AT WALLS
by Florence M. Pettee

"The thing savors of the incredible, Sibly. It isn't human. How can a man come to his death in so mysterious a way? There he sits, stark and stiff, in the cold gray light of the morning. Both doors into his study are locked and bolted. The windows just above the gray wall are securely screened and locked. I ask you, Sibly, what possible grounds you can have—you or the police—for suspecting murder?"
    John Sibly crossed a lank leg. He knew that Gresham, a private detective of considerable reputation, was only trying to draw him out. Inwardly, he smiled at the attempt, although he replied soberly enough.

"I look to foul play as the answer to the riddle of Harrison Clay's death because—I am his doctor."

"Well? Are you hinting at poison, since you have intimated that sudden death from organic disease was impossible?"

"I am not hinting at the *manner* of death. *I merely state that I know Harrison Clay came to his death by murder.*"

"Hm," murmured Gresham drily. "Well, the police are also working on that assumption. What more do you want? Why are you consulting me?"

"Because the chief, who is a good friend of mine, has told me *sub rosa* that the department is shortly to arrest the dead man's son, young David."

"Why David?"

"Unfortunately the young man has a high temper. When he was honorably discharged from service, he became set on a naval career. Now, Clay, senior, was keen for the young man to follow science—chemical research. He was rabid against the marine program. They had heated words over the affair, even the day before Harrison Clay was found, a corpse sitting rigidly in a chair before his desk in an entrance-proof room. Several heard the rash words, among which were hints of disinheritance in favor of his nephew, Percival Clay. On close bullying by the police, these witnesses have testified to the unfortunate scene between the dead man and his son. The police, completely balked at the way foul play could have been consummated, propose to show their rigorous investigation by arresting young Clay. Subsequently, they hope to worm out of him the mysterious way Harrison Clay was done to death."

"Just who testified to the police about the quarrel between young Clay and his father?"

"Let me see. There was the nephew, Percival, the old cook, Malinda, Mr. Arthur Armstrong, a scientific friend of the deceased, who was visiting at the house when the dead man was found, and Johnson, a servant."

"Hm," reflected Gresham. "Well, why your haste to prevent young Clay's arrest? Of course you don't believe him guilty. But I recall him as a husky fellow whom the incarceration in jail won't floor. Besides, this act of the police, provided young Clay is innocent, will draw a red herring across the suspicions of the real criminal, so to speak. What's your perturbation?"

John Sibly shifted uneasily. Then—"Hang it all, Gresham, I suppose you will call me an old fogey and all that. But it goes against this crabbed brain of mine to have this son of my old friend and patient hauled into jail as a suspect of patricide. I don't want David Clay so branded, even temporarily."

"Then—" suggested Gresham tentatively.

"I want you to get at the truth. *I want you to discover how Harrison Clay was killed and who committed the outrage.*"

Red Gables, the summer estate of the dead Harrison Clay, occupied some acres beside the surf in the aristocratic shore-colony. A red tiled wall shut in the stucco house with its scarlet roof. Red Gables itself loomed a bright red-topped pile close by the wall sheering down to the heavy surf. Harrison Clay's den and laboratory combined, where he lay dead, was situated on the first floor at the rear of the house overlooking the sea-wall which sheered up close.

Digby Gresham was admitted through the gates guarded by the blue-coats. The police department did not resent his introduction to the case. Rather did they welcome it. The strange death of Harrison Clay had disturbed them mightily from the moment they had been summoned by young Clay, who had already broken down the door and found his father lifeless.

Fortunately for Digby Gresham the coroner in charge of the untoward in that little summer colony was away. For the seaport had been heretofore a model, free from major or minor crimes. Much difficulty had been experienced in locating the coroner. Hence Digby Gresham congratulated himself on his rare good fortune in arriving in the death-chamber before the body had been disturbed—the body or its surroundings. Only a trusted inspector of the department had investigated there. And he had immediately posted a man outside the door with the orders that no one should enter, except by his permission.

So Gresham entered the somber house. Respectfully a uniformed man stepped aside, permitting him to enter the room of death.

With a quick eye Gresham saw the glass topped experimental benches, the intricate electrical equipment in the room, the vials, retorts and burners. For Harrison Clay was a private investigating scientist of unusual ability, albeit the investigations he pursued had been largely of a mysterious nature. Gresham's eyes traveled to the two lone windows. Although they were not closed, yet they were heavily screened with fine-meshed wire netting. And the screens were strongly locked on the inside, making ingress from the sea-wall without an impossibility. Then Digby Gresham's eyes went to the dead man sitting there.

In the swivel chair before the wide-topped desk sat Harrison Clay, rigidly, like some wooden martinet.

The figure leaned back against the chair, one hand lying across his knee, the other grasping the arm of the chair stiffly. The latter stood so close to the desk as to bring the knees of the dead man against its wood. The head slumped forward on the chest almost as though Clay were asleep. Only the eyes themselves, glassy and basilisk, belied this assumption. They seemed starting from their sockets as though their owner beheld some fearful apparition. Yet the dead man sat sidewise to the window with papers strewn over his desk. Beyond him yawned the wide fireplace.

Digby Gresham examined the flue. It was too small to permit even the entrance of a kitten. Yet there were other animals smaller than kittens which had been trained in Oriental countries to bring about subtle and insidious death. A monkey now—

Frowningly Digby Gresham turned to the stiff figure. He made swift and microscopic examinations. Yet the cubicle seemed unbroken. No tiny pin-point showed to whisper of some fine and poison-dipped point. Yet the coroner's autopsy would prove that fact more absolutely.

But if Harrison Clay had not met death by some such subtle poison, how had he, a man organically sound, come to his sudden, inexplicable death?

Intently Digby Gresham scanned the dead man's features. He looked at the papers spread out carelessly on the desk. Chemical formulae they were, betokening a man highly trained in such research. Swiftly Gresham went to the glass-topped tables. He looked over their contents expertly. For Digby Gresham was no mean dabbler in chemistry himself. His laboratory was one of the finest private ones in his own city.

Digby Gresham whistled softly. He strode back to the desk and the dead man sitting there.

Then the crime sleuth examined the doors meticulously. But no enlightening scratch rewarded him there. He studied the strongly locked and fine-meshed screens at the windows. They were absolutely without marks of tampering. Obviously, no poison-point could have been shot through them as had been done in the case of the Pulsifer poisoning.

How had Harrison Clay been killed?

For certain facts which Digby Gresham had already unearthed led to his absolute belief in the theory of murder.

Until the autopsy should disclose whether or not the stomach or the intestines showed traces of poison administered before Harrison Clay locked himself in his room, Gresham went noiselessly about the house and grounds.

Finally his tall figure climbed to the tiled top wall. There he continued until he stopped just outside the fatal room.

"No, sir," said Malinda, the cook, "I know the master couldn't have died at the hand of his son. David is quick-tempered enough, but not that hot-headed." A canny look sifted across her face. She whispered dramatically, *"I think the master killed himself."*

"Why?"

The woman moved restively. She picked uneasily at her dress. "B-be-because he's been acting queer o' late."

"Then why didn't the doctor notice it?" shot out Gresham.

"Oh, doctors!" flung back the woman scornfully. "What they don't notice would fill books! I've been with Mr. Harrison for years, and I know him. And he has been acting very nervous and excited of late. He would work far into the night, behind locked doors in that room of his. I think he went suddenly crazy from overwork and killed himself."

Narrowly Digby Gresham studied the cook. Why had she voiced the insanity theory and most surprising of all, suicide? Was it an offensive or defensive suggestion? Just what lay in back of it?

"How did he kill himself?" asked Gresham gently.

She shrugged. "He's got stuff in those bottles of his to kill a hundred men."

"But," insisted Gresham, "Dr. Sibly gave no intimation of a nervous breakdown, of coming mental trouble."

"Humph, *he* wouldn't. I wouldn't have him to a sick cat!"

"Then you don't think David Clay killed his father?"

Her eyes flashed balefully. "Of course not! Ridiculous!"

Thoughtfully Gresham next interviewed the servant Johnson. He was a short, florid man with straw-colored hair, wide blue eyes and a red complexion. He looked the part of English butler to perfection.

Johnson added nothing except a nervousness of manner which all those implicated in the affair displayed.

But the nephew, Percival Clay, was strong in his suspicion of his cousin.

"David was always hot-headed," he declared. "He'd fly off the handle at the least thing. Not that I'm hinting at anything," he interposed hastily, yet very clumsily, Gresham thought. "And the war, too, has blunted him to any form of death."

Percival Clay shivered.

"You were not in the service?" questioned Gresham quietly.

Percival Clay regarded him over his heavy-bowed spectacles. "Defective sight prevented my acceptance," he said stiffly.

Gresham's interview with Arthur Armstrong elicited nothing further. And David Clay himself only stoutly averred his innocence.

Then came the coroner's report.

"I find, Mr. Gresham," said that official, "no trace whatsoever of any known poison in the entrails of the dead man. Moreover, the skin discloses no scratch or suspicious prick where poison could have been intruded into the system in that manner. I confess that I am absolutely in the dark as to how Harrison Clay met his death."

Some hours later Digby Gresham received a bulky communication in answer to a hastily sent wire. And the long legal envelope bore the imprint of the government's official rank.

Then Gresham drove away to a neighboring city. There he was gone some hours. When he returned, some of the frowns had been smoothed from his forehead.

He called up the police headquarters and addressed himself to the chief of the department.

"Send over to my quarters a couple of men in plain clothes. Let them come heeled and with entirely dependable steel bracelets."

"What for?"

"I am out to take the murderer of Harrison Clay."

Shortly Digby Gresham, accompanied by the men from headquarters, parked outside the main door of Red Gables.

"Station yourselves in the shadows behind the portières here," ordered Gresham, for dusk was already heavy in the hall. "When I make the accusation and flash on the lights, you snap on the bracelets. Keep your man covered, for he is a dangerous one."

The two men from headquarters slid out of sight, although they were but three feet from Gresham's elbow. In the dim half-light the detective rang for a servant.

A little silence followed. A big car roared by.

Heavy footsteps came through the corridor. They paused just before Gresham.

"Yes, sir?" inquired Johnson. "You rang, sir?"

"I did," Gresham gestured alertly. *"I arrest you for the murder of Harrison Clay."*

Blinding lights dissipated the darkness as the two officers followed their instructions to the letter.

Johnson, white and hard-eyed, regarded the detective.

"Perhaps, sir," he said with his usual dignity, "you will explain what you mean. If it is a joke you are playing, it is a mighty poor one."

"It is no joke, Nicolai Dombrosky," retorted Gresham. "I have it on good authority that you have patented several admirable though diabolical devices for your government. I have specified knowledge as to the nature of these patents. Moreover, I can pretty well surmise *why* you killed Harrison Clay. A man of your stamp, still aiding your country by the inventions you have disposed of would be a bitter enemy of a man like Harrison Clay.

"For Clay perfected many admirable devices for the United States government, although these were done in secret and were quite unknown. Even at this time Clay was perfecting a new high-power explosive which could be manufactured at a surprisingly low cost and from common materials we have at hand. The formulae for this invention of which he apprised the government are missing from his private effects. But I found them, hidden away under the carpet in your room, Dombrosky.

"You felt a bit too secure, because nothing seemed to implicate you, and because young Clay was suspected. Harrison Clay's new explosive would have been a big boom to the dastardly archfiends you serve."

"B-but," interposed one of the men from headquarters, "I see *why* Clay was killed, but I can't for the life of me understand *how*."

Gresham answered, "One of this man's recently patented inventions on file in Washington is a pistol for shooting liquid gas—lethal gas. I have no doubt but that this weapon for shooting fatal gas was held against the screen in the open window and a charge of the death-dealing fumes shot into the room—killing Harrison Clay almost instantly. I was immediately struck by the appearance of the dead man. His eyes seemed strained from their sockets as they would when the lungs had suddenly been filled with suffocating and deadly gas."

The erstwhile Johnson started to answer.

"Don't deny it," interrupted Gresham, pulling something from his pocket. "For sewn inside the feathers of one of your pillows I found irrefutable proof of your guilt."

In his hand, Digby Gresham held forth a rubber gas-mask.

Black Mask was not the only top-line detective pulp to bring forth an alternative classic of the short persuasion. Both *Detective Fiction Weekly* and *Dime Detective* not ony published but cover-featured one, the former in 1934 (Anthony Rud's "The Feast of the Skeletons") and the latter in 1950 (Michael Morgan's "Charity Begins at Homicide").

The Rud mini-masterpiece, like his full-length payloads for Macaulay, stars that celebrated private dick, Jigger Masters. One of a series of Masters short stories written for *Detective Fiction Weekly* in the early thirties, "The Feast of the Skeletons," was ballyhooed on the cover of the August 25, 1934, issue as an example of "Strangest Crime." The crime it concerns is pretty strange, all right—a sort of clever reverse twist on the Yellow Peril theme Rud used to such stunning effect in *The Stuffed Men*, in that Orientals—specifically, Japanese—are the *good* guys. They're also the victims, and several of them die horribly—but what the hell, you can't expect *too* much compassionate innovation out of a pulpster working in those dark days of 1934.

Four emissaries of the Japanese government, who have come to this country to discuss ways and means of establishing peaceful coexistence with the United States, have mysteriously disappeared in the general vicinity of the Long Island estate of Ambassador Robert Gormely, where they were supposed to have met with members of the State Department. Not only that, but photographs were sent to the Japanese government following each abduction, each snapshot showing a long table set for a banquet, each one adding a new guest clad in dinner jacket, shirt, collar, and tie. But this is no ordinary banquet; it is one at which "sheer terror is toastmaster." For all four of the nattily attired figures in the last photograph are human skeletons.

Naturally the Japanese government is upset about this, and so relations between Nippon and the United States are badly strained. A fifth emissary, the staunchly pro-American Mr. Hakura, arrives to meet with Albert Drysdale of the Treasury Department. Since neither Drysdale nor the local authorities have made much progress in finding out who is making bunches of articulated bones out of Mr. Hakura's political comrades, Hakura proposes to take matters into his own hands by hiring a private detective—the internationally famous snooper, Jigger Masters.

But before a willing Masters can do much, a car in which Hakura and Drysdale are riding is forced off the road and two masked figures kidnap the dignitaries. Where have Drysdale and Mr. Hakura been taken? Jigger wonders. Could it be that "both bodies had been snatched for the grisly purposes of the skeleton-maker?"

Jigger's investigation eventually leads him to the Gormely estate, where he and his assistant, Tom Gildersleeve, find the entrance to a secret passage inside the garage. All sorts of exciting things take place in the subterranean passage, and in a branch of it that leads to a boathouse on Long Island Sound and that was "possibly . . . used to land speedboat cargoes of illicit liquor in the days of prohibition, though such acts were hard to reconcile with the upright, forceful character of the owner, Robert Gormely." Masters, separated from Gildersleeve, survives a gun battle and some hand-to-hand combat but is then whacked on the head and knocked out. And when he wakes he is in the underground lair of the organizer of the grisly feast, the "surgeon monster" who gets his jollies transforming Japanese politicians into skeleton dinner guests.

The skeleton-maker's name is Dr. Arnold Chadwick, and this is what he looks like:

> He was two or three inches above six feet, but so gaunt and sunken of cheek he looked even taller. He was hairless of head, and strange furrows, alternating purple and ghastly white, ran transversely across the dome of his high, narrow head. There were puckered scars in both his cheeks, and his ears had been shorn off close to his head.

Chadwick wasn't born resembling a cross betwen Frankenstein's monster and the Phantom of the Opera; nor had he always been a homicidal maniac. No, "this horrible looking specter had once been the personal physician-surgeon to a President of the United States!" But at that time he was also a traitor selling valuable information to Japan ("he was said to be a descendant of Benedict Arnold," which explains it at least to Masters's satisfaction). Then Japan had caught him selling *their* secrets to Germany, and so they tortured him by cutting off his ears and putting purple furrows on his head, and then returned him secretly to this country, where he was locked in a nut ward at Walter Reed Hospital. The ever-resourceful Chadwick escaped, however, and ended up at the Gormely estate (*he* was the one who built the secret passages, "in case his plans went wrong," though how he did it without Gormely or anybody else finding out is left to the reader's imagination), and his purpose in creating the feast of skeletons is to wreak vengeance on the two nations he hates by fomenting war between them. A devilishly diabolical scheme, eh?

The trussed-up Masters is soon taken into Chadwick's surgery, the place where "decaying human flesh was stripped from mortal bones." There, Jigger discovers Mr. Hakura (who, alas, is already dead) and an unconscious Albert Drysdale. But neither of *them* is to be the mad doctor's next dinner guest:

> "And now, for making a profession of minding the business of other men, you will meet the just reward of the snooper, Mr. Masters! You will be reduced to the essentials right now, and given place number five at my little dinner of death!" . . .

"Great God!" breathed Masters, not having to feign the horror in his voice, as he tried a verbal experiment to gain time, "you don't mean to *cut me up alive?*"

"Why not?" asked the surgeon nonchalantly. . . . "You will be a trifle too large to seem the skeleton of a Nipponese, but that cannot be helped. I had intended to have thirteen Orientals at my feast before it was finished; but I see, now that one snooper has found me out, that I shall never glimpse the other eight Japanese. So I must make shift with what materials come to my hand. . . ."

"Plunge in your knife . . . end it!" [Jigger] gritted.

"You were a white man . . . *once!*"

"Ah, don't be childish," gently censured the fiend.

Well, Masters doesn't get carved up, of course. He uses a bit of glass he's managed to pick up to saw through the lamb's gut that binds his wrists and then hurls himself at the skeleton-maker. A terrific fight ensues, which Jigger ends by breaking the fiend's scrawny neck. Tom Gildersleeve helps take care of Chadwick's henchmen, and order is restored not only to the Gormely estate but to the political arena, where friendly relations between Japan and the United States are reestablished—for a few years, anyway.

Melodrama of a much different sort is the substance of Michael Morgan's "Charity Begins at Homicide" (*Dime Detective*, September 1950). The setting is Hollywood, and instead of mad doctors, skeleton feasts, and goofy plans to foment war, the devilishly diabolical scheme here is much more down-to-earth: a gang of murderous big-con artists is out to bilk a large-scale charity campaign called the Fund for Needy Children. And the hero is not a renowned snooper of Jigger Masters's nonpareil abilities but rather a somewhat bumbling amateur sleuth named Bill Ryan.

Michael Morgan, as you'll recall if you've read *Gun in Cheek*, is the author of that spectacular alternative masterwork *Decoy*. He (or rather *they*, Michael Morgan being the collaborative pseudonym of C. E. "Teet" Carle and Dean M. Dorn) is also the author of yet another Alternative Hall of Fame novel, *Nine More Lives*, which we'll examine at some length later in these pages. Bill Ryan stars in all of the entries in the Michael Morgan *oeuvre*—the two novels mentioned above and a handful of long novelettes in *Dime Detective, Mammoth Detective,* and *Hunted Mystery Magazine* in the late forties and early fifties. Ryan is a movie stuntman with an eye for the ladies and a penchant for homicide who often must use his stuntman's wiles to get himself out of—and sometimes into—dangerous situations that crop up during his avocation as an unwitting detective.

Alternatively speaking, "Charity Begins at Homicide" is the best of the shorter works featuring Ryan. It plunges our reluctant hero into all sorts of hot water (some cold water, too, in which he is almost drowned)—all as a result of his relationships with a woman named Merna Powers (who works for the Fund for Needy Children), the wife of dipso film director Wally Wells, several corpses, and the big-con artists mentioned above; and it culminates in a wild and woolly scene in San Pedro Harbor in which Ryan, with police sanction and assistance, drops from a helicopter onto the gang's "floating hideout," a yacht called the *Tippy Lou,* in order to rescue Merna from a fate worse than death. This feat of derring-do he somehow manages to perform on a night so windy the crooks on the yacht don't hear the chopper as it hovers close enough overhead for Ryan to drop off a rope ladder onto the deck. Some stuntman! Some brave hero! Some inspired nonsense!

The distinctive Michael Morgan prose style, which reached such heights of marvelous absurdity in *Decoy* (it soars pretty high in *Nine More Lives,* too, as you'll soon discover), is clearly in evidence here. The epigraph to this chapter is one of the highlights from "Charity Begins at Homicide"; here are a few of the others that help to make this a Hall of Fame short story.

> She'd never been on a [movie] set before, she explained with a voice that had the same sort of ripe promise which comes from thumping a cool mid-summer watermelon.

> His voice was so oily it would repulse water.

> *"Bill Ryan,"* I said bitterly [to myself], *"why don't you get your brains counted? You see a girl with real class whom you want to know so badly that your saliva glands*

*pain . . . so what do you do but insult her and send her
out of your life even before she's at the threshold of being
in it."*

If sarcasm was molasses, I'd have been covered with goo.

Arlene was dead. The handle of an ice pick said so. It was
all that showed above her body. The remainder was buried
in her chest. The presence of it protruding from the cool
flesh had an appearance of finality.

[Ryan, having been hit on the head]: A million violins
screeched on one horribly high note and the house blew
up inside my skull.

Merna . . . thrust out her arm and swept the desk lamp
onto the floor. The room blanked into a crash of darkness.

His voice went back to slapping my head from one side to
another.

Thus Florence Mae Pettee, Anthony Rud, and Michael Morgan,
and some of their efforts for those glorious pulp-paper magazines of
long ago—just a few of the many treasures to be found, no doubt,
among the thousands of criminous stories that appeared in their now
brittle and crumbling pages.

The pulps are dead. Long live the pulps!

6

"Loaded To The Gunwale With Superpowered Quake-Stuff To Make Your Withers Quiver!"

Inspector Barnard's latest and most sinister quest is another test of his superbly intelligent scrutinies. His assignment is the capture of a killer, known in the press and in Scotland Yard as the Ear Hound because he hacks off an ear from each victim. . . .

The Ear Hound's seventh victim is found—"And it must be his last!" commands the Chief. The case goes to Inspector Barnard after another man is reported to have been driven insane by it. Sergeant Trotter and his famous old bowler hat lend their assistance to Barnard. The ancient bowler in this case, having served well for unexpected purposes, meets its doom—in an episode that is a positive pinnacle of nerve-battering achievement.

—From the dust jacket blurb for
Sinister Quest by T.C.H. Jacobs (Macaulay), 1934

Riddle me this: What series of continuous writings in the mystery field have all-too-often been outrageous, overexaggerated, inaccuracy-filled, and unfair to the poor reader?

Answer: Why, publishers' dust jacket blurbs, of course.

Blurb-writing is a minor art. Frequently, however, those denizens of publishing offices who engage in it are poor weeds in the literary garden, and the fruits of their labors are on the deformed and wormy side. They use too many superlatives. They give away too much of the plot. Or they misread (or don't read) portions of the book and include plot elements that are incorrect, perhaps aren't even present—at least not in the book they're describing. They misname characters. They use dubious grammar, dubious syntax, and dubious judgment. And sometimes, when the blurb-writing denizens are frustrated fiction writers, their prose takes on a rather luminous shade of purple. Adjectives flow like cheap wine; so do adverbs and descriptive nouns, not to mention similes and metaphors of uncommon vintage.

Occasionally, as with novels and short stories, some or all of these traits combine to produce a blurb of alternative significance. Inasmuch as I've created the Alternative Hall of Fame, I see no reason I can't also create a special annex for the display of these virtuoso blurbs. This chapter is it.

As with novels, short stories, and prose nuggets, there are different types of blurbs (and blurb writers). Some impress you with their blithe audacity, as in the following written by someone in the employ of the London publisher, Jarrolds, for a 1946 novel entitled *Make the Corpse Walk* by Raymond Marshall (a pseudonym of the British imitator of American hard-boiled fiction, James Hadley Chase).

> Kester Weidmann, a half-crazed millionaire, believes that his dead brother's corpse can be reanimated by Voodoo, and contacts Rollo, crook night-club proprietor, who has negro employees. Rollo, seeing a fortune in the deal, plans to arrange a Voodoo seance. Kester's chauffeur, who is under a debt of gratitude to Kester, steals the body in order to prevent Rollo from obtaining it. Celie, Rollo's mistress, is also involved in the plot, and Susan Hedder is planted at Rollo's club by Kester's chauffeur to watch Rollo.
>
> After many thrills there is a grand game of hunt-the-slipper with the corpse for a slipper. The magnificent finale is worthy of *Hamlet* and the excitement is maintained throughout.

Here's another example, from the American edition (Henry Holt and Company) of a 1937 novel by a British mystery author:

> There arrives a time in the life of every detective story writer when he surpasses himself and his colleagues and

produces a high-powered novel that cannot be equalled by any of the other offerings of the season. This eventful moment has arrived for Francis Gerard, and *Fatal Friday* proves itself to be not just another mystery story but a genuine masterpiece in its field.

Other blurb writers take the opposite approach: low-key, straight-foward—almost dull, in fact. But those with an alternative bent manage to slip in a quiet zinger that makes you sit up and take notice. The blurb concocters at Phoenix Press were especially adept at this, as the following for *Murder's No Accident* (1949) by A. S. Fleishman demonstrates:

Max Brindle had crossed the Pacific merely because a lumpy brunette had visited him in San Diego three weeks before, and had offered him the inducement of a steamship ticket and more money than he could afford to turn down. Now, in Shanghai, he still had no idea of the job he was supposed to do, except that he was to start out by getting in touch with a certain Matthew Sand. His first attempt to see the mysterious Mr. Sand was unsuccessful, and shortly thereafter his mind was distracted from his quarry by the discovery of a corpse attached to a flagpole outside his hotel window.

Phoenix's blurb writer(s) wasn't always at the top of his/her form, however. Every now and then, such as in the following from the jacket of Wallace Reed's *No Sign of Murder* (1940) he/she—having read too many Phoenix mysteries, no doubt—indulged in the same sort of specious logic the authors themselves were all too often guilty of.

Clarabelle Bates died peacefully in her sleep without apparent reason. Even an autopsy failed to reveal the manner in which her living body had become a corpse. Obviously, since not the victim of any malady which could be diagnosed, the woman had been murdered.

Not only logic but coherency can sometimes fall by the wayside in the white heat of blurb creation, the result being a nugget of garbled nonsense such as this one for Vivian Meik's *The Curse of Red Shiva* (Hillman-Curl, 1939):

> "You will gasp for mercy for your children as I have cried for mine, and only the striking blade will be the answer. Behold! By Red Shiva I curse you!" A knife gleamed in her hand as it flashed downward and buried itself in her heart.
>
> More than a century and a half since those words were uttered by a beautiful Indian slave to Peter Trenton, adventurer. . . .
>
> But now, after five generations, Sir Peter Trenton was found under Westminster Bridge, brutally murdered, a gold mohur tightly tied around his neck.
>
> Sir Derek Balliol had guessed the significance of the series of murders—but he was killed before he could speak! Only Verrey was left . . . and against him were pitted the cunning powers behind the newly-awakened race consciousness of the East.

The petard that hoists another breed of blurb writer is the desire to be too clever, too avant-garde, in his or her approach. Coherency suffers in this type of blurb, too. Not to mention accuracy. The following is a perfect example.

The discovery of a lost plane
Heads the action in this
Exciting new mystery.

Starring Zebulion Buck and Jim Dunn,
Experts, in disguise, in the study of
Avalanches, the
Story concerns the theft
Of a large sum of money and murder of a
Nosy prospector.

Fortunately Dunn and Buck are
On the spot to assist in
Rounding up suspects—not to

Mention fighting forest fires.
Uncovering local intrigue, or contracting
Rocky Mountain Spotted Fever.
Deeds of derring-do provide high
Entertainment for all.
Read it for fun

Right: the novel's title is *The Season for Murder*. (The author is Hugh Lawrence Nelson, the publisher Rinehart, the year 1952.) But anyone who reads it won't find Zebulion Buck or Jim Dunn expertly studying any avalanches (they're Denver private eyes), nor will they find either man assisting *anybody* in the contracting of Rocky Mountain spotted fever.

Still other blurb manufacturers like to emulate the style of the novel they're writing about, especially if that novel happens to be told in a slangy sort of prose. Not being true fictioneers, however, they sometimes fail to get the patois just right, so that their similes and metaphors come out slightly skewed. That is what happened to the poor soul who wrote the come-on for Paul Haggard's *Death Talks Shop* (Hillman-Curl, 1938):

> A murder mystery which roars along on all cylinders to a breath-taking denouement; characters who live, love, rob and kill under the shadow of impending disaster; dialogue as hard as icy pavements, as real as a sock on the jaw; cascading, tumultuous humor as brash and brazen as tomorrow's tabloid—these are the guts of this top-flight, daffy, memorable thriller.
>
> Who rubbed out Perry Hammett, tycoon and man about town? Who deposited a good-night slug in Richard Tobias? Who snuffed out Peg Lamont, a gal who knew all the answers? These are some of the riddles which acid-mouthed, genial Mike Warlock, star reporter of the *Daily Globe* sets out to solve.

Here's another in the same vein, from the jacket of a 1952 Dutton "Guilt-Edged Mystery" by Sam S. Taylor, which features the sleuthing activities of hard-boiled private eye Neal Cotten:

> Investigations, of whatever kind, often lead to murder, as well as *vice versa*, and slot machines sometimes turn up more than merely lemons. The proof of these adages is offered, with dividends, in *No Head for Her Pillow*, a fast, exciting mystery that is almost as tough as a forty-cent steak.

I haven't taken a bite out of my copy yet, but if I ever do I'm sure I'll find that the blurbster wasn't exaggerating.

Another approach in the fabrication of jacket copy is the one which focuses on the book's cast of characters rather than on the plot itself. This approach works well when the cast is composed of colorful and unusual folk—alternatively well in this sparkler for *Boss of the Rafter C*, a 1937 Western mystery by Jay Lucas (Green Circle):

> Greg Lawson thought that the man who had never traveled didn't amount to much. He left Montana for the Mexican border, which he had heard was the wildest country left—his partner, Slim Hammond, had some sort of cow outfit down there. It took Greg about ten minutes to find that things were far too wild and tough to suit him. He had meant to be a spectator, and not the central figure expected to tame the whole countryside single-handed.
>
> That was just the job that big, quiet, handsome Greg found on his hands. His nerve—and cleverness—in doing it surprised nobody more than himself: no one had expected it of him but Rose, Slim's sister, to whom he promptly became engaged. Even that had its complications: There was Faquita, the fiery mexican dancer of the Purple Cactus, and also Six-Shooter Nan, the wild, red-headed little Mormon gunwoman who seemed to hate him worse than sin.

And through it all, like an evil mist, looms the strange, cultured, mysterious killer known as English Dick. . . .

Some publishers had better alternative blurb writers than others, of course. Two, as we've seen, were the lending-library houses, Phoenix Press and Hillman-Curl. But for consistently fresh, inventive, and zany jacket copy, the best by far was Macaulay. Somewhere in the bowels of 381 Fourth Avenue, New York City, in the early to mid-thirties, there was a man or woman of rare talent who toiled in obscurity and who will—sadly—forever remain anonymous. But this super-blurbster's work lives on, each of his/her writings bearing the unmistakable stamp of one person's genius; and it is only fitting and proper that some of these minimasterpieces be enshrined here, where they can be fully appreciated.

For *Calamity Comes of Age* by Gregory Baxter (1935):

> The young lady whose twenty-first birthday fell on April 9th and who received an unexpected present of a Balkan doll came of age at a calamitous moment. At the center of a nest of furious intrigues, she stands dazed and mystified by the crossfire of plots, to a heavy accompaniment of violence and murder.
>
> According to the notice in the agony column of the *Times*, she would learn something to her advantage by communicating with Box 801. The advantages seemed extremely dubious and remote. If not imminently fatal. According to Scotland Yard's Inspector Daniels the doll's potent political ramifications are vital in European chanceries. And according to Peter Osborne the young lady's birthday is being abused by these distressing affairs, since she is more precious and important than the doll. The first calamity interrupted Peter's serious golf, and it was he who accidentally broke the doll and proved its emptiness. The aid and protection needed by the lady at the age of calamity, Peter was anxious to provide.
>
> A thick mystery stirred by many clever, malevolent hands makes a sharp-clicking story, tense from the descent of the first murder victim to the suicide and confession

wind-up. A piece of sound workmanship in the pursuit of the happiness of trembling panics and alarms, with the proper density of mystery, and with smart sleuthing, romantic undercurrent, and urbane interludes of amusement.

For *The Laughing Peril* by H. L. Gates (1933):

The little yellow Chinese image with a laughing face, when it first appeared on John Farley's desk, robbed him of his memory of years of narcotic investigation in the Far East. It lured Sylvia, his fiancee, into the doll house of Hong Fong, merchant of best grade almond-eyed beauty. It shocked her mother into paroxysms of mental torture. It made a demon out of the beautiful Chinese girl, Chia Sung, except that its powers were dead where they crossed the power of her own hopeless love.

The laughing peril is a symbol of murder, but more especially of subtle terrors that robbed victims of their wills. Behind it is a master mind that is going insane, working with diabolical ingenuity to avenge the wrong he fancies has been done to his ancestors. He would marry a white girl to a half-human monster, he would treat a Chinese girl with obscene, inhuman tortures, he would work for the destruction of the whole white race by his gigantic international scheme for the use of kiff and hashish. With such an oriental demon John Farley fights at close quarters, and the cold sweat runs in torrents. Be prepared for horror in full strength, as the laughing peril drives strong men and women to maniacal madness.

For *Silent Terror* by T.C.H. Jacobs (1937):

The terror surrounding the murder of a well-known daughter of joy is of the ominously quiet kind. Inspector Ruggles Radford, summoned from his favorite cocktail bar, could find no marks on the body. Possibly the woman was hypnotized and ingeniously strangled.

Collaborating with Ruggles on this case is his friend, Dr. Dick Shannon, a lively, enterprising young man. Dick somehow had the notion that the queer looking anthropologist and the young lady whom they saw in the bar, as well as the counterfeit bill Dick received, could be linked up with the murder. The underworld angles indicate traffic in drugs, women, and illegal forms of engraving. The dance hall girl whom Dick tries to pump yielded no information, but she also came in under the reign of terror. The tracing of evidence and the capture of the entire gang provide action and sheer fright, up to the maximum of a thrill fan's capacity.

For *Murder Could Not Kill* by Gregory Baxter (1934):

If there is a man whom murder could not kill, he must bear a charmed life, have miraculous powers, or play into phenomenal luck. If there ever was a man whom murder wanted to kill, that man was Robin Foster. He blundered right into a murder, and then with almost unpardonable audacity, persisted in butting in on the plans of the high command in sumptuously profitable murder.

Robin Foster witnessed a murder accidentally and, rushing to the aid of a terrified lady, received a memorable poke in the face. It sent him in a dizzy spin from a running board and allowed the murderer to escape, but it fixed in his vision the image of a knotted fist and a forearm with a curious scar. And it was only the beginning of even more memorable blows to come.

Probably he would have dropped the affair if the distressed lady had not proved so alluring, gracious, sympathetic, and distinguishedly beautiful. She quite broke up his customary nonchalance. But if he had dismissed the matter, he would have missed a string of the biggest gasps of his life and an exceedingly curious knot of mystery surrounding the private affairs of Miss Laurette Dexter, her murdered father, her father's avowed enemy, and the suave, distinguished Mr. Peter Lessing to whom Laurette is affianced. Moreover, he would have missed murder that could kill one who once gave death the slip and thereupon became presumptuous in his special advantage. If Robin Foster had turned down his chance to embroil himself in these jeopardies and to bid for the affections of the delicious Laurette, the reader would have been deprived of a magnificent bout with all the chilly emotions.

And finally, this anonymous blurbster's crowning achievement— and the greatest of all the alternative blurbs—this one for *The Rum Row Murders* by Charles Reed Jones (1931):

This is an up-to-the-minute mystery. Not only does it take all your spinal nerves over the jumps, but it also makes you feel that you are wire-tapping in one of the latest politics-cum-gangster scandals. And it gives, in the grand manner, an indelible picture of life and piratical warfare on board a rum boat anchored on the high seas off the stern and rockbound coast.

A Congressman is put on the spot. A new weapon of murder is invented. The police catch the wrong man and interrupt a charming romance. A young detective pays with his life for learning too much. A police inspector hustles cans of "alky" on a rum boat. A hairy ape is reported prowling through the halls of a Boston hotel near the dreaded death room. The survivors of a band of hijackers hang from a yard arm, and ultimately the mutilated bodies of their executioners are washed ashore.

Inspector Jimmy Conway is the one who has to dodge miraculously through the maze of danger to get the dope on the rum row murders. He is the one who finally escapes death in the hotel death room, plugs the killer, and reveals the weapon that worked through a keyhole and other fabulous mechanisms.

Loaded to the gunwale with superpowered quake-stuff to make your withers quiver.

7

Sex, Sex,
And More Sex!

She shut me up. The best way a woman can. Rainwater smell got in my nostrils and her full, sweet mouth was mashing down on mine, sending electricity running through all my wires. I got my arms around her and meshed her with my arms. We melted like a molten rivet into an I-beam.

In the dim light of the room, we pulled apart. But we were still as close as consecutive weekdays.

—Michael Avallone,
Meanwhile, Back at the Morgue, 1960

Firmer than a handshake, more sensuous than a lust-crazed python, softer than melted marshmallow, hotter than original sin, suggestive as the mind of a censor, Andromeda's muscles talked to me in body English, and I listened and responded, with every red-blooded hormone in my body. . . .

It was peristaltic pleasure personified, it was hot and happy and wild and wanton, it was the most, the ultimate, the living end, the far cry, the distant dream, the turbulent terminal of all mortal experience.

—Clyde Allison
Agent 0008 Meets Modesta Blaze, 1966

Sex first reared its pretty head in crime fiction in the twenties. Until that time, detective stories—indeed, nearly all mass-circulated fiction—was squeaky clean. Boy met girl, boy sometimes kissed girl, but that was as far as personal relationships were allowed to go

114

in print. Fictional marriages were consummated, fictional babies were conceived in such strict privacy that even the most prurient-minded reader was given nothing whatsoever to pique his imagination.

The advent of Prohibition and the flapper era changed all that. The twenties was the decade of the first sexual revolution. Men and women threw off the shackles of the Puritan ethic and set out to prove that, the bluenoses notwithstanding, sex could be interesting if not downright pleasurable.

Writers, naturally, took advantage of the relaxed attitudes toward sex (though not without considerable hassles from self-styled moral crusaders in Boston and other parts of the country). Sinclair Lewis, James Branch Cabell, Fitzgerald, Hemingway, Gertrude Stein, and many others among the prevailing *literati* seized the opportunity to deal frankly and honestly with sexual matters. So it was only natural that progressive crime writers of the period did the same, if in a somewhat more restrained manner when it came to the intimate details of the mating game.

It was Dashiell Hammett, that great innovator, who first brought sex to the attention of mystery readers. The relationship between Sam Spade and Brigid O'Shaughnessy in *The Maltese Falcon* (1930) is nothing if not sexual—and a highly charged sexuality at that. Early on in the novel Brigid says to him, "I've thrown myself on your mercy, told you that without your help I'm utterly lost. What else is there? Can I buy you with my body?" Whereupon Spade "kisse[s] her mouth roughly and contemptuously," and then sits back and says, "I'll think it over." And later, in a scene full of intense if understated passion:

> Her eyelids drooped. "Oh, I'm so tired," she said tremulously, "so tired of it all, of myself, of lying and thinking up lies, and of not knowing what is a lie and what is the truth. I wish I—"
>
> She put her hands up to Spade's cheeks, put her open mouth hard against his mouth, her body flat against his body.
>
> Spade's arms went around her, holding her to him,

muscles bulging his blue sleeves, a hand cradling her head, its fingers half lost among red hair, a hand moving groping fingers over her slim back. His eyes burned yellowly.

End of chapter. Even by today's standards that's fairly warm stuff, the more so for what it implies rather than what it states. The clinically graphic sex scene has yet to be written that can stir the reader's biological juices more thoroughly than any he can conjure up in his own imagination.

Hammett also pioneered risqué dialogue in crime fiction. When *The Thin Man* was published in 1934, its publisher, Alfred A. Knopf, cleverly enticed new readers by stating in a New York *Times* ad: "I don't believe the question on page 192 of Dashiell Hammett's *The Thin Man* has had the slightest influence upon the sale of the book. It takes more than that to make a best seller these days. Twenty thousand people don't buy a book within three weeks to read a five-word question." Which of course had another ten thousand or so wanting to know just what that five-word question was. The following exchange of dialogue between Nick and Nora Charles incorporates it:

". . . Tell me something, Nick. Tell me the truth: when you were wrestling with Mimi, didn't you have an erection?"

"Oh, a little."

She laughed and got up from the floor. "If you aren't a disgusting old lecher," she said.

Very bold and sophisticated for its time, this repartee; *nobody* had ever mentioned an erection in popular fiction before, except in reference to a tall building. Equally daring and titillating was such other *Thin Man* dialogue as a wife referring to her philandering husband as "chasing everything that's hot and hollow." Despite Knopf's disclaimer, the sexual content of the novel was a major factor in its success. (Risqué dialogue of a somewhat cruder nature enhanced the film version as well and contributed to the ongoing popularity of Nick and Nora at the box office. At one point in the film, when a team of police detectives is searching the Charles' hotel suite, looking for evidence they think Nick might be witholding, Nora [Myrna Loy] points at one of the cops and says to Nick [William Powell], "What's that man doing in my drawers?" Nick's response is an open-mouthed gawk at the camera.)

While Hammett was introducing sex to the readers of mystery novels, pulp publishers were busily displaying it to readers of popular magazine fiction. Gaudy, full-color pulp covers (and black-and-white interior illustrations) depicted women in various stages of undress, often tied up and/or being terrorized by bug-eyed monsters, slavering fiends with whips and chains, or tough-looking mugs brandishing guns, knives, hatchets, clubs, hypodermic needles, garrotes, jars of acid and poison, and any number of other lethal weapons. Until the mid-thirties, the package promised more than the stories themselves delivered—although in the twenties *Weird Tales* did occasionally offer stories dealing with such topics as necrophilia. From 1934 to the advent of World War II, some pulps delivered exactly what their cover and interior art promised—and then some.

One such group of magazines was the "Spicys," the offspring of a Delaware-based outfit that rather hilariously called itself Culture Publications, Inc. Beginning in June 1934, Culture introduced *Spicy Detective*, *Spicy Mystery*, *Spicy Adventure*, even *Spicy Western*. In addition to standard pulp fare—fast action, wildly imaginative plots—the Spicys featured as much sexual innuendo, voyeurism, and heavy breathing as the law of the time would allow. Male–female encounters (and euphemism-laced prose) of the following sort were *de rigueur* in each story.

My arm looped around her waist. I drew her close, slid my hand up her body to the swelling sheen of her breasts.
"You can't say 'no'!" I panted. "I must have you!" Frantically, I glued my mouth to her lips. For a moment they remained tight shut and cold. Then, as though some movement of my hand over her melting curves had given the spark to her emotional tinder, her lips parted and she

went limp against me. Immediately I was caught and lifted to exotic heights of whose existence I had never dreamed. Her mouth became a writhing well-spring, fused to mine by its own searing heat; a sweet, soul-destroying succuba. (Arthur Wallace, "Passion Before Death," *Spicy Mystery*)

Then I got a surprise. She swayed toward me, wrapped her gorgeous arms around my brisket, fed me a succulent sample of labial fireworks. I could feel her firm breasts cushioning against my chest, throbby, pulsating. "Dan . . . dearest!" she moaned.

My instincts took a long lead off third base. I lifted her, carried her toward the divan on the other side of my living room. . . . As soon as I got my kisser unsucked from hers I panted, "You can dish it out, sweet stuff. Can you take it?" And I caught her in a bear hug, got my mitt fastened on a shoulder strap of the swim suit. . . . Then I let my kisses stray southward along her sleek shoulders. She quivered, locked her arms around me. "Lover . . . !" (Robert Leslie Bellem, "Death Dance," *Spicy Detective*)

This sort of thing had a great many red-blooded males under the age of twenty-five panting, fantasizing, and locking themselves in bathrooms all over America. It was both tame and innocent, however, compared to the kind of jaded sex the "weird menace" or "shudder" pulps were dishing out during the same period. The stories in such magazines as *Terror Tales*, *Horror Stories*, *Dime Mystery*, and *Uncanny Tales* were the sort the Marquis de Sade might have relished—stories bearing such titles as "Love Comes from the Grave," "Bodies Born for Slaughter," "The Pain Master's Bride," "Dead Mates for the Devil's Devotees," and "Bride of the Stone-Age Ripper." The contents of the stories reflected both the titles and illustrations, often to stomach-churning proportions, as in these passages from "Where Beauty Dwelt in Terror" by one Donald Graham (*Uncanny Tales*, March 1940):

Then I saw the fiends begin to caress the girls' bodies with bestially roving hands, committing incredible indecencies on the innocent young maidens, salaciously pawing those twisting, protesting young forms. . . . Several of them were busy lighting a large fire in the center of the dirt floor, heaping buckets of coal over the kerosene-soaked wood that had been piled there. Meantime, others had stripped down two of the prettiest girls hanging by the wall. With whips these two youngsters were forced to get on all fours, then lie flat on their stomachs, head to head. . . .

Now the dozen other girls were taken from the rack, all of them as naked as the day they were born, and some of them modestly tried to cover their nakedness with their arms as they were pushed into the center of the arena. . . .

The dozen girls were to be made to fight a tug of war, with two living bodies forming the center of the rope! But as the unwilling victims picked up their opposite ends of the rope, I saw that the horror of the thing went even further than that! As the whips slashed down on the girls' bare backs, and as the ropes grew taut under the sudden strain, I saw the living victims in the center of the rope lifted clear of the floor—*and carried sideways so that their bodies were suspended directly above the bed of flesh-shriveling coals in the center of the room!* (Italics Graham's)

The narrative goes on like that for another several hundred words, getting nastier and more sadistic by the paragraph—the *ne plus ultra* in sadomasochistic fantasies. It was just such fiction as this that led "public decency" organizations to bring pressure to bear on Culture and other pulp magazine chains (primarily through the U.S. Postal Service, which threatened to revoke the magazines' second-class mailing privileges), and that eventually killed off, or at least drastically altered the focus of, the weird menace and Spicy titles. During the last ten years or so of the pulp era (1942–1953), sex and/or sadism seldom entered into the story lines of magazine crime fiction except by inference.

Despite Hammett having opened up the mystery novel to fictional intimacy, surprisingly few of his contemporaries took immediate advantage of the relaxed attitude toward sex in print; and of those that did, nearly all of whom were of the hard-boiled school, the approach was pallid indeed by comparison to Hammett's. Most publishers seemed disinclined to allow overt sex into their mysteries. There was, however, one notable—and very short-lived— exception.

That exception was an outfit called Valhalla Press, which published one sexy mystery in 1936: *Passion Pulls the Trigger*, by Arthur Wallace. (The back jacket panel of this novel announces a second Valhalla mystery, *Killer's Caress* by Cary Moran, but this book seems never to have been released.) Valhalla was evidently a pulp-related sexploitation venture, inasmuch as its "Authors' Committee" (listed on an inside page of *Passion Pulls the Trigger*) consisted of such names as Robert Leslie Bellem, E. Hoffman Price, Arthur Wallace, and Jerome Severs Perry, all of whom were regular contributors to the Spicy pulps. Further evidence, if any is needed, is the similarity in sexual content and approach of *Passion Pulls the Trigger* to that being offered in the Spicys.

The novel features the lurid activities of private eye Val Vernon, which begin with the murder of an attractive heiress on a Manhattan street corner—a girl who just happens to be nude under her tweed coat. The dust jacket blurb gleefully ballyhoos this fact, and goes on to proclaim:

> With probably the most startling opening chapter of any murder-mystery book yet written, Arthur Wallace weaves a plot with threads of seduction, sin and sanguinary murder. Passion not only pulls the trigger to wipe out the voluptuous actors in this drama, but serves as a motive for crime.
>
> The trail Val Vernon follows leads from the death corner to a Broadway theatre, to a mansion on Long Island, to the haunts of dope fiends, to dingy rooming-

houses. Time and again, the lure of flesh almost proves his undoing. Lust is matched against cunning and the thrill battle rages until the last page.

PASSION PULLS THE TRIGGER is *not* a book for neurotics.

No, indeed. On the other hand, neither is it a book for sex-starved, prurint-minded folks looking for a hot time in print. The sex here is pretty mild stuff, really.

Val stood by while she slipped out of her skirt. A skin-tight peach silk loin cloth encased her delicately curved hips and the flesh fullness of her upper thighs. Val swallowed hard. Some day, if he ever knocked off a case that had some dough hooked on it, he'd marry Betty Reynolds. Now he had to content himself with playing around.

He kept his eyes on her exciting figure while she pulled on a grass skirt. It was too much for him just looking at the sleek, litheness of her body. His fingers itched to touch and his lips to caress. He stepped up behind her, slipped his hands under her armpits and clasped them around her. . . .

The thrill of it all shot down to the pit of Val's stomach. Her hands covered his and pressed them hard on the coned badges of her femininity. He could feel the throbbing pulse-beat of her flesh and the warmth of her curves against his thighs.

She drew her mouth away slowly, letting the dampness linger. "I *must* dress, Val, darling," she panted. "After the show tonight? Huh?"

There was no ignoring her red, moist lips. Val mashed his mouth against them. They parted and met his hotly, avidly. Val could feel her breasts soft against his chest. He put his hands on her hips. The warmth of them dampened his palms.

Before he knew it they were down on the couch. "I went for you the first time I saw you!" Bunny gasped.

Val's hand fell on her knee. Bunny's dress bunched above the rolled tops of her stockings. The smooth skin of her thighs gleamed white.

"Kiss me!" she panted. "Love me!"

She slid down further into the confines of the couch. Her long limbs, made more seductive by sheer hose, were columns of alabaster roundness. Val's mouth went dry. He knew he had to resist the pulsating passion of her. It was going to be hard.

Those are the two most erotic scenes in the book. Poor Val Vernon never does get laid!

This big-tease approach may be one reason Valhalla Press failed to last long in the literary marketplace. Another reason—the main one most mysteries published up until the end of World War II are rather sexless affairs, according to Marie Rodell, Duell, Sloan and Pearce's mystery editor of the period and the author of *Mystery Fiction, Theory and Technique* (1943)—was that "the morality of the average mystery fan is apparently pretty strait-laced. He will countenance murder, but not sexual transgressions." Rodell says further in her how-to treatise:

Sexual perversions, other than sadism, are definitely taboo. And sadism must be presented in its least sexual form. Homosexuality may be hinted at, but never used as an overt and important factor in the story. An author may, in other words, get away with describing a character in such fashion that the reader may conclude the character is homosexual, but he should not so label him. All the other perversions are absolutely beyond the pale.

Even references to normal sex relationships must be carefully watched. Except in the "tough" school, unmarried heroines are expected to be virgins, and sympathetic wives to be faithful to their husbands. (A tearful and truly repentant Magdalene is sometimes possible.) A certain amount of sexual joking between married characters is permissible, so long as it is not crude and does not use any

Anglo-Saxon monosyllables, nor refer too directly to the sexual act. And of course the entire list of possible clues, motives and methods dependent on the natural functions, or on the sexual act, are out of the question.

My, how times have changed! As late as 1942, the attitude of mystery writers toward women and sex could be laughably unsophisticated—even in a so-called hard-boiled novel. Consider the following, for instance, from Britisher John Bentley's American tough-guy imitation, *Mr Marlow Takes to Rye*:

> The giant again laid a hand on Hazel Lawes. This time, his enormous fingers came to rest on the front of her dress, near the throat, clutched the material and pulled.
>   Her scream drowned the sound of ripping cloth. Next instant, the top of the dress was in rags, exposing bared shoulders, a lace-trimmed satin underslip, held up by thin shoulder straps.
>   "You follow the idea, Marlow?" Forbes's tone was cynically contemptuous. "We just repeat the process until you either reveal the hiding place of those jewels, or Miss Lawes is completely naked. I'm quite sure your innate gallantry will assert itself before many minutes have passed. You'll never let her suffer the indignity of parading before us in the nude."
>   The swine was right. He knew I'd cave in long before Steve's greedy, obscene eyes defiled her loveliness.

When mystery writers *did* write about sex in those days, their approach could be downright rhapsodic, even when they were dealing with nothing more erotic than a kiss. This is abundantly true of the great alternative writers—our old friends C. E. "Teet" Carle and Dean M. Dorn, for instance, in their first novel as by Michael Morgan, *Nine More Lives* (1947):

> Our first kiss. It, alone, mattered in my life. For at least a couple of years, we clung to that first kiss, as though the

ending of it would be the awakening from a dream. My
hands came away from her face. My left slid under the
curve of her neck and continued until her head was
cupped in my elbow. I began to straighten up, carrying her
with me. She lay in my ams, her hands cupping the back
of my head, pressing it downward savagely. We were a
molded unity and there was no breath for either of us.

We had to break it. The human body can endure only so
much. I let her face drop away from mine a few inches,
and her hands relaxed their pressure on my head. We
breathed deeply. My eyes opened and fondled her closed
eyelids. I kissed her quickly a dozen times, then paused.

Her eyes opened. "Hi, baby," I whispered.

"Hi, you big louse."

My hands whipped up from under the bed covers, caught
her shoulders, pulled her down on top of me. My arms
encircled her body, fingers moving over the fine-weave of
a sweater. I pressed her to me, rolled over so that she lay
across my hips, her back against the bed. I pulled my
shoulders out of the blankets, put my face above hers,
kissed her eagerly. She was impassive. Her lips were as
unresponsible [sic] as the back of a hand.

Teet Carle, who did most of the writing in his collaborations with
Dorn, was also a master of postcoital dialogue:

". . . . I'm cheap, Bill. I'm not a nice person. I
wouldn't have let you if . . ."

I was across to her side, holding her. "There isn't a
cheap inch on your body."

She looked up at me. "Bill, believe me, it never
happened before. I'm not a pushover."

"Cookie, there's a thing known as love at first sight."

I kissed her. She asked, "Tell me, Bill. You didn't
come to my place just because you knew I'd be easy,
because you thought I'd want you so much I'd hide you
out, because it was your only chance?"

I shouted, "Hey, the chops are burning."

Two major changes in the approach to sex in crime fiction oc-
curred in the late forties. One was the publication of Mickey
Spillane's *I, the Jury*, in 1947; the other was the advent of the
paperback original.

There is nothing soft or gentle about Spillane's approach to
fictional sex—indeed, very little that is even pleasurable. The
women Mike Hammer encounters and beds are tough—most would
just as soon kick him in the balls as they would fondle the same part
of his anatomy—and all too often treacherous and deadly. And of
course his attitude toward them is equally hard-boiled. When his
lover Charlotte turns out to be a murderess at the end of *I, the Jury*,
Hammer deals out the same justice to her as he would to any male
thug or crook: he puts a .45 slug in her belly. And when, dying, she
asks him how he could have done this to her, he says coldly, "It was
easy."

This rough-and-tumble attitude toward sex, with its sadomasochistic overtones, was a refinement of the more overt sadism of the
weird menace pulps of a decade earlier (and there have been further
refinements unto the present). It was so popular with readers that a
great many writers imitated it over the next twenty-odd years,
especially those who toiled in the area of the paperback original.

The promise of voyeuristic sex, as much as the cheap cover price
(twenty-five cents for most titles throughout the fifties), was what
sold millions of originals to a primarily masculine audience.
Whether standard-sized paperbacks published by such "legitimate"
mass-market houses as Gold Medal, Dell, Avon, Lion, Popular
Library, and Ace, or digest-sized books brought out by flash-in-the-
pan entrepreneurs under such unsuccessful imprints as Falcon
Books, Phantom Books, Original Novels, and Rainbow Books,
their cover art was generally as lurid and suggestive as that of the
pulps. In the main, they utilized the "peekaboo" approach: women
depicted either nude (as seen from the side or rear) or with a great
deal of cleavage and/or leg showing, in a variety of provocative poses. Often enough those sexy poses were tempered—or enhanced, if you happened to be of a certain bent—by guns, knives,
and other deadly weapons. Their titles, too, were often mixtures of
sex and violence: *Murder Is My Mistress*, *My Love Is Violent*,

Naked Fury, Love Me—And Die!, *Strip for Violence*, *Let Me Kill You, Sweetheart*, *Whip-Hand*, *The Sadist*, *The Raper*. The same is true of their cover blurbs: "She screamed—but he just kept coming at her . . ." and "She was young and lovely and evil as hell—and I knew from the moment we met I would never get enough of her" and "There was invitation in every lovely curve of her body—an invitation right to the morgue" and "He was stretched on the rack of a corrupt and alien love."

Despite their packaging, however, these and other softcover crime novels published by Gold Medal et al., were primarily standard, if violent mysteries with the sexual content added in varying amounts as spice. And not all of their writers slavishly imitated the Spillane approach to intimacy. Some toned down the sadistic and /or ultramacho aspects; some eliminated them entirely. Others, such as Richard S. Prather, intentionally added elements of ribald humor.

A few authors, happily enough, added elements of ribald humor that *weren't* intentional, and thus fashioned alternative sex-scene classics.

Nothing seems to move writers to greater eloquence than describing either (1) the female anatomy, in particular the bosom; (2) the various aspects of sexual foreplay, as we've already seen demonstrated by Michael Morgan; and (3) the sex act itself. Here are a few nuggets mined from softcover originals published over the past thirty-odd years.

> Her soft flesh rippled up at me. She let it ripple. She uncrossed her legs and the robe fell open still further. Her knees were round and maddeningly pink. The nakedness of her inner thighs graduated enticingly, sensuously slow up to the danger zone. (Michael Avallone, *The Crazy Mixed-Up Corpse*)

> She laughed and the best parts of her jiggled, sort of on a slope. . . . She . . . continued to [laugh] as she slipped into her dressing gown. All sorts of things kept peeping out at me. And believe me, like I said before, she had the things to peep with. (Earl Norman, *Kill Me in Shinjuku*)

She urged me closer, the invitation plainer than if engraved on vellum. I grinned, released her hand, and leaned toward her. Her arms circled my neck and drew me down. A moment later hot, wire-tinged lips were giving me the kind of kiss which makes hair sprout on bald-headed men. I leaned into it, enjoying the surge of unexpected wattage. (Milton K. Ozaki, *Maid for Murder*)

It was a pass all right. A pass with horns on and no matter what kind of cold fish she was she recognized the big fisherman reeling in her lips. I held her vised and planted her mouth deep into my soul. (Michael Avallone, *The Fat Death*)

I put my arms around her and drew her close. She didn't resist. Then her cool arms were around my neck and her warm breasts were digging into my chest and she was kissing me like a French horn in reverse. (Robert O. Saber, *Sucker Bait*)

She was pulverized. As if she had been running all day. Her whole body had that numb tingling feeling that always followed their lovemaking. Slowly, her heartbeat came down to somewhere around normal and the small beads of perspiration stopped excreting with such speed. (Peter C. Herring, *The Murder Business*)

She was breathing hard, firm breasts rumba-ing in the field of [her] Kelly Green [sweater]. (Michael Avallone, *The Hot Body*)

There was music in her ankles, rhythm in her hips, and melody in her brain. And many fires to be quenched. Carmody could not believe that those wide liquid eyes had ever been reserved, lash-guarded. . . .

Lydia's kiss was greedy, mouth to mouth, not lip to lip. . . . Deftly, lightly, he lifted her legs from beneath and at the same time, caught her at the waist. With fine timing, he wafted her up and closed in on her as she rose to chest level. (Hamlin Daly, *Case of the Cancelled Redhead!*)

I looked at her breasts jutting against the soft fabric of her dress, nipples like split infinitives. (Max Byrd, *Fly Away, Jill*)

Of course, not all women in paperback originals were made as lusty or voluptuous as those in the above novels. Nor were all the protagonists portrayed as quite so virile. Some, in fact, are downright unsure of themselves when it comes to sexual matters—unsure, even, of their own body parts. One such refreshingly *un*virile character is Kenn Davis's black San Francisco private eye, Carver Bascombe, as witness the following passage from his most recent case, *Melting Point*:

> She looked directly into his face, the desk lamp throwing irregular shadows onto his lean brown face. Sharon's brown eyes were soft, like molten chocolate drops. Carver squirmed under such a direct stare. Did he still have an erection? He closed his eyes. No, not fully erect. Did she notice? He hoped not.

If the legitimate mass-market paperback houses offered mysteries spiced with sex, the reverse was true of such soft-core porn publishers as Merit Books and Novel Library (both published by Camerarts out of Chicago), Pad Library (Agoura, California), and Vega and Ember (San Diego). Sex was their main commodity, and for the most part the titles and cover blurbs on their criminous (and other) novels made no bones about it.

Camerarts's specialty was the dominant-male, Mike Hammerish approach to sex, as some of its mystery titles indicate: *Dammit, Don't Touch My Broad!*, *Passion Has No Rule Book*, *Playground of Violence*, *Unbelievable 3 & 1 Orgy!*, *Honey Blood*, *Torture Love-Cage*. Their cover copy was even more explicit, as in the following from Glenn Low's *Honey Blood*: "Guys—there's a big illustration on this page [brawny guy, naked to the waist, holding a voluptuous woman in a see-through blouse high over his head] for a big, big man's book. But remember: the one thing that always guarantees you big, exciting manly shockers is this," and there follows a big red arrow angling downward, ostensibly at a logo that reads "Novel Book" but in fact at the front of the brawny guy's pants, where the faintest suggestion of a bulge can be discerned.

Camerarts's writers—among others, Jack Lynn (creator of the ultramacho private eye Tokey Wedge), Bob Tralins, Con Sellers, Mike Skinner (who rather interestingly was black), Jack Savage, Glenn Low, Arnold Marmor, Jerry M. Goff, Jr.—were pretty straightforward in their handling of fictional sex. They wrote it the same way their heroes indulged in it: fast, rough, and raw. Every now and then, though, a little of the eloquence of their more legit brethren slipped in for the delight of us connoisseurs.

The hard tips of her breasts shown through the thin pajama top like giant-size pencil erasers. (Jack Lynn, *Broad Bait*)

Her fingers opened her blouse, then unhooked her brassiere, lifting the warm garment up over the quaking, accentuated ovals. The bra lay up over them, and he felt its fabric touch his forehead in contrast to the smooth breasts that bobbed by his searching mouth. (Bill Anthony, *Animals*)

Her naked breasts pointed at me like a double dare. (Quint Arnold, *Erotic Awakening*)

Her mouth opened hungrily and we started a delicious game of tongue tag. This went on for some time, and the ecstasy button on both of us was pushed in all the way. (Steve Lee, *Uninhibited Females*)

God! I thought. In her dance she incarnates passion by conveying the two halves which compose it. . . . In this instant she is truly a beautiful woman because she looks like womanhood. . . . Indeed, I thought, Dawn spoke with her whole tremulous body undulating to her fingers—all in rhythm, as the sea runs up and down the

beach and is never at rest, but seems to obey a general line
of curve. (Jerry M. Goff, Jr., *Rocco's Babe*)

The blonde stretched flat on her back. Hips bouncing.
Thighs quivering. Toes beckoning. And . . . she fero-
ciously massaged her own breasts, and the nipples rose
like pink silos bursting with harvested emotions. (Louis
Fisher, *Wild Party*)

Pad Library, on the other hand, went in for sleaze of a milder and
more disguised sort. Its books carried such sedate titles as *Security
Risk* and *Devil Girls* and were a showcase for the literary endeavors
of Ed Wood, Jr. Yes, that's right, the very same Ed Wood, Jr., who
gave us such immortal film classics as *Glen and Glenda* (the
heartwarming story of a crack-brained transvestite, whose first
incarnation was as a novel called *Killer in Drag*) and the
magnificent Bela Lugosi swan song that some experts consider the
single worst film ever produced, *Plan Nine from Outer Space*.
Wood, as you'll note from the following excerpt, was every bit as
alternative a prose stylist as he was a filmmaker.

Without taking her lips from his, she rose from the chair
and when she stood facing him, she put her arms around
his waist and he around hers, and they locked into an
embrace which would not be satisfied until they had
searched out each other's secrets. . . .
    They melted to the demand of lust and her blue mohair
cardigan fell from her shoulders to lop itself over the chair
she had been seated on. When they walked across the
stage toward a dressing room there was only one thing in
mind—Lust—The domineering factor of life. . . .
    And they took each other in the cold dressing room.
And when they were finished, there were few secrets left
for them to explore. Their eyes met and their mouths met,
and they were in tune to each other for that one, brief last
gasp as they expounded to each other. (*Security Risk*)

And finally we have Vega Books and Ember Library, published
by Corinth Publications of San Diego. (Corinth, you may remem-

ber, was the outfit that got itself sued out of business in the late sixties for reprinting pulp novels featuring such super-heroes as the Phantom, Secret Agent X, Operator 5, and Dusty Ayres without bothering to secure permission from the copyright holders.) Its approach to fictional sex was the graphic one—as euphemistically graphic as the law would allow in the mid-sixties. And what it specialized in was the rather odd combination of "serious" homosexual novels and wild and wacky heterosexual spy spoofs.

The spy spoofs were written by someone calling himself Gene Cross, which is also the name of the narrator (*The Wild Mare Affair*, *The Tigerlily Affair*), and by Clyde Allison (William Knowles), the undisputed master of the soft-core porn novel. The Allison titles— eighteen in all, published between 1965 and 1968—are unabashed parodies of James Bond. They feature the outlandish exploits of the otherwise unnamed Agent 0008, mankind's only hope against the power- (and sex-) mad female operatives of SADISTO and KRUNCH; they bear such titles as *Sadisto Royale*, *Platypussy*, *Agent 0008 Meets Modesta Blaze*, and *Agent 0008 Meets Gnatman*; and they are the ultimate not only in soft-core porn novels but in goofy satire: by turns raunchy, mad, silly, ingenious, childish, horribly sexist, and very funny.

Allison was nothing if not inventive. Only he could have devised a sex scene which utilizes a trapeze high above a packed circus arena, some incredible aerial acrobatics, a conjoined plunge into a safety net, and certain astonishing trampoline antics. I can't go into specifics; this is, after all, only a PG-rated book. But you get the idea.

And only he could have devised climactic scenes such as this one from the rather tamely titled *Lost Bomb*:

> Things looked confusing. There was, I decided while sitting astride Elephantra [a gigantic Indian elephant], who was still waving the naked blonde in the air above her, as the five nude KRUNCH girls ravished their way through the crowd, while the machine gun stuttered shatteringly and bullets flew everywhere, as the helicopter continued clattering around above us with its rotors

sending ten million in small bills flying in all directions over the berserk crowd, there was, I concluded, clutching the Ming vase under my arm, only one thing to do.

And I did it.

I had Elephantra make an illegal left turn off Fifth Avenue and urged her to flee the scene.

As we crunched through the milling, hysterical crowd, I heard . . . the distant voice of the *Village Vice* drama critic deride, "Boo! Hiss! Highly derivative!"

Allison, as the above indicates, was fond of puns, literary references, film references, all sorts of satirical asides to the reader, and private jokes which surely escaped the notice, not to mention the comprehension, of ninety-nine percent of his readers. Not only is the following an example of his literate playfulness, it also wins hands-down the Pronzini Award for Crime Fiction's All-Time Greatest *Coitus Interruptus* Scene.

The phone rang.

Anha swore shockingly in Swahili [she's multilingual], rolled over and up, answered her phone.

"All right," she snarled, "so I'll close the venetian blinds, if it bothers you that much. You know, you don't have to stare out the window. All right, I don't want my doorbell to ring. I'll close them!"

She slammed down the phone, strode to the windows, snapped shut the blinds while cursing fluently in Sanskrit.

"Nosey neighbor across the street?" I inquired.

"I'll say," snapped Anha. "You'd think he disliked females, the way he carries on every time I throw an orgy with my blinds open. The fat slob. He's so overweight I honestly don't know how he manages to climb four stories to his orchid room twice a day."

"Maybe he has an elevator, whoever he is," I suggested.

"Maybe," conceded Anha. "I like everything about living in the West Thirties except that stout jerk who lives across the street." (*The Lost Bomb*)

As for Allison on his favorite subject, here are a few representative samples:

> "Well," whispered Modesta, "if sex doesn't sap your strength—here . . ."
> Something tinkled at my feet.
> I picked it up. A key.
> "It's the key to my metal bikini," murmured Modesta. "The metal loin cloth, that is. You don't need a key for my metal bra, it has combination locks. You just twiddle with my knobs."
> "Any time . . ." I viriled, moving toward her. (*Agent 0008 Meets Modesta Blaze*)

> Her breasts were twin towers of sexual power, dual cupolas of quivering femininity . . . twin rounded peaks of swaying rapture, creamy hemispheres of fun flesh tipped by shell-pink aureoles from which sprouted deep crimson nipples. . . . I sheathed my teeth with my lips and gently bit and chewed her glee globes while my hands stroked the flowing length of her roller-coaster-curved torso. (*The Sex-Ray*)

> "Ahhhhhhh!" she sighed, as I plunged like a ramrod into the glorious gun-barrel of her loaded loins. (*Agent 0008 Meets Modesta Blaze*)

In the seventies and eighties the depiction of sex in the mystery and suspense novel has become increasingly more clinical—all manner of sex, from the tender to the violent to the depraved. Nothing is left to the imagination these days, which is no doubt the reason fictional intimacy has become something of a bore. Taking all the mystery out of sex is like taking all the mystery out of a detective novel: what you've got left is a bunch of clear-cut details leading to an obvious conclusion, and therefore no damn suspense.

Nevertheless, it is precisely because of its graphic and clinical nature that the Alternative Sex Scene To End All Alternative Sex Scenes achieves that lofty distinction. This "erotic" masterpiece was authored in 1972 by Roland Puccetti, an expert in mind–body problems affiliated with the Philosophy Department of Dalhousie University in Nova Scotia, as part of his novel *The Death of the Führer*—one of those "Hitler is still alive!" exercises in serious nonsense. In this one, it is postulated that Adolph did not really die in his Berlin bunker in 1945, that through warped Nazi ingenuity and the wonders of modern medical science the Führer's evil brain was saved from extinction and secretly lives and plots on.

No writer present or future could ever hope to surpass the passages which follow. No writer in his right mind would even hope to try. They are truly the ultimate, shining example of sex rearing its *ugly* head in crime fiction—a scene so mind-boggling that it must be quoted more or less in its entirety to be fully savored.

Here, then, the Alternative Sex Scene To End All Alternative Sex Scenes:

> I forced myself to look at her face. It was twisting and turning too, the eyes closed and her lips parted in a moan. No, it wasn't a moan. It was a single word murmured over and over again: BITTE, BITTE, BITTE. I began whispering in turn, slowly, to match the strokes of my body, the impact of moist flesh on moist flesh. It became a weird incantation as I plunged on and on.
>
> "Gerda oh my darling Gerda oh can you know what this means to me to have seen you wanted you now to have you like this really it is the greatest day of my life it is as if I came over the castle wall to die and woke up in heaven and you know Gerda it may sound silly but every time I was near you even at the tea party this afternoon and now tonight I felt yes it is silly but I felt in the presence of the Führer my beloved can it be he is somehow still with us and near us oh Gerda I am as certain of this as intuition can make it tell me darling am I right oh Gerda how my happiness would be complete if I could just see him again and hear his voice I don't care how he has changed Gerda is he not in this castle have I not perhaps even met him and did not know it only you I am sure can tell me yes tell me who he is. . . ."

Her fingers dug into my arms with sharp nails, her back arched spasmodically, she started to pull me deep down into a bottomless pit. Somewhere within my body a train of cold liquid left its station, gathered speed with relentless fury and plunged on to its destination.

Gerda's eyes opened widely now. The pupils looked dark in the fire glow . . . and somehow beyond them and behind them there was a deep rustling of Teutonic forests, of shadowy predators roaming in the night. Only then, at the instant of our climax, did I see suddenly etched in my brain the dust-laden map in the Führerbunker with arrows slashing into Berlin. . . . Only then did I raise my trembling, terribly tired fingers to her head, slide them under the golden hair and feel the bony ridge across her skull. Only then did her lips part to give the fateful cry.

"ICH BIN DER FÜHRER."

8

Big Brother Is Watching

". . . I say, Fitzhugh, why not go to the club? Nobody could touch you at the club!"

Fitzhugh's lips twitched queerly.

"I—er—I imagine I'd be asked to resign if a gang of Chinese murderers came into the club after me."

—Murray Leinster,
Murder Will Out, 1932

When you prospect for alternative gold, as I wrote in Chapter 3, you're liable to find it just about anywhere. I meant that literally. Look long enough and often enough, and you can unearth not only nuggets but an occasional bonanza hidden away in the mountains of *good* crime fiction by *good* writers—the work of some of the best writers in the genre, in fact.

Every author—especially if he or she (1) started young and oh so innocent and (2) has created a large body of work—suffers a blind lapse now and then, when he/she not only constructs something of blush-making dimensions but compounds the felony by allowing it to be published. (I quoted *my* biggest alternative nugget in the preface to *Gun in Cheek*; inasmuch as I was born without masochistic tendencies, I am not going to repeat it here. Go look it up if you're interested.) Still, we ought to know better, even in the early stages of our careers. Eh? Professionalism and all that sort of thing.

This chapter, then, is by way of a small chastisement of each of those nonalternative writers who have slipped a time or two over the years. And a warning to the rest to take extra care with your similes, your metaphors, your descriptive passages, your dialogue. One small misstep could land *you* in a book of this sort. Big Brother is watching.

We'll begin with that rarest of alternative strikes, the Hall of Fame classic composed by a writer who has otherwise distinguished himself with a body of good work. Fortunately in this case, the writer is not (or was not) a specialist in mystery and suspense fiction, nor is his distinguished body of work in this field. His speciality, rather, was science fiction, to which genre he contributed such innovative short stories as "First Contact," "Doomsday Deferred," and "Exploration Team," and such novels as *Murder of the U.S.A.* (1946), an interesting blend of s-f and the deductive mystery in which the protagonist solves the enigma of which country dropped three hundred A-bombs on U.S. cities.

Name: Murray Leinster, a.k.a. Will F. Jenkins.

Alternative classic: *Murder Will Out* (1932).

In the early years of his long and productive career, Leinster wrote several uninspired mysteries (and several rather mediocre Westerns as well). The first and best of his crime novels was *Scalps* (1930); the second was *Murder Madness* (1931). *Murder Will Out* was the third. Unlike the first two, this glittering treasure trove was not published in the United States; only John Hamilton Ltd. in England saw fit to bring it out. What made Hamilton see fit is not clear, unless it was felt that they, like so many others of the period, could cash in on the then-great popularity of Sax Rohmer and Dr. Fu Manchu.

Murder Will Out, you see, is a Yellow Peril novel . . . sort of. It's not the same type of Fu Manchu pie baked by Tom Roan in *The Dragon Strikes Back* (see *Gun in Cheek*) or Anthony Rud in *The Stuffed Men*; the recipe here is one of Leinster's own special devising. And an epicurean pie it is, too.

Here are the ingredients:

A fellow named Fitzhugh (rich, white, and terrified) asks his friend Leonard Staunton (rich, white, and heroic) for help. Seems he is being "blackmailed" (actually it's an extortion plot) by a Chinese secret society that keeps sending him notes signed with elaborate purple hieroglyphs—that is, an "ideogram in the archaic form of Chinese writing, which now is reserved for wall-mottoes, book-titles, and the like." The notes demand that Fitzhugh fork over one hundred thousand dollars; the latest one says, cryptically, "To-night at Midnight." Understandably, this has Fitzhugh gabbling a bit. Staunton, in his sympathetic fashion, tells him that he's "nervous as a Follies girl with clothes on!" According to Leinster, Fitzhugh's hands "quivered like a tuning fork," which surely indicates a very high level of agitation.

Staunton says he'll help and sends his pal off to the protective confines of their mutual club. Then he hies himself out to Long Island, where his fiancée, Jeanne, her naval officer brother, Jack, and her father, Senator Baldwin, just happen to be planning a Chinese garden party at the family estate. It is at the estate, Wyndale, that things begin to heat up: Staunton receives an anonymous telephone call from a Chinese who says that "Mist' Fitzhugh will be executed at twelve o'clock to-night," and immediately leaves for Manhattan, having deemed this personal message much more sinister than the purple-hieroglyph notes and Fitzhugh's quivering hands. Jeanne and Jack decide to follow when another purple-hieroglyph message is delivered to them. While speeding along toward New York, Jeanne notices that a car is following her little roadster; Jack isn't too worried at the outset, though: "So it is," he says. "But since we are ahead of it, it would seem to be necessary that it should be behind us."

But then the following car speeds up, seems to be trying to overtake them. A frantic chase ensues, during which one of the tires blows out—the result of an assassin's bullet, Jeanne thinks. She manages to stop the car safely. As she does, "the other car came roaring up, braked wildly, and half-rolled, half-skidded to a stop." A bunch of Chinese guys pile out of it. And Jack, brave fellow that he is, piles out of the roadster with his trusty revolver in hand.

"Stick 'em up!" he orders. "Put your hands up or I'll begin to blow holes in some of you!"

Well, the Chinese guys stick 'em up. And one of them says, "Please. We are poor acrobats and have little money for to rob, also being paid by cheque. Please!" See, it was all a mistake; they aren't really members of the Society of the Purple Hieroglyph, just the entertainers from Senator Baldwin's Chinese garden party who are miffed at not having been paid in cash so they could cheat the IRS.

Lunacy of a different sort reigns in Manhattan, where Staunton tries to save Fitzhugh from his midnight date with death. Just as it seems he's succeeded, Fitzhugh is kidnapped by a Chinese taxi driver—and his body is later found with the head blown off by a shotgun blast. Enter Captain Morgan of the NYPD and a stout stranger who identifies himself as Lieutenant Condon, British Secret Service, Shanghai, China. During a meeting of these minds (such as they are) in Staunton's office, another purple-hieroglyph note turns up unexpectedly. How *do* these messages keep appearing in unlikely places? Could it be . . . Oriental magic?

More lunacy, if not more magic, ensues: Condon gives Staunton a letter which he says was in the pocket of Fitzhugh's jacket and which Fitzhugh must have written earlier that night, before he was kidnapped and had his head blown off, because "he felt sure he was going to be killed." It asks that he be buried in Woodlawn Cemetery the following midnight with Staunton as one of the pallbearers. Everybody agrees that this is a pretty queer request; but that doesn't stop them from going to the graveyard to carry out Fitzhugh's last wishes. Jeanne goes along, too, for no good reason, and tries to lighten things up, "to be ribald," by looking at the undertaker's man and saying, "He has—he has such a lovely graveside manner."

In the midst of the eerie proceedings at Woodlawn, a doctor named Mansfield—a collector of porcelains whose presence at the burial Fitzhugh specifically (and for no explained reason) requested—spots a card in one of the floral offerings that has been made of "roses and carnations, queerly dyed" to represent a purple hieroglyph. The card says, "In the midst of life we are in death," which is a little vague and not very sinister; so the wily Orientals, evidently realizing their mistake, follow it up with another card that contains a somewhat more cryptic message: "One o'clock tonight."

What happens at one o'clock? Why, Doctor Mansfield is poisoned by a cigarette whose burning paper and ash form a purple hieroglyph (neat trick!). Ah, but Mansfield doesn't immediately succumb; there's still hope for him, Condon informs Staunton, because the poison is something called "Flower of Oblivion . . . one of the opium group" and there is "an absolute and positive antidote."

Mansfield weakly (and conveniently) claims to have the antidote in his rooms in Brooklyn, toxicology being his field of expertise, so they all rush out to Flatbush in a desperate attempt to save his life. When they arrive Mansfield uncorks a bottle filled with clear liquid, swallows the contents, and announces with relief, "Beat 'em! That—that will work like magic." But he's wrong. The canny villains have gotten there first and substituted water for the antidote: instead of being saved, the doctor keels over and Condon pronounces him defunct.

The scene shifts back to Wyndale, the Baldwins' Long Island estate, but not before Mansfield's body mysteriously disappears and still another purple-hieroglyph note turns up. This one says: "Mr. Leonard Staunton is informed that in part because of his meddling in the affairs of the Society whose symbol is below, he will shortly receive the orders of the Society as to what sum he is to pay, and how he is to pay it. He is informed that it will do him no good to appeal to the police, and that if he behaves in an undesirable fashion, Miss Jeanne Baldwin will be executed to convince him of the necessity of obedience."

What to do, what to do? More cryptic messages. More anonymous telephone calls. More hand-wringing. What to do, what to do? Decision: Senator Baldwin calls in the "Federal Secret Service," not to mention Captain Morgan, Lieutenant Condon, a passel of New York State troopers, *and* four private detectives—a small army to guard Wyndale from an invasion by the Society of the Purple Hieroglyph. One of the Feds says confidently, "You're guarded, Senator, a good deal more carefully than the President of the United States.

Sure. Right.

Two more notes materialize, one demanding that Staunton appear at a pagoda on the estate grounds, where "the Head of the Society will appear before him and communicate to him the orders of the Society as to the sum he is to pay and the manner of its payment." Before Leonard goes to the pagoda, while Condon is out prowling the grounds (where the Feds et al. are likewise on patrol), explosions and a fire occur inside the main house; everyone rushes in, thinking the Chinese villains have somehow managed to breach security, but of course it's only a ruse to draw everyone's attention away from the pagoda. When Staunton finally does go there he finds a bloodstained dagger, Condon's cigar (but no sign of the lieutenant), and the inevitable purple hieroglyph.

Still another communication instructs Staunton to bring five hundred thousand dollars to the last buoy of the Ambrose Channel outside New York Harbor and to do so by motorboat (as opposed to swimming, perhaps). Staunton reluctantly agrees. And Senator Baldwin reluctantly raises the dough.

It is on the harbor, on a dark and stormy night, that the exciting climax takes place. A second speedboat approaches Staunton's craft, occupied by three men. One of them, speaking in Chinese dialect, demands the money. But Staunton and Jack Baldwin have a surprise ready for them instead—a little magic of their own. It so happens that Jack (a naval officer, remember?) has convinced his commander to bring the S-35 submarine they're serving on to the rendezvous. The sub looms up out of the water so fast that the three Chinese in the speedboat have no time to escape (*some* submarine!). Sailors and marines quickly capture them.

And you'll no doubt be flabbergasted, if not actually prostrated by amazement, to learn that the three men *aren't* Chinese after all. *"Unmasked now and standing shamefacedly in the bright electric light in the belly of the submarine . . . were Fitzhugh, Mansfield, and Condon—the three dead men, very much alive!"* (Italics Leinster's.)

They were the ones leaving all the notes around for each other to find; *they* were the dastards behind the extortion scheme. Just the three of them. Three evil white guys masquerading as Celestials under the guise of a phony Society of the Purple Hieroglyph.

Now you know why Leinster's Yellow Peril recipe is so unique. What he so cunningly cooked up here is an Oriental-villain pie which does not contain a single Oriental villain!

The main plot ingredients of *Murder Will Out* are not the only ones that make it such a savory dish. Leinster's prose lends plenty of spice. For instance, there is his cauliflower ear for Chinese dialect:

> "We just sell Senator Baldwin li'l piecee porcelain of Pen-Ho, ma'am."

And his passion for adverbs to modify the word "said"—in particular the adverb "comfortably," which he was fond of using in some rather curious contexts:

> Leonard said comfortably:
> "My bootlegger has committed a quite pardonable gin this time. I'll get you a drink."

> "A long cool drink is what you need," said Leonard comfortably. "This weather is enough to make anybody nervous. It is hot as the devil!"

> "I'm on leave," Condon added comfortably, "and this is not official business with me."

> "I said," said Condon comfortably, "that I had evidence. I found Mr. Fitzhugh's body this morning."

> "Just a moment, Mr. Staunton," he said comfortably. "At what time did you come in?"

> "Do you realize," he asked comfortably, "that both of us—you and I—have now attracted the attention of the Society of the Purple Hieroglyph?"

> Lieutenant Condon smiled drily.
> "Perhaps," he said comfortably, "they think it will make it more difficult for us to interest the police."

"Why," said Condon comfortably, "we've gone over the pagoda almost with microscopes. No one is hidden there."

And his (repetitive) descriptive powers:

Over all the house a deep silence brooded, and over the wide-spreading gardens the infinite peacefulness of a summer night held sway. There was the chirping of innumerable insects, which formed a sustained shrill clamor without pause or alteration of tone. . . . The mutter of motor-cycle engines on the roadway outside was an anomaly, to be sure, but over the star-lit garden paths small bats flitted noiselessly, and somewhere nearby a whipporwill repeated its unspeakably monotonous cry, and the stars in their course blinked and twinkled in their customarily inane fashion.

Then the peace and quietness of Wyndale was shattered indeed. It seemed for a moment as if the shrubbery itself were on the move. The stars blinked down inanely at men running madly, desperately, toward the house.

And his portrayal of young love:

Leonard did kiss her. But the romantic rapture that had made them both so idiotically happy just before sundown was replaced by a tense anxiety which was no less romantic, but was much less comfortable.

And finally, his perfect grasp of the setting of his story:

The normal audience for the departure of a speedboat, the capsizing of a canoe, the irritated cranking of a motor, or any other diverting activity in this section [of New York City] is in the neighborhood of two hundred and fifty people.

And here I thought New Yorkers were blasé about *every-thing*. . . .

Alternative classics by respected writers being as rare as they are, I'll fill out this chapter with several "good gold" nuggets of various types and sizes.

In the category of Fractured Similes and Metaphors:

> In spite of his weathered appearance he looked like a drinker. (Raymond Chandler, *The Lady in the Lake*)

> Even Captain Woofer had excused their failure to keep the dates with Internal Affairs. But Captain Woofer was still monomaniacal, and would have gladly nailed a gold piece to the mast if he thought a reward would harpoon the swine who had been tormenting him so mercilessly. (Joseph Wambaugh, *The Glitter Dome*)

> And I think it's interesting, if irrelevent, to note how a person out on the sidelines of a certain chain of events can make so great a dent in those events without even trying. (Max Allan Collins, *The Baby Blue Rip-Off*)

> My life was an ice floe that had broken up at sea, with the different chunks floating off in different directions. Nothing was ever going to come together, in this case or out of it. (Lawrence Block, *Eight Million Ways To Die*)

> Darius' voice was tight as a drumhead, dripping bitterness like acid from a cracked battery. (George C. Chesbro, *City of Whispering Stone*)

> She pointed an arm as long as a windmill's across to a yellow stucco house that in some odd disintegrated way looked not unlike herself. (Leslie Ford, *Siren in the Night*)

> It was a full summer in Boston and the heat sat on the city like a possessive parent. (Robert B. Parker, *Taming a Seahorse*)

The category of Anatomical Oddities:

She lay on her back, arms and legs akimbo. (Ed McBain, *Ghosts*)

A quick smile shot through Thorne's eyes. (Leslie Ford, *Siren in the Night*)

Big Brennan, badge pinned to the light summer jacket over his cream-colored shirt, stood with his hands on his hips, gunbutt jutting, and pushed his Stetson back on his head. (Max Allan Collins, *A Shroud for Aquarius*)

The category of Strange Phenomena:

And with this he stopped short, mopped his forehead with his handkerchief, and polished the lenses of his pince-nez with absent fingers. (Ellery Queen, *The French Powder Mystery*)

About him, the maple-wood furniture of suite seven stood shivering in the chill of a December morning. (Earl Derr Biggers, *Seven Keys to Baldpate*)

The category of Author Omniscience:

Staying out of the hot clutches of the Mafia might be the most difficult accomplishment of his checkered career, but if he could survive that cliche he might be able to outlast anything. (Leslie Charteris, *Vendetta for the Saint*)

The category of Narrative Hooks, First-Sentence-of-a-Novel Division:

Cyrus Hatch aroused himself. (Frederick C. Davis, *Let the Skeletons Rattle*)

The category of Whacky Word Choices:

Constable Lee had one of his shoes off and was thoughtfully pouring its boatload of water onto the floor. (William Marshall, *Perfect End*)

"But we must first, while there is still time, exercise the malign being that is Gilles de Rais so that he can no longer menace the world of the living." (Stuart Towne [Clayton Rawson], *Death Out of Thin Air*)

The category of Specialized Knowledge, Handgun Division:

[Lieutenant Freevich] had fired almost a complete round of ammunition. (Hugh Pentecost, *The Steel Palace*)

The category of Unintentional Puns:

"Plaza 3-7918," Emily read aloud. "Henry, doesn't that ring a bell?" (Margaret Scherf, *The Green Plaid Pants*)

Then, once out of the town, there seemed to be nothing but the endless landscape of snow and trees, the occasional lorry, or a car heading back towards the last town, or great monster log-bearing trucks, lumbering in either direction. (John Gardner, *Icebreaker*)

The category of Dubious Claims, Language Division:

We spent the next few minutes discussing the fact that Miss Larsson was fascinated by private detectives because she'd learned English with the help of *Alfred Hitchcock's Mystery Magazine*. (George C. Chesbro, *City of Whispering Stone*)

The category of Medical Marvels:

[Cult leader] Simeon Taylor was killed—beheaded and left to die on a roadside in a Southern town. (Hugh Pentecost, *Sow Death, Reap Death*)

The category of "Huh?":

She had a full bosom like a breastplate, looked at her watch impatiently. (Michael Collins, *Freak*)

And finally, the category of Dream Sequences (and winner of the Pronzini Award for Best Alternative Nugget by a Major Writer):

Gerald Whittaker dreamed he was standing in a muddy plain. It was smooth, dark gray ooze. The landscape was flat and even and empty, the sky sullen with fast rushing clouds. The clouds were gray too, a dirty gray with ragged fingers, and they came so close overhead he wanted to duck. And they came from behind, sweeping off to the far horizon, running away.

Gerald Whittaker was all alone in his landscape. There was not so much as a broken sapling, not so much as a dried leaf. And a cold wind was wailing. He could hear it now, the hollow moaning that from time to time rose to a keening shrill of anger.

The wind came from his rear too, and it drove the clouds like whip-lashed horses. (Hillary Waugh, *Parrish for the Defense*)

9

Confessions Of A B-Movie Junkie

Bad alibi like dead fish—cannot stand test of time.
    —Charlie Chan in
    Charlie Chan in Panama, 1940

Even now, automobile and assistants outside loaded for trip to distant city . . . uh, automobile loaded, not assistants.
    —Charlie Chan in
    Dark Alibi, 1946

One of my shortcomings, as has been pointed out to me on more than one occasion, is that I have an addictive personality. I can't do anything in moderation; overindulgence is my middle name. Give me one potato chip and I'll eat the whole bag. Give me one alternative classic and pretty soon I'm not only wallowing in the things, I'm writing books about them.

It's no different with B-grade crime films from the thirties and forties. Many of which, if you didn't already know it, are filmdom's version of alternative classics. I've been hooked for years on those grainy, flickering, black-and-white Bs—in particular the ones featuring series sleuths: Mr. Moto. Torchy Blane. The Saint. The Falcon. Boston Blackie. The Crime Doctor.

And Charlie Chan, the most insidiously addictive of them all. Ah, Charlie Chan. . . .

I don't remember the exact date I saw my first Chan film, though I do remember the title—*Charlie Chan on Broadway*—and that it was sometime during my impressionable, formative years. The willingness for experimentation was rife in me in those days; I had already had my first beer and my first unclean thought. So when a friend invited me to his house one afternoon while his parents and siblings were out, to try my first Chan, I accepted with nervous anticipation. We sat in his darkened living room, and for an hour and a half we tripped out on the combined effects of Warner Oland (the best of the screen Chans, who reprised his role sixteen times before his untimely death in 1937), Keye Luke (Chan's Number One Son Lee in eight early films), Douglas Fowley, William Demarest, Marc Lawrence, and Lon Chaney, Jr., in a brief but psychedelic walk-on. I marveled at Charlie's wisdom, I giggled at Lee's bumbling attempts to become a master detective like his father, I sat damp-palmed as the suspense built to its climax. I even guessed the identity of the murderer.

I was hooked.

At first, though, I could take Chan or leave him alone. He was plentiful in those days; you could get him just about any Saturday afternoon, and often on weekday evenings, too. Sometimes I would go three or four months without even *wanting* a fix, much less needing one. Still, on an average of one Saturday a month I would find myself cinematically stoned before the tube. I didn't even mind the commercials; they only heightened the delicious anticipation at what lay ahead, the rush I would receive when, for example, the lights went out (as they often did in Chan films) and another corpse turned up.

Then, in 1970, I moved to Europe to pursue my writing career, and for three years I did not see a single Chan film. Most of the time it wasn't so bad; I had plenty of other things to occupy my time and my mind. Oh, I admit that I felt the craving now and then, and that on one trip to New York I became sulky and abusive when plans to watch *Charlie Chan in Monte Carlo* went awry. But all in all, those three years were not difficult. For I knew that someday I would move back to San Francisco, and that when I did Charlie and Lee and Number Two Son Jimmy and Birmingham Brown and all the rest would be waiting there for me.

Only . . . they weren't.

Things had changed drastically in San Francisco during my absence. Minorities had gathered a unified strength and were being paid attention to by, among others, the program directors of the various television channels. The Chinese community felt that the Chan films were a sham, owing to the fact that the great Chinese detective had never once been portrayed by a Chinese. (The two Orientals who played him in silent films, George Kuwa and Kamiyama Sojin, were Japanese; all the others—E. P. Park, Warner Oland, Sidney Toler, and Roland Winters—were Caucasians.) They felt that although Keye Luke, Victor Sen Yung (Jimmy), Benson Fong (Number Three Son Tommy), and Frances Chan (daughter Frances) *were* Chinese, the characters they played were little more than foils and buffoons, and that the Chinese way of life and thought were badly distorted by these depictions. And the black community felt that the antics of Birmingham Brown, as portrayed by Mantan Moreland, and of his cousin Chattanooga, as portrayed by Willie Best, were racial stereotyping at its most offensive. All with just cause, of course. They were *right*, the Chinese and the blacks, and never mind that the Chan films were a product of a different if less enlightened time and could be viewed by some of us as entertainment in spite of their shortcomings.

Never mind, too, that some of us *needed* those films.

Those dark months of 1973–1974 were when my craving began to get out of hand. I bought a powerful antenna for my TV set so I could pick up a San Jose UHF channel that occasionally, being far enough south of San Francisco to embolden its ownership, showed a Chan film. But then I moved to a different neighborhood, and no manner of antenna could pick up the San Jose station. (This was in the days before cable hookups, remember.) My desire increased twofold. I would travel around to the homes of friends and relatives, arriving at opportune times and casually suggesting that we "watch a few minutes of one of those old, you know, Charlie Chan movies" that "just happened" to be on. And I wouldn't take no for an answer either.

There's no telling what might have happened if it hadn't been for the advent of the video recorder. This wonderful machine was my salvation. Oh, not at first; at first, as you might expect, it seemed a Chan addict's dream come true—a means of providing myself with a permanent, inexpensive, and inexhaustible supply of his cinematic adventures. I bought some tapes here and there and made arrangements with a friend in Washington, D.C., where many of the Chans were being shown on a regular basis, to tape others for me. Before long I had forty-two of the forty-seven Chan films made between 1926 and 1949. And before long, too, I was lying blear-eyed in front of the flickering tube for days on end, watching one film after another, some of them again and again and again, until—

Until there was no longer any rush, any kick, any high.

Until I began to lose interest.

I knew all the plots by heart, down to the minutest detail in those of my favorites—*Charlie Chan at the Circus, Charlie Chan in Reno, Charlie Chan on Treasure Island.* I could recite lengthy exchanges of dialogue verbatim. I knew the exact moment Rita Hayworth (then billed as Rita Cansino) would make her entry in *Charlie Chan in Egypt*, her first film role. I knew that Boris Karloff would get shot in the head near the end of *Charlie Chan at the Opera* and that he would miraculously survive. I had timed to the second the appearance of Erik Rhodes in *Charlie Chan in Paris*, so I could tune out what is surely the *worst* drunk act ever committed to film. I knew that *Charlie Chan on Treasure Island*, with Cesar Romero and Douglas Dumbrille, not only had the best script of all the Chan movies but also had the best atmosphere; and that the one with the *worst* script and atmosphere, other than the six Roland Winters debacles made on minuscule budgets in the late forties, was *Charlie Chan in Rio*—a film exactly one hour in length, fifty-nine minutes of which contain nothing of any interest. Yes, and I knew something else, too, something very few people alive today know: the exact wording of nearly every aphorism and pithy observation uttered by a screen Charlie for the enlightenment and amusement of millions since 1931.

I had, truly, ODed on Charlie Chan. And as a result, I had kicked the Chan habit—or, more properly, *it* had kicked *me*!

I'd be a liar if I said that I've never backslid just a little, never watched a Chan film since. I have, but only on rare occasions, only as a detached observer, only in the company of others, and only one at a sitting. I'm not afraid of becoming addicted again; but I am afraid of reliving *all* those familiar plots, hearing *all* that familiar dialogue. It's bad enough that even now, with no effort whatsoever, I can recall the wit and wisdom of Charlie Chan from more than fifteen of his screen cases. . . .

The Black Camel, (1931)

Always harder to keep murder secrets than for eggs to bounce on sidewalk.

Sometimes very difficult to pick up pumpkin with one finger.

Cashimo, you are zebra—sport-model jackass.

Soap and water can never change perfume of billy-goat.

Only very clever man can bite pie without breaking crust.

Charlie Chan in Paris (1935)

Joy in heart better than bullet.

Many strange crimes have been committed in sewers of Paris.

Charlie Chan in Egypt (1935)

Cannot believe piece of carved stone contain evil—unless dropped on foot.

Charlie Chan's Secret (1936)

Most precious gift to be able to cross bridge to honorable ancesters before arriving. (?)

Punch in ribs more desirable than shot in back.

Charlie Chan at the Circus (1936)

Facts like photographic film—must be exposed before developing.

Hm, very peculiar. Man already married announce engagement to trapeze lady.

Evidence like nose on anteater—very plain.

Charlie Chan at the Racetrack (1936)

Most murders result from violence—and murder without bloodstains like Amos without Andy.

Charlie Chan at the Opera (1936)

When fear attack brain, tongue wave distress signal.

Charlie Chan at the Olympics (1937)

Truth like football—receive many kicks before reaching goal.

Letter like banana—outer skin must be removed before contents revealed.

Charlie Chan on Broadway (1937)

Mud of bewilderment now begin to clear from pool of thought.

Murder case like revolving door—when one side close, other side open.

Charlie Chan in Honolulu (1938)

When money talks, few are deaf. (E. F. Hutton himself must have watched this film.)

Have humble impression psychiatry of no value when brain cease to function.

Pardon, gentleman, was of opinion this cabin only occupied by corpse.

Opinion like tea leaf in hot water—both need time for brewing.

Charlie Chan in Panama (1940)

No heart strong enough to hold bullet.

Dividing line between folly and wisdom very faint in dark tomb.

Murder Over New York (1940)

Canary unlike faithful dog—do not die for sympathy.

Aid from Number Two Son like interest on mortgage—impossible to escape.

Kitchen stove most excellent weapon—good for cooking goose.

Chan: Number Two Son recognize (Hindu) assailant? Number Two Son: No. They all look alike to me.

Dead Men Tell (1941)

Corpse have no place on honeymoon.

Charlie Chan in Rio (1941)

Interesting problem in chemistry: sweet wine often turn woman sour.

Pretty girl, like lap dog, sometimes go mad.

Castle in the Desert (1942)

Man who walk have both feet on ground.

Lovers use element of surprise . . . also criminals.

Guilty conscience like dog in circus—many tricks.

Offspring [Number Two Son] sound like chip off old chopstick.

Dark Alibi (1946)

Skeletons in closets always speak loudest to police.

Son Tommy is noisy woodpecker on family tree.

For time I nurse theory—very excellent theory—but now instead of nurse, I fear theory need undertaker.

Tommy, you sit down so much you get concussion of brain.

No experiment is failure until last experiment is success. (?)

Shadows Over Chinatown (1946)

Mutilation is usual pattern when motive is murder for profit.

Confucius say, "Sleep only escape from yesterday."

Perhaps voice from dim past may lift curtain to oblivion.

Private detective like influenza epidemic—he cover wide territory but do very little good.

I may no longer carry the Chan monkey on my back, but there's no question of my unshakable addiction to other B crime films— series and one-shots alike. I own upwards of a hundred and have watched scores more on borrowed tapes and on the Late Late Show. If that doesn't make me an expert, it at least allows me to offer an informed opinion when I'm asked such vitally important questions as: What is *the* alternative B classic, the worst crime melodrama ever made?

My answer: Any film starring Bela Lugosi, take your pick. But if you back me into a corner and force me to select just one, it would have to be *Scared to Death*.

This dog among dogs was made in 1947 by an outfit calling itself Golden Gate Pictures, Inc., and is (here's a bit of trivia for film buffs) Lugosi's only appearance in a color production. Why Golden Gate Pictures and the producer, William B. David, wanted to make it in color is not clear. Neither is the color; it was filmed in something called "natural color," which is a blatant euphemism for watery and sort of faded-looking. Why Golden Gate and William B. David wanted to make the thing *at all* is beyond comprehension.

What makes *Scared to Death* such a magnificent piece of alternative filmmaking is not Lugosi, who doesn't have much to do in it except slink around in bushes swirling his cape, and as a result is somewhat less hammy than usual. Nor is it the rest of the cast, which with a couple of exceptions isn't too bad; the other featured players include such B crime/horror veterans of the thirties and forties as George Zucco (everybody's favorite mad doctor, typecast again here), Douglas Fowley (some people's favorite wisecracking newspaper reporter, ditto), Nat Pendleton (not too many people's favorite dumb cop despite his roles in a couple of *Thin Man* flicks, ditto), and Joyce Compton (nobody's favorite dumb blonde except mine, ditto again). Nor are the photography, the direction (by Christy Cabanne), or the "production values" to blame—although each does contribute its fair share. No, the real genius behind

Scared to Death is somebody named W. J. Abbott, who invented the storyline and wrote the script.

Abbott's muse must have been either drunk or badly hung over when he sat down to create this thanksgiving turkey. The story makes precious little sense, and what there is of it is as riddled with holes as the villains in a Fearless Fosdick caper. Characters act and react to situations and other stimuli with no more logic than the populace of Harry Stephen Keeler's private universe. And the dialogue . . . well, you can literally see Zucco and some of the other vets trying not to cringe when uttering, or listening to others utter, some of Abbott's more inspired witlessisms. Even Lugosi, who would later sink to even greater depths in Ed Wood, Jr.'s stunningly awful *Plan Nine from Outer Space* (mercifully, his last film), seems a tad embarrassed by his role in this Looney Tunes production.

How alternative is it? Well, to begin with, the story is narrated by a corpse. The opening scene takes place in the "autopsy room" of the Central City morgue, where the body of a young woman is stretched out on a table. Seems nobody has any idea of how she died, so the coroner and his assistant are getting ready to carve her up in order to find out. But before they commence, the coroner muses as follows: "And yet . . . one often wonders what could have caused the last thought that was cut off by death. If it were spoken now, what would it be . . . ?" Whereupon some weird music starts up (there is a lot of weird music in *Scared to Death*, all of it comprised of the same seven or eight discordant notes), the camera moves in for a close-up of the corpse, we hear her voice—presumably from the Great Beyond—and bingo, we're into an extended flashback of the events that led to her demise.

All these events take place in the house of the supposedly mad and sinister Doctor Van Ee (George Zucco)—a combination living quarters, clinic, and one-time insane asylum. There are no exterior shots of the house, the grounds, or anything except some bushes (usually with Lugosi lurking in them) seen through the living room window. We're talking *low budget* here, most of the production money having gone into the pocket of the con artist who sold Golden Gate Pictures and William B. David the "natural color" film. Also on hand are Dr. Van Ee's son, Ward (played by either

Roland Varno or Angelo Rossitto, it isn't clear which and it doesn't matter anyway); Ward's wife, Laura (or Laurel or Laurette, as she is also known now and then), histrionically portrayed by Molly Lamont, who is in fact the imminent corpse on the slab in the Central City morgue doing the voice-over narration; a mysterious patient of Dr. Van Ee's named Mrs. Williams (it isn't clear who plays her, either), who is "decked out like she's going to a horse show"; a private patrol officer, Bill Raymond (Nat Pendleton), "who's always hanging around hoping somebody gets murdered" and who is present to provide some dubious comic relief (he got kicked off the Central City homicide squad for shooting up a dressmaker's dummy instead of a murder suspect and he's real anxious to have his old job back, which isn't likely because in the first place he's incredibly stupid and in the second place he wears a derby hat that makes him *look* even stupider than he acts or talks); and the maid, Lilly Beth (Gladys Blake), whose job it is to snoop around, act as a foil for Raymond's moronic dumb-cop routine, get herself hypnotized so she looks dead, and try to stay in character in a scene where Raymond props her up against the wall with one hand sneakily groping her left breast.

Are you with me so far?

Pretty soon Dr. Van Ee's sinister cousin, Leonide (Lugosi), shows up. He is supposed to be an illusionist with a checkered past; he is also purported to have been an inmate of the place when it was a nuthouse and to have "engineered an immense number of secret passages through which guards could watch inmates at night," until finally he took one of these passages "into the outside world" and was next heard of running around Europe. With him on his return to the old homestead is his "inseparable companion," a deaf-and-dumb dwarf named Igor (no kidding), who has no plot function whatsoever—unless you count scurrying around a lot, almost tripping a couple of people, and trying to look sinister at more or less opportune moments. The other two main characters, and nominal "heroes," don't put in an appearance until the halfway point. These are reporter Terry Lee of the Central City *Times* (Douglas Fowley), who insists on pronouncing the word "homi-cide" as "homo-cide"; and his fiancée, Jane Cornell (Joyce Compton), "who is good for dull days in a man's life." Jane is even dumber than Bill Raymond, though in a much more lovable way, and is considerably more attractive: she has blond hair, a cute mouth, a nice figure, and she doesn't wear a derby hat.

The "story" and the "action" revolve around a revenge motive from the past, involving the fact that Laura/Laurette/Laurel was once the dance partner of a guy named René in France before or during the war. Seems they did this swell improv routine called the "Dance of the Green Mask" in the Green Room of the Parisian Something-or-other (the word is spoken only once, in voice-over narration—not the corpse's, the murderer's at the "climax"—and is so badly pronounced that you can't understand what it is or even what it might be no matter how many times you listen to it). Then something terrible happened: Laurette/Laura/Laurel betrayed René to the Nazis as a spy because she hated him even though he was good and kind, and then sent him a green scarf to put over his eyes when he was shot at a concentration camp; only he wasn't shot, he "had ideas of his own" and escaped somehow, but Laurel/Laura/Laurette didn't find that out until much later, after she'd come to this country and first got a job as a singer and then coerced Ward into marrying her on a dare so she could get all the Van Ee money and, not incidentally, the house with the secret passages that used to be an insane asylum.

Are you *still* with me?

Well, now Laurette/Laurel/Laura has been getting mysterious letters from abroad and is worried that somebody is (1) trying to drive her bonkers, or (2) intends to murder her most foully, or (3) both of the above. She's especially fearful of green masks and blindfolds, because of the scarf that she sent René in the concentration camp when she thought he was going to be executed by the Nazis. And she becomes even more terrified when she receives a package containing a severed head—a dummy's head, as it turns out, from "a group of Dr. Van Ee's anatomical specimens" locked in the cellar—and bearing a cryptic warning in green ink on the *outside* of the package: "Look for the man with the green mask."

Things really start to pop at this point. Doctor Van Ee gets whacked over the head in his office, for no reason that is ever explained. Leonide commences lurking in the bushes outside. Igor runs around tripping people. A weird, disembodied, bilious-green mask keeps appearing and disappearing at the same living room window—sort of like a green Halloween mask attached to the end of a stick. One time it seems about to fall off the stick, but the camera deftly cuts away in time so that you can't be sure. Some shots ring out, for no reason except that shots are *supposed* to ring out in B melodramas like this. Lilly Beth gets hypnotized "by mental telepathy" into trying to place a green blindfold over Laura/Laurette/Laurel's eyes and then falls down and Doctor Van Ee says she's dead, even though he knows she isn't. Leonide lurks in the bushes some more. The weird mask keeps flashing people from outside the window, to the tune of more weird music. Doctor Van Ee gets hit on the head again, this time out in the bushes (evidently to prove that they are not just Leonide's domain). Leonide appears from inside a secret passage and swipes Lilly Beth's "corpse." Raymond gets drugged and tied to a chair. Leonide unhypnotizes Lilly Beth. The lights go out and come back on again. A strange foreign voice seems to issue from behind the living room walls. And then—

Then Laurel/Laura/Laurette, who has herself been placed in a hypnotic trance, is ordered by the strange disembodied voice to put on the green scarf blindfold, which she does and which causes her to scream and fall down dead. Whereupon everyone scurries about in a frenzy, until Raymond goes out into those same damn bushes and with no struggle at all puts the arm on Mrs. Williams, the mysterious woman who made the earlier appearance decked out like a horse show patron. Only Mrs. Williams isn't really a woman at all but a guy in drag, and not just any guy but René, he of the Dance of the Green Mask with Laurette/Laurel/Laura in the Green Room of the Parisian Something-or-other who was betrayed by Laura/Laurette/Laurel but who miraculously managed to escape the Nazi firing squad so he could come to Central City and wreak his revenge.

The final scene takes place in the "autopsy room" of the morgue, where the kindly old coroner tells Terry and Jane and Bill Raymond that Laura/Laurette/Laurel was literally scared to death. Laurel/Laura/Laurette's corpse doesn't have any comment to make on this, her voice-over narration having ended abruptly about two-thirds of the way through the picture, just before René/Mrs. Williams started *his* voice-over narration. More of the same weird music, up and out. The End. *Voilà!*

No, not quite. To absorb the full flavor of *Scared to Death*, you must experience some of W. J. Abbott's splendiferous dialogue. Here are a few of the more interesting lines and exchanges.

> LAURA: I know what's going on here. Someone's trying to scare me out but it won't work, see? Here I am and here I'll stay until I rot.
> DR. VAN EE (cryptically): I'm afraid there's more truth in that than you might expect.

> LEONIDE (upon meeting Bill Raymond): Sir, there is an air of inquiry about you that immediately offends my deepest nature. There's something suggesting Scotland Yard, the French Sureté, the Italian carabinieri, the Turkish polizei. In short, sir, I think you're a *cop*!

> LEONIDE (to Ward): My boy, trouble and I are (pregnant pause while he holds up two entwined fingers) like this!

> LEONIDE (mugging fiercely in an off-angle closeup): Laurette, Laurette . . . I'll make you a bet . . . the man in green will get you yet!

> BILL (bursting into Laura's bedroom after hearing her scream): To the rescue, ma'am! Who done it? Which way'd he go?
> LAURA: Get out! Get out!
> BILL: I just heard you yell. I was hoping it was a murder, at least.
> LAURA: Get out of here! You have no business here!
> BILL: But you don't understand. I'm supposed to be here. That's what I'm being paid for. You see, I'm Bill Raymond, private cop in this neck of the woods. I was hoping we'd have a little murder or something happen around here so's I could solve it and get my old job back at Central Homicide. Nothin' personal, of course.

LAURA: You and Mr. Ward are pretty thick, aren't you?
LILLY BETH: Thick?
LAURA: Yes—like your head!

BILL: Dere I was . . . outside her room, minding my own business . . . listening at the keyhole—
DR. VAN EE: I don't think that falls into the realm of your duties here, Raymond.
BILL: But Doc, there was screams inside. You gotta admit it's within the longitude of my profession to make an investigatory reaction thereto. . . . Jeez, what am I sayin'?

TERRY (to Jane): Baby, I'm gonna miss you an awful lot when I grow tired of you.

BILL (soliloquizing when he thinks Lilly Beth is dead): Poor Lilly Beth. I kind of hinted that I needed a murdered body, but . . . gee, I didn't think she'd take it personal.

LEONIDE (to Dr. Van Ee): My dear Joseph, the principle of hypnosis isn't as simple as you would make them believe. It requires long and patient study. But I will risk the wrath of the unknown . . . and use my great knowledge.

TERRY: Think hard, now. You saw a green mask—
JANE: Oo! It came out of the wardrobe.
TERRY: Like a moth?
JANE (claps her hands): Yes, darling, just like a moth! Aw, how clever of you! It was just like a great big moth . . . (Pirouettes gaily) . . . and it flew around and around and around—
TERRY: Please! Don't make yourself any dizzier than you already are.

I can't help wondering: What would Charlie Chan have made of all this enlivened nonsense?

"Man who hook self on alternative classics," he might have said, "like Number One Son who have hallucinations he is great detective. Even small mind terrible thing to waste."

10

Titles, Anyone?

Death Takes a Stroll Down Memory Lane

Murder Invites Some Friends Over for a Few Beers
—Mythical titles
I wish someone had used

Have you ever noticed how many dumb titles there are on mystery and suspense novels?

The history of the genre is littered with them. Most are of unimpressive dumbness, to be sure, but there are some that achieve alternatively zany heights. This being the case, it seems to me there ought to be a small display of these, too, in the Alternative Hall of Fame annex. That's one of the benefits of creating your own hall of fame. You can put any damn thing in it you want.

Many of the outstanding dumb titles appear on criminous works published in the thirties and forties; and in turn many of these begin with the word "death" or the word "murder." Back in those days, publishers were insistent upon mysteries *looking* and *sounding* like mysteries, so that potential readers wouldn't mistake one for, say, a treatise on the mating habits of the Mediterranean fruit fly. They and their editors wanted mystery titles to be simple, colorful, provocative—even to the point of employing sometimes outrageous puns. Therefore they used (and overused) such words as "corpse," "blood," "case" (as in *The Case of the Beckoning Dead*), "clue," "riddle," "secret," "terror," "sinister," "mystery," "death," and especially "murder" (which S. S. Van Dine reportedly once nominated as the strongest word in the English language).

But there are only so many ways to incorporate such words into a short and colorful title, at least insofar as keeping the title within the bounds of literacy. As a result, some authors and editors let themselves get carried away to ridiculous extremes in their search for a catchy title. Such as in anthropomorphizing "Death" and "Murder"—endowing each with physical and vocal abilities that, instead of hooking the reader, can inspire a comic reaction in the mind of one such as yours truly.

This is what I mean:

Death Goes Window Shopping. (Looking for layaway plans?)

Murder Joins the Chorus. (One, two, three, kick. One, two, three, kick.)

Death Plays the Gramophone. (Golden Oldies like "Lights Out," "A Scythe Is Just a Scythe," and "Cruisin' Down the River Styx.")

Murder Does Light Housekeeping. (But I'll bet it doesn't do windows.)

Death Serves An Ace. (And John McEnroe throws another on-court tantrum.)

Murder Goes to College. (Where it shoots off its mouth and graduates Magnum Come Louder.)

Death Tears a Comic Strip. (No sense of humor.)

Murder Seeks an Agent. ("I got this little image problem, see, and I thought maybe you could arrange some positive PR . . .")

Death Turns a Trick. (The Unhappy Hooker.)

Murder Greets Jean Holton. ("Hi there. What's *your* sign?")

Death Takes the Bus; Death Drives; Death Rides a Train; Death Rides a Sorrel Horse; Death Rides a Camel. (Fear of flying?)

Murder Gives a Lovely Light. (By flicking its Bic?)

Death Wears a Copper Necktie. (Tacky, tacky.)

Murder Has No Tongue. (A mute point.)

Death Stops the Manuscript. (From doing what?)

Murder Makes Us Gay. (Gee, I always thought it was either genetics or personal preference.)

Death Kicks a Pebble. (No bucket handy?)

Murder Makes a Man. ("Behold, Igor! *Now* all we need is a living brain!")

Death Paints a Picture. (Free-hand or by-the-numbers?)

Murder Leaves a Ring. (In the bathtub? Around the collar?)

Death Calling—Collect. ("No, operator, I will *not* accept the charges!")

Murder Plays an Ugly Scene. (Break a leg, Murder.)

Death Wears Pink Shoes, Death Wears Red Shoes, Death Wore Gold Shoes. ("So what do you think, Imelda? Shall we try on just a *few* more pairs?")

Murder Rents a Room. ("Don't you have anything with southern exposure?")

Death Designs a Dress. (Shroud control?)

Murder Was My Neighbor. (There goes the damn neighborhood.)

Death Takes the Joystick. (*Everybody's* doing drugs these days, it seems.)

Murder Lays a Golden Egg. (Thus pissing off the goose, who figured he had a lock on the job.)

Death in the Fifth Position. (Best argument I've ever heard for sticking with the missionary position.)

Corpses, too, have come in for titular abuse from overzealous writers and editors. As in the following:

The Corpse Spells Danger. ("D-a-n-g-e-r. Not bad for a dead guy, huh?")

The Corpse That Spoke; The Corpse That Talked; The Corpse That Walked; The Corpse That Traveled. (I wish I had half as much pep and vitality.)

Corpse de Ballet. (Oh yeah? Let's see one do a pas de deux.)

The Corpse Came C.O.D. ("Mabel, you been out shopping again? There's a delivery guy here with the biggest damn package . . .")

Corpse for a Client. ("Listen, mister, I'm not a mind reader. I can't help you if you're gonna sit there looking deadpan.")
The Corpse in the Camera. (Not only a clever hiding place, but an amazing feat of personal engineering.)
A Corpse for Kofi Katt. (Krazy's sister?)
Corpse in Handcuffs. (Insult to injury.)
The Corpse in the Cab. ("I don't care what your problem is, bud, you pay the goddamn fare or you don't get out of this hack.")
The Corpse in the Elevator. ("Going up? What floor, please?")
The Corpse Moved Upstairs. (And good riddance, too.)
The Corpse on the Flying Trapeze. ("Oh, look, George! Look! He's not even going to use a safety net!")
The Corpse Came Calling. ("You don't mind my dropping in like this, do you? It's just that I've been *dying* for a cup of coffee.")
The Corpse Is Indignant. (And who's got a better right to be?)
The Corpse Said No. ("And I meant it, too. You just have no sense of *timing* . . .")

And here are the worst of the rest, including some of the more interestingly silly pun titles.

All Killers Aren't Ugly. (Nope. Some are cute as lace pants.)
Another Mug for the Bier, Bier for a Chaser, Three Short Biers. (Come to think of it, I'll have a Heineken.)
Baby Don't Love Hoodlums. (She don't love good grammar, neither.)
Blood for Breakfast. (I prefer toast and coffee, myself.)
Brain Drain, Brainfire, Brainwrack. (What you get from reading too much alternative fiction.)
Breath of Murder. (A condition even Listerine can't cure.)
Clean, Bright, and Slightly Oiled. (Me on Saturday night.)
Don't Just Stand There, Do Someone. (The author of this title, preferably.)
The End of the Mildew Gang. (Spring cleaning in the underworld?)

Enter the Corpse; Enter Two Murderers; Enter Three Witches. (Exit Pronzini.)
Felo de Se? ("Hell, no! What are you, some kind of pervert?")
The Fifth Must Die! (I'll drink to that.)
Flash of Splendour. ("That's what *he* called it, officer. I call it just plain disgusting.")
The Girl with the Dynamite Bangs. (And a short fuse to go with them?)
Honey, Here's Your Hearse! ("It's very nice, dear, but . . . well, I was hoping for something a little smaller and sportier . . .")
I'll Fry Yet. (Vow made by a fired short-order cook.)
In the Grip of the Dragon. (Tong-tied?)
It Always Rains on Sunday; He Hanged His Mother on Monday. (Well, that explains it.)
It's Always Too Late To Mend. (Darn it.)
Justice Peeps Over the Handkerchief. (So that's what that blindfold really is—life's snotty noserag.)
Kill Him Quickly, It's Raining. ("And I forgot to roll up the windows in the car.")
Lady, Shed Your Head. ("I'd rather garage it instead, if you don't mind.")
Last Rites for the Vulture. (But his family will carrion without him.)
The Mind Benders; The Mind Killers; The Mind Poisoners. (Those in charge of network TV programming.)
The Mouse Who Wouldn't Play Ball. (Another greedy jock looking to renegotiate his contract.)
The Painful Predicament of Sherlock Holmes. (Hemorrhoids?)
Poisoned Fang. (What happened to Phyllis Diller's husband.)
Rope for an Ape. (Monkey business.)
She Ain't Got No Body. (So how can she hold her head up in public?)
Softly Dust the Corpse. (Heloise's Household Hint #1763.)
Stiffs Don't Vote. (No, but some stiffs get voted *for*.)
The Swinger Who Swung by the Neck. (Gallows humor.)

The Thing That Made Love. ("Oh, mother, it was awful! I'll never, *never* go out on another blind date as long as I live!")
Vegetable Duck. (Quacked corn?)
What To Do Until the Undertaker Comes. (Take a nap, watch TV, play Trivial Pursuit, read an alternative classic. . . .)

11

Hail To The Chief!

But in that flying, fleeting instant, I got the message.
The urgent telegram. The Red Alert. The Forget-Me-Not.
The SOS. The May Day.
The Change of Heart. The Reversal of Motive . . .
I've changed my mind, Helen Friday's eyes said.
—**Michael Avallone,**
The Hot Body, 1973

There are notable alternative writers, and outstanding alternative writers, and great alternative writers.

And then there is Michael Avallone.

Avallone: The Fastest Typewriter in the East. Avallone: Author of some 220 novels from 1953 to the present, nearly all of which are paperback originals. Avallone: Creator of Ed Noon, private eye extraordinaire. He's the greatest of them all by a wide margin. The giant among giants.

The top of the heap.

The nonpareil.

The chief.

Nobody else can touch him, not even with a ten-foot pole.

Or any other cliché.

What makes Avallone number one, numero uno, the leader of the pack? What makes him the Alternative Writer of the Century? Lots of things. All the reasons there are.

And then some.

He is the patriarch of point-belaboring.

The master of the malaprop.

The overload of wonderful one-liners.

The nabob of non sequiturs.

The savant of silly similes.

The sultan of screwy said substitutes.

The Amazon of absurd alliteration.

The captain of cliché.

The duke of the daffy, the powerhouse of the preposterous, the Hercules of the haphazardly hilarious.

In other words, the one to be reckoned with.

The Big Guy.

You can't read an Avallone novel without finding a plot of high alternative standards *and* at least a dozen passages of such alternative brilliance that they sparkle like gold fillings in the molars of a mess of small-time mugs. Dialogue, description, introspection, action, reaction, and the sock finish—he can do it all.

And he does.

Every time.

Some of those times he outdoes himself, usually when he's dealing with one of his favorite subjects.

Baseball.

Old movies.

Patriotism and/or right-wing politics.

Breasts.

Nobody writes about breasts the way Avallone does, with such flair, such reverence, such passion. Not that he neglects thighs, of course. Or calves. Or hips.

Or faces.

Eyes, nose, cheeks, lips. Even ears. Described lovingly, eloquently, innovatively.

The feminine phiz in all its glory.

The fact of the matter is, Avallone likes dames. And so does Ed Noon. Beautiful dames with big bazooms. Especially *glamorous* beautiful dames with big bazooms, such as Hollywood and Broadway actresses, fashion designers, and the wives (and mistresses) of important politicians, not excluding an expresident.

Ed Noon is very horny private richard. The horniest. But that isn't all he is, not by a long shot. On the contrary and *au contraire*.

He's also as tough as they come—a red-blooded, fast-shooting, wisecracking, ball-busting PI in the grand tradition of Spade and Marlowe and Mike Hammer. There's no situation he can't handle. No obstacle he can't overcome. He's seen it all, done it all.

He's been there and he knows the score.

When to throw the high hard one and when to whip in a roundhouse curve or the old changeup.

When to hit-and-run and when to pull the straight steal.

When to swing for the fences and when to lay down a sacrifice bunt.

When to crap and when to get off the pot.

In the early days of his career, back in the McCarthy era, Noon was a loner working out of his "mouse auditorium" of an office on West Fifty-sixth Street in Manhattan. Later on he acquired larger, spiffier offices on West Forty-fourth, as well as a beautiful black secretary with big bazooms named Melissa Mercer. (Wait a minute. The big bazooms aren't named Melissa Mercer. That's the *secretary's* name. The big bazooms don't have a name, other than big bazooms and a lot of euphemisms that mean big bazooms.) Melissa taught him about civil rights, not that he was ever prejudiced against people of the Negro persuasion. He even took Melissa as a lover to *prove* that he isn't prejudiced.

Big bazooms are big bazooms, no matter what color they are.

Finally, in the later stages of his career, Noon was given the greatest honor of all for a patriotic dick: a job as special investigator for the President of the United States, working on cases too tough for the FBI and the CIA to handle. Like the case of the Doomsday Bagman, who always follows the president around with a black satchel containing the blueprints and code patterns for an all-out thermonuclear war.

And the case of the loaded baseball at Shea Stadium.

And the case of the underwater empire run by a band of man-eating females.

Tough cases like that.

The president even had a special phone installed in Noon's office, so he could call Ed directly whenever trouble was brewing. A red-white-and-blue hotline, to summon our true-blue hero to fight the Reds. In a white heat.

Noon has had to kill a lot of people over the course of his many investigations, though never in cold blood and never without just cause. But he doesn't like to kill. It hurts him when he's forced to squeeze the trigger on his .45, because underneath his rough-and-tumble, devil-may-care, anything-goes, go-to-hell-and-up-yours exterior, there beats the heart of an old fashioned romantic.

An idealist.

An incurable nostalgiac whose favorite song is "I'm Just a Cockeyed Optimist."

His idealism never wavers, even when his eyes are full of gunsmoke. Even when the Grim Reaper threatens to render him blotto, finished, null and void, a Zero on the Big Board.

Even then.

A sentimental slob and a cockeyed optimist—that's Ed Noon in a nutshell.

Two nutshells, actually.

Three if you count the horniness.

And the toughness makes four.

Ed Noon is far and away Avallone's most impressive creation, having begun his career in 1953 with *The Tall Dolores* and having carried on through twenty-nine additional cases, the last being *Dark on Monday* (1978). 1953 to 1978. Twenty-five years.

A quarter of a century.

A silver-anniversary career.

But Noon's capers comprise only a small percentage of the Fastest Typewriter's impressive output of novels. Avallone is also the father of the Man from AVON and the Satan Sleuth. The chronicler of three Girl from U.N.C.L.E. capers featuring April Dancer, a dozen (as by Stuart Jason) starring the Butcher, and three detailing the exploits of Nick Carter. The novelizer of numerous screenplays and TV scripts, among them such notable full-length films as *A Bullet for Pretty Boy Floyd, Charlie Chan and the Curse of the Dragon Queen*, and *Friday the 13th Part III*, and such TV shows as "Mannix," "Hawaii Five-O," and "The Partridge

Family." The author of twenty-five Gothic suspense novels under the pseudonyms Priscilla Dalton, Dorothea Nile, Jean-Anne de Pre, and—yes—Edwina Noone. And the creator of scores of other novels on a wide variety of themes.

Some 220 novels altogether, in less than thirty-five years.

That's a lot of paper under the bridge.

And a lot of alternative classics.

The following seven novels, six of which feature Ed Noon, are just a small percentage of those worthy of inclusion in the Alternative Hall of Fame. Their plots and their star-spangled prose are ample evidence of Avallone's genius, his Herculean stature, his preeminence.

His greatness.

This is the Big Guy at work. Read 'em and marvel.

And pay homage.

It doesn't get any more alternative than this.

The Crazy Mixed-Up Corpse (1957)

In which Noon gets involved with the murder of the young daughter of a Chinese laundryman, a fur-bearing, gun-bearing blonde who "wears clothes nakedly," a crazy Texas oilman named Carver Calloway Drill, and a strip-teaser who peels to the sensual strains of "The Hucklebuck."

> I'd been disgusted with the morning altogether and getting a police call on top of everything was the straw that all camels beware of. Including private eyes.

> I went down like a lead balloon as five hundred pounds of something smashed me in the right side. Went down, twitching and kicking with a million needles working on me like a sewing machine. Pain skyrocketed through me like a bolt of lightning and the tops of the buildings overhead rushed down to meet me.

> The color of the month for the laundry tickets was green, green as my gills felt.

She stopped and rammed her painted fingers into hips as curved and full as a horse's flanks. . . . Her eyelashes reached out to grab me.

My head hurt, my side ached and my eyebrows felt like they were AWOL.

When the last note of the piano ended "The Hucklebuck" and [strip-tease dancer] Holly Hill threw one last soul-smashing grind to the rafters where the male cockroaches must have exploded with frustration, the applause was deafening. It was like a first night with Barrymore doing Hamlet in front of a bunch of people who believe all playwriting began and ended with Will Shakespeare. Well, it was Shakes all right.

Penny Darnell pouted at her Scotch.

"Your tongue is hanging out and I feel unnecessary. She makes me look like a clothespin."

"You can hang me up to dry any time, baby."

One of her breasts bobbed into view like a cantaloupe rolling off a display in a fruit store.

[She swung] a whiplashing right hand . . . and Penny Darnell's face vibrated on her shoulders like a smacked dinner gong.

The grand piano that somebody had dropped on my head played on and on. The noisiest concertoes and orchestrations in the books. And none of it baby or grand. All crashing, clamoring, colliding notes. And loud, loud, LOUD. Then the crescendoes suddenly stopped and my head hummed like a giant-sized tuning fork. My ears felt like two enormous tines.

His glower was on full blast now. And the bend in his nose almost ironed out.

"Okay," she sighed. "Rush off and do what you have to do. . . . But you will remember the address, won't you?"

"Cross my forty-fives and hope to die." We kissed. Kissed and clung like autumn leaves on a wet walk in Central Park.

Carver Calloway Drill . . . towered above Tom Long's chair like a Macy's Thanksgiving Day balloon.

I . . . swung myself around and sat down on the divan and twisted her lovely, naked body until she was staring at the floor with her magnificently curved, white buttocks staring up at the ceiling like two blank white eyes, two symmetrically exact hills gleaming in the sunlight.

His breath was hot and sweaty.

Meanwhile, Back at the Morgue (1960)

In which Noon, synopsizing in his own words, is hired by "a Broadway showman looking for the lead in his coming play. There are three, maybe four, attempts on his life. Four finalists for the role are terrorized in an elevator. A great star who wants the part for herself is mysteriously murdered. And then out of the blue, the night, and nowhere a tall, beautiful girl marches in . . . and says, 'I am Annalee. I was born to play *Roses in the Rain.*' Wouldn't you be suspicious? Wouldn't you say the plot was sickening as well as thickening?"

My mouth dropped about six feet, into my shoes.

Her breasts strained at their moorings.

"Your book was interesting, true. Made quite a splash, true. But it was a curiosity piece, a freak. Like astrology or tea-leaf readings. Or beer suds."

I sat forward in my chair and placed my left shoe against the black buzzer jutting out from one inside corner of the desk. You can't see the buzzer from the front of the desk. It's a cute trick, really, silly for a grown man, but it scares the hell out of anybody who doesn't know about it.

Directly behind Marcus Manton, the car horn installed in the clothes closet by the sink went off with an ear-shattering honk. An old retired submarine skipper had installed it for me as payment for locating his missing daughter in the big city.

Forget about chickens. The chick that walked into my office that cold night was designed to make men feel like roosters. She was something to crow about.

I smiled at her, trying to take the miracle of her apart slowly, piece by piece. First there was the calendar-girl perfection of her. White skin, a cloud of black hair framing an oval face. And height. It seemed like yards of height, but I settled for five-feet-six without heels. . . . She smiled so I could count her dazzling teeth. I saw eyelashes a foot long and eyes with all the colors of the rainbow in them.

I showed Marcus my Missouri leer. The one that didn't believe anything it heard, little of what it saw.

Her smile evaporated slowly. Like the moon easing behind a white cloud.

"Tsk, tsk," I frowned.

The smile came back. The smile that would have laid nine good men and true out in a neat pile ready to die for her.

Fran Tulip remained where she was—in the center of the office, the center of attention. An unseen spotlight had her riveted and pinpointed. She might have been standing under a halo of changing colors and moods. She knew how to stand.

I suddenly noticed her clothes. They hadn't seemed very important up to that point. A tightly belted woman's trench coat that showed off her figure the way a four-alarm fire displays the warehouse it's burning to the ground.

Karl Leader's pointed beard bobbed with his smile.

Her appeal stopped dead on its nouns.

Dimly, I thought of vacations and Tahiti and painting. I
didn't believe that stuff about the half-naked brown-
skinned babes for a minute, but it would be nice. Gun
smoke in the nostrils was beginning to get me.

Sweat was dancing its wet adagio on my forehead.

The Bedroom Bolero (1963)

In which Noon moves into his new offices on West Forty-fourth
Street, hires Melissa Mercer as his secretary, and becomes entangled
with a psycho who strangles young nude women, all of whom have
weak hearts and double-initial names (e.g. Alice Albin)—strangles
them in red-painted rooms beneath cheap colored lights arranged in
a Q design while listening to the slow, sinuous beat of Ravel's
Bolero on portable record players, after having first dosed them (the
young nude women) with generous amounts of cantharides (Spanish
fly to you). Why the psycho does all this earns Avallone motive-
cum-laude honors. Also involved in this marvelous muddle is a
Bohemian nightclub called the Green Cellar, a ghoulish performer
known as Evil Evelyn Eleven, a mysterious fat guy named Mr.
Orelob (get it?), an apparently homosexual waiter who keeps trying
to hit on Noon, and a bang-up final chapter entitled "Farewell to a
Maniac."

> [My] heart closed its eyes, lay still, and died. The torch
> [I'd been carrying for her] vanished in a pool of mud and
> went *gluckkkkkk*!
>   "What do you know about the *Bolero*?"
>   "Come again?"
>   "The *Bolero*. Ever hear of it?"
>   I composed myself.

> I must have been a little looped by then. I remember the
> bottle was half-empty or half-full, depending on which
> state of physics is the truer one.

[The dead woman's] nudity was upsetting because she had had one of those perfect figures where the stomach wall is flat, the hips taper like two halves of a medicine ball and the breasts poke confidently beautiful into the world of men. The body was white, something that may have had to do with dying, but seemed more an indication that the woman had been fair all over.

I left 77 Riverside Drive close to nine o'clock that Thursday night. I wasn't a block away from the place, on foot, when I realized I was trying to walk home which wasn't exactly logical considering that my home address like my office was brand new.

". . . Don't you know how Evelyn Eleven is?"

In a world in which there are people called Robert Six, Johnny Seven and an actress once chose to call herself Helen Twelvetrees, I had no axe to grind.

Her voice was quiet, not raised one octave above the graveyard but there was no arguing with her voice. It reeked of command as well as clamminess.

She looked as cute as a mustard seed in a tight green dress.

Her sigh flooded my ear.

My size nine black shoe shot out from the launching pad of the wall like a guided missile and buried itself in the outer space of the groin of the man in the middle. . . . The sudden long howl that exploded out of his throat was like a rocket of triumph bursting radiantly in my ears.

I kept cranking my head like a maniac avoiding those punishing punches to my head. I had to give with the guy hanging onto my arm or the next sound I would hear was the arm bone connected to the shoulder bone going pop like the weasel.

Her eyes were wide, the nose was a lovely hawk and her mouth was well-formed.

I had a brief whiff of the wet violets and fragrant perfume of her personality.

You had to hand it to her. She was Black Magic and a Greek chorus of Tragedy with all its nuances and fine exhortations of everyone's subconscious.

Applause Niagara-ed around the room.

"Howie," I tsk-tsked.

"Really," she reallyed in a voice made unreal by the sudden acquisition of freedom and a hefty divorce settlement.

"Yes," he sweated.

She wasn't dead. She was alive in a way that set the nape of your neck on edge.

He was a breezy, stout man with cheery features and extrovert personality when he said good morning and made small talk. But as soon as he got down to the heart of the matter, the man of science and textbooks came out of hiding. His entire demeanor halted and shifted into gear which made Monks blink at the Jekyll-and-Hyde transformation, but it lent a gravity of belief to his story that no amount of records and statistical notes could have made more impressive. I listened too.

He looked at me guardedly and the breezy demeanor vanished under his chair.

There IS Something About a Dame (1963)

In which Noon runs afoul of a guy named Memo Morgan who won two hundred grand on a TV quiz show by answering such questions as "Where are the Hebrides located?" with such replies as "Off the coast of Ireland." A genuine mnemonic genius, no? Other characters include a nutty Shakespearean actor, a crooked private eye, and some willing (and not-so-willing) dames. The plot revolves around an undiscovered (missing, lost) Shakespeare/Christopher Marlowe manuscript—and revolves, and revolves, and revolves. . . .

He was a cool apple all right and looked as if he'd picked the tree to fall from.

I should have been thinking about other things. Like how long does a man live after a .45 slug rips a hole through his lower abdomen? And why shoot a man through the gut anyway unless you wanted him to suffer real bad? Or is Life just a succession of sappy accidents after all and none of us are [sic] exactly geniuses when it comes to directing our own breaks? Of course, I had no warning to think about those things. But I should have been thinking anyway.

His eyeballs suddenly rolled and the show was over for him. I caught his head before it bounced off the marble floor of the Ritz lobby. I checked his pulse. Faint but still there. A kind of unconsciousness had taken charge.

The [thief] could have been anyone. . . . He could have been a Martian for all I knew about him.

But why would a Martian shoot a hole through an ambulance tire, then hang around to retrieve the bullet?

"Christ," he said like the devout Catholic he was.

I sprawled into the worn swivel chair and nothing but memory churned around in my thinkbox. Like the light switch going on, the TV show where Morgan had won all that dough flashed before my memory. The office was quieter than Silent Night.

I didn't know it then but a real big key to a door I didn't even know existed was staring me in the face. But not having a deal in the game yet, the idea died in my head under several thousand layers of blurry subconscious.

I was tired. I dragged myself out of the chair, trudged over to the leather couch and spread myself out evenly like a rug.

The whine and pound of the deadly lead [from a machine gun] rattled the office like a clumsy tambourine.

Then just like the commercial on an absorbing TV drama, it stopped. The sudden silence put my teeth together in a painful clinch. But I just lay where I was, hardly breathing, heart kicking like a mule against my ribs. In the darkness where all sounds seem larger than a breadbox, my imagination was leapfrogging over the unbelievabilities.

My bewilderment took on a couple of new glands.

His deep chuckle was controlled, mirthful and full tilt.

I could only hope I wasn't walking into a machine gun like a clay pigeon.

"There are several large holes in the structure [of the story] that won't stand up if I lean on them."

The tangled chaos of the whole evening was drawing to a close.

The Voice muttered an oath and pressed the trigger of the .45 which, for that split-second forward push of my palm, was still leveled directly at my stomach. *Click!* My rioting heart heard the noise and did a flip flop of ecstasy as my short left hook thudded off the Voice's right shoulder which had reared protectively.

The footsteps didn't walk right in. They stopped outside the door and knocked.

A sneer curved her face.

Sir Stewart had gone rigid in his chair. As if his dream of a lifetime was walking the plank.

My head still hurt but I got my eyes open by putting one foot on each lid and prying up toward the sky.

I could feel my muscles start to panic, try to crawl all over my body, but I made them stop.

There's something about being tied up that paralyzes your sense of freedom.

Missing! (1969)

A Noonless right-wing fantasy disguised as a political suspense novel, in which President-elect Robert Winslow Sheldrake mysteriously and inexplicably disappears on the eve of his inauguration, throwing the country into a turmoil. Who is running things? The old, tired Democratic regime? The Republicans, under Vice President-elect Martin Alcott? The Demos are portrayed throughout as a bunch of weaklings and fools; the Republicans, and in particular Sheldrake, are deified as America's "saviors." (One of the ways in which Sheldrake plans to "save" the country is to escalate the war in Vietnam.) The explanation for the president-elect's sudden disappearance is semihilarious in its absurdity and also contains a dandy bit of *deus ex machina*. A subplot concerning the attempted assassination of VP-elect Alcott has an even dandier bit of *deus ex machina*—or rather, in this case, *deus ex squirrel*. All in all, a very nutty novel indeed.

> In mini-skirts or out of them, like the two-piece ensemble of skirt and Sloppy Joe sweater, albeit of the finest cashmere, she was a stunning young lady.

> Terry [Sheldrake's daughter] was like a proud young stallion with nervous thoroughbred lines; Sheldrake was cool, seasoned and almost weatherproof. But in the mold, the dye of heredity, lay the identical chin, the straight nose, the wide-set, serious eyes, the lean parallel of masculinity and femininity that still somehow sets one human being off as a woman, the other as the man.

> He didn't fit anymore; he didn't belong. He was as out of step as the cakewalk.

> There were still people to thank, congratulate and conspire with for their unstinting and very necessary help in

building the steamroller that had launched Sheldrake toward the Presidency.

For all their matching smiles, Thomas Teller and his wife, Clara, had been arguing. You can tell by the withdrawn pallor of the former Vice-President's face.

She was proud of her breasts. The bra wasn't built that didn't have its cups filled to contain her.

At no one time in the nearly two-hundred-year history of the United States had the eyes of its citizens witnessed such an assault on the senses.

There was no longer any rain. The gleaming, shining streets of the nation's capital were scrubbed clean by the heavenly tailors, but heavy, buffeting winds swept down from the north and in its purifying, icy wake, insanity, bedlam and hysteria stood up to be counted.

"One thing more we cannot rightly rule out," Kinley amended his remarks. "A man, acting strangely and far off his norm, can have a lot happen to him in the five minutes he is out of everyone's sight. Suppose Sheldrake bumped his head on a door, or cracked himself with a shoe falling off a closet shelf—well—there's a possibility, too. We have to look into every angle because if we don't find out what happened to him real soon, this country could go to the dogs."

Benson was prune-faced and durable as a sequoia, but you could always see the eagles in his eyes. . . . He was no lily of the valley.

General Hilary Benson called for a five-minute break. The table didn't make a move to break away. No one had to go to the men's room and somehow the problem had rooted everyone where they sat.

Di Mallella laughed again and his cigar barrel-rolled in his mouth.

It was a precedent-shattering kind of stillness.

The Senate was as silent as the Grant Memorial on Sunday. You could have heard a Republican change votes.

The nurse, tall, silent, starchy, administers another needle into a defenseless left arm as it lies fanned out over the coverlet of the bed.

The Fat Death (1972)

In which Noon deflowers a beautiful virgin fashion designer; has his mind boggled by a guy calling himself the Slim Saviour who drops leaflets on New York City telling people to "Beware the Fat Death, Don't Eat Yourself into the Graveyard"; gets smacked around by a couple of tough Italians, one of whom is a "pint-sized female with startling dark eyes and a bust right out of Vesuvius"; watches a porno movie starring the virgin he deflowered; survives a fire; and once again announces with self-effacing charm that "the plot thickens and gets worse all the time."

It was really her nose that got me. It was ruler straight with the barest pinch of reality in the nostrils.

[The seven-foot-tall man] sat down, a long drink of ink under control.

The right arm that left his shoulder should have been labeled greased lightning.

He had recovered from the knockout with class and no complaints but he didn't react too kindly to my prying into his unconscious pockets.

Monks grunted. . . . "He didn't last longer than two seconds. [Stabbed in] the heart. Bull's-eye. The blade didn't touch a bone.
    "A coronary conclusion," I said.

Her eyebrows climbed like lovely sparrows.

We stopped kidding around. Her eyes collapsed and my face broke as we melted together.

Alberta Carstairs had won the day. The private detective sitting next to her with rainbows in his eyes and fever in his blood didn't ask her a single valid question about a murder case. I should have remembered my business but I didn't. I was too busy estimating the depth of blue in Alberta's eyes and the degree of tonality to her fresh, vibrant skin.

My face was a poker game. It told her nothing of what was eating me down to the bare bones.

Her movements were almost lethargic, charged with that sensual laziness that might precede the brief interval before the enjoyment of one's most abandoned dreams are about to be realized.

Her breasts were rising and falling like a sighing wind.

The eightball that all Negroes live behind had blinded her common sense.

Her gasp almost blew the door down.

Before I could protect my defenseless skull, somebody found a nice convenient place on it to park something heavy. Real heavy. It felt like all the cedar chests in Grand Rapids, Michigan.

"Si!" she screamed, the words [sic] a torrent of high-pitched fury from the depths of her soul.

She stared at me quietly, her violet eyes almost glazed. There wasn't a ripple of anything on the waters of her face.

His craggy face suddenly looked as ineffectual and as malleable as butter.

The Hot Body (1973)

In which our esteemed president sends Noon to Fort Lauderdale to prevent Helen Friday, "the wife of an American ex-President, the widow of a man assassinated while holding office, the former First Lady of the United States," from carrying out a mad plan to defect to Cuba. Noon is at his most ineffectual here, poor lad; he lets a couple of Castro's goons (and Helen Friday, too) mistreat him rather badly, and instead of saving the day himself, has it saved for him by the fortuitous arrival of none other than Robert L. Fish's Brazilian cop, Jose da Silva (disguised as a "jet *piloto*"). The real brilliance of the plot, however, lies in the fact that more than half of the book (seventy-one pages) takes place in La Friday's Lauderdale hotel room! Proof positive that the Big Guy can pull off any sort of fictional coup when he sets his fertile brain to the task.

> Pulling back quickly, a fluttering arm gestured toward me and then disappeared. Nerves taut and keeping my brains together, I took the cue and marched in. Eyes peeled, hands close to the heat I had to carry and it only took a second.
>
> Unbelievably, I heard the rustling sounds recede backwards, lost the scent of her aura, her personality. It was as if I could really feel the empty space behind me. I waited, not daring to turn, not wanting to break the slender, hairline mood and rhythm of the entire room. The total set piece between us. Woman-with-gun-holding-up-man-in-quiet-hotel-room-five-floors-above-the-Lauderdale-real-estate.
>
> Beretta behind me, twin double-derringers in front of me, I was boxed in better than I ever had been before.
>
> By two perfect strangers, to boot. That was a kick.

He had all the hallmarks, the staples, that characterizes
the secret agent species.

Miguel de Domino tied me up.
And gagged me.
Like he had promised, it was the meanest tie of them
all.
I'd never been tied like that before.
The Marquis de Sade would have been proud of him.
In or out of the Spanish Inquisition. The man was an
expert.
There was something new under the Florida sun. A
rope trick.

The gag cloving to the roof of my mouth, filling my jaws,
tasted no better than it had. Chandler's classic plumber's
handkerchief came back with a vengeance.

Helen Friday was already well on her way to Fort
Lauderdale Airport. And I was stuck in Room 443 where I
might rot until anyone came to do the room.

The sound [of a telephone falling off a table onto a carpet]
was something like hearing *The Stars and Stripes Forever*
in the middle of a prisoner of war camp. Along with a
cease-fire announcement.

There are many things that are confounding and confusing
about this cockeyed caravan they call Life but the
topmost, pinnacle feature has got to be the utter unpredic-
tability of everything.

We are a long time dead, when we're dead.

[The man with the gun's] mouth gaped . . . his instincts
recoiled.
    It was only for a second or two, the barest fraction of
diversion. But for the man who is waiting for an opening
like that, any opening at all, it was more than enough. It
was a veritable bonanza. A coffee break.

When the woman is Helen Friday and she has what Helen Friday had, there is only one thing that can be held out to a man as the greatest gift. The beyond-price token of gratitude. That *something* that made Adam lose his fig leaf.

Below us, far below, was nothing but the endless blue-green of the Atlantic Ocean. One of the big drinks. Enough water to sink the entire population of the world. And then some.

No person's death diminishes you as much as your own does.

You can tell John Donne I said so, too. Him and his tolling bell.

Hail to the chief!

12

The Alternative Hall of Fame, Part II; Or, "Inspiration Splattered Me In the Face Like a Custard Pie"

I cold-eyed him back, my mind chasing its tail around in my skull trying to measure him for the right pattern. He was a type of dick I'd never met. He wasn't following Lesson I in the police manual's chapter on grilling suspects. I'd have felt better if he'd huffed onion breath in my face and gouged my eyeballs.
> **—Michael Morgan,**
> *Nine More Lives*, 1947

Holliday smiled, a dead man's grin, all teeth and anguish. In his hands the Uzi looked like some deadly kitchen instrument, the latest thing in noodlemakers gone wrong.
> **—Arnold Grisman,**
> *The Winning Streak*, 1985

Way back in Chapter 1, as you'll recall, I inducted a number of novels published between 1910 and 1940 into the Alternative Hall of Fame. In this chapter, the inductees will be novels published from 1945 to 1985. As with those earlier enshrined, these classics "shine like a balefire in the dark forest of mediocre mystery, dull deduction, and static suspense." Boy, *do* they!

Three Short Biers, JIMMY STARR (1945)

Murray & Gee, the short-lived Culver City, California, publisher that gave us Milton M. Raison's splendid mysteries (among them *Murder in a Lighter Vein*, about which see *Gun in Cheek*), is likewise responsible for two of three detective romps by Hollywood publicity agent and gossip columnist Jimmy Starr. Murray published Starr's maiden effort, *The Corpse Came C.O.D.*, in 1944. This novelistic silly-symphony was filmed three years later under the same title, with George Brent and Joan Blondell, which fact may have encouraged Starr to write *Three Short Biers*, another silly-symphony that was never filmed. Nor could it have been, except perhaps by the Marx Brothers in conjuntion with the Society of Little People.

This and Starr's other two mysteries (the third, *Heads You Lose*, was brought out by Frederick Fell in 1950) showcase the antics of a tough, wisecracking newspaperman named Joe Medford, "Hollywood's Number One Reporter," a.k.a. "Cinemaland's Cunning Casanova." Medford chases as many babes in his adventures as he does clues (with remarkable success), and downs bucketsful of Martinis and such other concoctions as the combination of milk, ground coconut, and a double jigger of rum. And he narrates each case in a brash, breezy style typical of Hollywood mystery novels of the period—a style spiced by Starr's own brand of dumb repartee, inventive said substitutes, and vaudevillean humor. As in these examples from *Three Short Biers*:

> "Well, boys, this is your unlucky day. I'm hungry!" she said, biting a piece out of the large menu. "Shucks! I always like menus when they're toasted, or they are delicious when accordion-pleated with crushed cherries."
>
> "Pardon me while I call up the insane asylum and reserve a room," Sam flipped and got up to use the phone.

"You know anything about midgets?" I asked.

"I had an Austin once," she said.

"Sweetie Pie, I'll wait for you until the cows come home—and then we could have cream with our corn flakes in the morning, couldn't we?"

"Swell, Baby," I said, "stir up a bucket of Martinis and I'll be there in a jiffy."

"I thought you drove a Chrysler," she flipped.

"Oh, if you want to get corny," I said. "You're driving me nuts!"

"Now that I have acted as hotel mistress for your strange friends, may I have my key?"

"You don't mean that. I might find some other strange friends."

"You annoy me!"

"No, you annoy me—it's more fun that way."

"Joe, you're impossible!"

"You're lovely."

"I'm a fool!"

"I know, but you're a lovely fool."

"Oh, go on your silly picnic! I hope the ants eat you up!"

"Do I look like a peanut-butter sandwich?"

Medford and Starr are alternatively delightful in all three of their homicidal capers, but in this mighty midget of a novel they have their finest hour. For midgets is what *Three Short Biers* is all about. A trio of them to be exact: Ena, Meena, and Mina, the Diminutive Dolls of Divertissement. And a short bier is what each of them gets before the final curtain on this slapstick farce rolls down.

Now why, as one of the other characters asks Medford, would anybody want to knock off a midget? Especially three female circus midgets who are "lending their singing and dancing talents to Busby Blanchard's lavish musical, 'The Devil's Angels,' the story of two wealthy Texas girls who took over their father's circus and got government permission to present it at the various army camps." But that's just what is happening. Ena is the first victim, found hanging some seventy-five feet above the soundstage at Silverstein Studios with a wire twisted around her little neck. Meena is dispatched not long afterward, also by means of strangulation. And that makes it obvious that Mina, too, is marked for a date with the Grim Reaper.

All sorts of other bizarre and frenetic happenings thicken the plot stew. Before the first murder a fun-loving director named Madison Samson, a.k.a. "Mad Sam," who liked to play practical jokes (such as "annoying writers at the studio by padlocking wastebaskets to the lapels of their coats, then . . . throw[ing] the keys in his swimming pool"), hired a broken-down actor named Clinton Hogarth to deliver a trio of "caskets for kids" (i.e. miniature coffins) to Busby Blanchard. Then, after Ena's death, Mad Sam himself is killed in an apparent automobile accident that turns out instead to have been murder by rifle shot. The three short biers inexplicably disappear. Medford, who is a pal of studio boss Moe Silverstein and therefore just happens to be on hand at the time of Ena's murder, begins poking his snout into both cases—a nose job that does not sit well with such minions of the law as police dick Dick Martin, D.A.'s investigator Harry Dunn, and coroner's assistant Docky Wocky Corrigan. Joe also manages to run afoul of (and to later play foul with) a gorgeous rival reporter named Debby Long.

When Meena is strangled Medford is again on the scene, arriving just in time to get himself conked on the head and weakly framed for her murder. One of the missing caskets turns up in Blanchard's garage. The last remaining midget, Mina, along with her normal-sized companion and nurse, Nell Rand, is spirited away by the fuzz to Dr. Abbott's sanitarium in Glendale for safekeeping. But another coffin soon turns up there (or is it the same one from Blanchard's garage?), and Joe then kidnaps Mina and Nell from the sanitarium to save them from the murderer's clutches. After which he rents an armored car (!) for Nell and the midget to live in (!) while he continues on his quest for answers. (At the rental agency where he obtains the armored car, the clerk at first looks at him askance, silently questioning Joe's motives. Whereupon Medford utters a now-famous disclaimer: "I am not a crook," he says.)

Back at Silverstein Studios, publicity director Norman Burns is poisoned by a bogus benzedrine capsule containing bichloride of mercûry. The three missing caskets turn up on the floor of Medford's office at the Los Angeles *Evening Post*. Back at the studio again, somebody tries to ventilate Joe's head with a bullet after Joe sees a strange woman skulking around the dead Burns's darkened inner sanctum. Down the coast, the armored car is forced off the road by the same mystery woman, a deliberate "accident" in which poor Mina is killed (and for which Medford, who thought up the screwy armored car angle, takes no responsibility whatsoever).

Finally, in a superbly conceived anticlimax, the mystery woman is captured offstage and revealed to be Sarah Denton, Burns's secretary, who in reality is Madame ZigZag, "the Modern Annie Oakley," a former circus trick-shot artist who "took her name from her peculiar zig-zag type of shooting." Her motive for all the carnage? She became mentally unbalanced when her six-year-old daughter died of an infection caused by a gunshot wound, the result of one of the Diminutive Dolls of Divertissement (who were also working in the circus at that time) having accidentally discharged the mother's six-shooter; and so she (Madame ZigZag) set out to bump off the midgets one by one in glorious retribution. She murdered Samson because Clinton Hogarth, the man Mad Sam hired to deliver the three short biers to Busby Blanchard, is in fact Madame ZigZag's exhusband. "Although they had been divorced since shortly before the death of their daughter, Hogarth was trying again to woo his wife. That was why the cruel Samson had picked Hogarth to deliver the caskets. Sarah obviously resented Samson's interference and his knowledge of her past, so he, too, was marked for death." She murdered Norman Burns purely by accident, the poisoned benzedrine capsule being intended instead for Joe Medford, whose meddling was leading him too close to the fact that Sarah Denton/Madame ZigZag was only pretending to be a publicity director's secretary so she could carry out her little vendetta. As for the disappearing and reappearing coffins, that was all Hogarth's doing: "He was in deep now, and evidently thought he could get in good with Sarah by helping her."

If you think none of this makes any sense whatsoever, you're right—it doesn't. And that, of course, is why *Three Short Biers* is a perfect Alternative Hall of Fame novel.

Still and all, I can't help feeling that Starr missed a bet—the crowning touch—in having Hogarth be Madame ZigZag's partner-in-crime. A much better choice, not only as casket-stealer but as the actual murderer of the midgets, would have been Moe Silverstein, the studio boss. From an aesthetic point of view, he'd have been absolutely ideal.

I mean, who better to dispose of Ena, Meena, and Mina than Moe?

Nine More Lives, MICHAEL MORGAN (1947)

Several years ago, in an article for *The Armchair Detective*, I made the somewhat rash statement that Michael Morgan's second novel, *Decoy* (1953), was "the worst mystery of all time." Three or four alternative classics that have come to light since offer powerful challenges to the preeminence of *Decoy*. Nevertheless, that marvelous paperback original is certainly *one* of the great alternative novels—and its authors are indisputably among the very first rank of exalted purveyors of alternative prose.

"Michael Morgan," as noted earlier in these pages, was the collaborative pseudonym of C. E. "Teet" Carle and Dean M. Dorn. The Messrs. Carle and Dorn were at one time Hollywood publicity and promotion agents for such studios as MGM, United Artists, Paramount, and 20th Century-Fox. Teet Carle, in fact, was director of publicity at Paramount for ten years and rubbed elbows not only with the likes of Bogart and Gable but with the likes of Dashiell Hammett and Raymond Chandler (Jimmy Starr, too, no doubt) during their Hollywood stints. It was after World War II that Carle and Dorn began their crime-fiction collaborations, and *Nine More Lives* (later published in paperback as *The Blonde Body*) was the first fruit of their labors.

Nine More Lives is a wholly different Hollywood mystery from *Three Short Biers*. Like all of the other Carle/Dorn stories, it features Bill Ryan, the movie stuntman with an eye for the ladies and a penchant for homicide, who must utilize his stuntman's training to escape all sorts of cliffhanger situations cleverly devised by Dean Dorn (who did most of the gimmick creating). As Teet Carle has rightly pointed out, Ryan was the world's first stuntman sleuth, preceding Lee Majors in "The Fall Guy" by some thirty-five years. Ryan, however—by his own admission on more than one occasion—is not terribly bright. He blunders into and out of all sorts of improbable situations and as a detective remains on a par with those paragons of ineptitude, Charlie Chan's Number One, Two, and Three Sons.

The improbable situations Ryan blunders into in *Nine More Lives* involve a mysterious Mickey Finn, the bump-off of a blond babe from Chicago, another stuntman, a film director, three thugs named Chiller, Algie, and Blackie, a beautiful blond "press dame," blackmail, and such spectacular stunts as Ryan leaping off the roof of an apartment building in a single bound and Ryan escaping a raging flood while tied up in the middle of it.

But none of this is what makes *Nine More Lives* a Hall of Fame novel. It is the radiant prose of Teet Carle, who did most of the writing. In the article for *The Armchair Detective*, and again in *Gun in Cheek*, I said that Carle was a "poet laureate of the absurd." And indeed he is. His similes, metaphors, one-liners dazzle the eye, stimulate the mind, linger in the memory. Only the Chief, Michael Avallone, has concocted nuggets to rival the alternative beauty of the dozens to be found in *Decoy* and the following from *Nine More Lives*.

Her voice had little bubbles in it, like it was dancing with her thoughts.

Her quick intake of breath was as strong as a travelling man eating soup during a ten-minute train stop at a Harvey House.

She came to life. Gone was the bubble, however, and the tingling businesslike coolness and, likewise, the come-uppance of the vocal chords.

And, damn it, that old urge for her was crowding my body to subway capacity.

She had my goat so firmly, I felt like bleating.

I pulled a smile out of my beard.

He grinned and dimpled his lips like a thread sagging between two thumb tacks.

I finished my drink, had another pair and was about to add a fourth when a big blonde body hove into sight and kept on hoving until it blocked out my view of anything else.

I jerked my head erect. My brain was behaving like a stuck record. That was crazy. The old think organ in the gourd was always. . . . Well, it was always. . . . What the hell was it always?

Then, there was light and my eyes were open and I was staring at blue sky. Only it wasn't sky. It was a blue ceiling, and my brain was up there, bouncing crazily against the plaster. . . . My head had expanded in all directions, and I felt its sides pressing against the walls of the room. My tongue was as large as an elephant's leg.

My head was clear enough now to let me clutch a fistful of anger.

He dropped a hunk of eyelid over his frozen left optic.

Hoping to pull his neck out a little farther so I could see what collar fit him, I tossed him a bone.

He shut off the lip-service and I watched his tongue do a cat-under-the-rug around his cheeks.

Walmers nodded slowly and hung a fixed stare over my ears. He tried to smile, but the cold in his peepers froze up the attempt.

A bead [of sweat] started at the edge of his thin hair, rolled slowly down the side of his face like an old lady picking her way across the street.

I snapped my head erect. The movement brought a sharp pain at the top of my head. It ran straight up to a point, the pain did. Wow! That conk on the noggin had made me pin-headed.

His eyes were deep-set, but they sparked out of their cavernous settings like red-hot rivets in a bucket.

Inspiration splattered me in the face like a custard pie.

This was a wagon of the law, and those men slipping hurriedly from it, exerting caution and alertness, were flatfeet.

For the second time in an hour, pin-wheels made a motordrome of the inside of my skull.

The Velvet Fleece,
LOIS EBY AND JOHN C. FLEMING (1947)

Lois Eby and John C. Fleming were yet another dynamic duo of uncommon alternative skill. According to the dust jacket on one of their novels (*Blood Runs Cold*), they were Hoosier first cousins whose "first novel, written via the mails across the country, proved so successful that Mr. Fleming joined Miss Eby in Los Angeles to continue the partnership." The partnership produced upward of a dozen novels, five of which were mysteries published between 1944 and 1952, and numerous radio plays and B-movie scripts. If their straight novels, radio scripts, and screenplays are the same caliber as their mysteries, I regret never having read, heard, or seen any of them; they, too, must surely provide a feast for the connoisseur.

The Velvet Fleece is the Eby–Fleming *magnum opus*. It tells the tale of a trio of con men, Silky and Dice and Rick Fagan (a.k.a. The Featherbed Kid), who set out to bilk a California war-widow and her city manager father out of a hundred thousand dollars. Fagan is "dynamite with the dames," which is why Silky picked him as "the come-on for the fix" in Hart City, "a perfect sucker town." Posing as a buddy of the widow's husband, Fagan turns on the charm to win her confidence and eventually her affection. Only then *he* begins to fall for *her*, and at the same time starts getting ideas about double-crossing Silky, the boss of the operation, and running a solo scam. Further complicating his activities is a slick twist named Tory Pizarro, who happens to be Silky's moll but who has been bedding down with Fagan on the sly. When she turns up unexpectedly in Hart City, the results are as predictable as they are volatile.

What we have here is one of those "crime doesn't pay" extravaganzas that might well have been subtitled "The Fall of the Featherbed Kid." Fagan narrates it all in a sort of grifter's slang—or what Eby and Fleming seem to have considered grifter's slang. What self-respecting con man, after all, would call a twist "Angelpants" or refer to a fink as a "dirty earwigger"? An unpremeditated murder is what finally collapses the Featherbed; he and Silky and Dice walk smack into a trap arranged by the wised-up widow and her old man, and before long he finds himself squatting in the gas chamber at Alcatraz, in a scene right out of a thirties gangster film starring Cagney, Bogart, and Pat O'Brien as Father Duffy. . . .

What's that? Alcatraz was a *federal* penitentiary, you say, and no executions were held there during its thirty years of operation? Condemned murderers in California have always been put to death at San Quentin? Well, you and I know that, but Eby and Fleming evidently didn't. Fagan "crosses the threshold into God's eternity" at Alcatraz, and that's that.

What Eby and Fleming *did* know was how to mix metaphors. They were, in fact, a couple of virtuosos at this alternative feat. Consider these among their more sterling efforts:

> I saw him puff up like a toad. Nothing like soft butter for a biscuit like him. This baby was made to order for our game.

> I had to keep his attention. If he looked around at Dice sitting there trembling, with that gaffed-fish look on his pan, our goose would be cooked.

> Did I say nice dames were dynamite? Well, take a nice dame that's a redhead too, and you have an atomic bomb! Three kisses and I was on the ropes. She looked a little drugged herself.

> Slowly it began to penetrate that something was really wrong. She wasn't throwing things. She wasn't blowing

off any steam. Automatically my mind called signals to block that kick.

Metaphor mixing was not their only narrative talent, however. Not by any means. They could turn a phrase, too—right over on its back.

> The waves of violent enthusiasm bouncing around that room had me walking on bubbles.
>
> Charley practically scooped out his tonsils in his gulp.
>
> His smile wasn't confined to his mouth, but extended in a ruddy glow over his square face.
>
> I guess I was supersensitive, but his voice sounded to me like a very small chariot with its brake set against the pull of four blooded stallions.
>
> She watched a bird hedge-hopping along a shrub outside.
>
> Owens was hardening like a good cement mix to the decision he'd made.

The Hoosier cousins were also adept at the profound observation:

> The human mind is a hell of a funny thing. It's like a stagnant pool with layers of the conscious on top, the subconscious below. During the night [my] subconscious had come to the top.

And physical description, especially of twists:

> She had a mop of hair that looked like somebody had touched a match to.
>
> The moon had come up. It platinumed her face above the black of her coat, and highlighted that mop of gold she used for hair.

She was built on rangy lines but the slick tailored suit made them look swell. She wore no rouge but bright red lips.

And, finally, the ingenious said substitute.

"Sure," I yessed him.

The Face of Stone, SYDNEY HORLER (1952)

Sydney Horler was, as they used to say in the old days, a caution. An outspoken caution, a priggish caution, a racist caution, an elitist caution, and an alternative caution.

A self-styled guardian of British morals, a xenophobe of startling dimensions, a tireless self-promoter, and a deplorer of sexuality in literature (although he himself wrote about sex extensively late in his career), Horler was the perpetrator of such endearing comments as: "The majority [of 'mentally sadistic sex-novel readers'] are women, very few men read the unhealthy novel"; "France has always been to me a country where . . . the two principal characteristics were the savage avarice of the average peasant and the all-pervading smell of urine"; "[the work of Dashiell Hammett] is crude to the point of mental disgust"; and "I know I haven't the brains to write a proper detective novel, but there is no class of literature for which I feel a deeper personal loathing." Between 1921 and his death in 1954, he churned out more than 150 novels, short story collections, plays, and nonfiction books, including more than 100 mystery and suspense novels. Most of his crime fiction features Secret Service agents (Bunny Chipstead, Tiger Standish) and dastardly villains of the megalomaniacal ilk (Paul Vivanti, "The Master of Venom," "The Voice of Ice"). All of his work, almost without exception, is of such a singular virtuosity of style and content that it has earned him such encomiums as this one from critic LeRoy L. Panek: "[Horler was] an egregiously bad writer even by the less than exacting standards of the popular novel."

Sydney's criminous stocks-in-trade were many and varied. He

devised some of the most illogical and inane plots ever committed to paper—plots involving fanatical Germans, Fu Manchu–type mad scientists, evil cults, venal dwarfs, man-eating "death bushes," and slavering "Things." He loved to "give old man coincidence's arm a frightful twist." He concocted masterful epithets ("You skunk! You rotten swine of a skunk!"); sometimes garbled the English language with the same élan as Michael Avallone and Michael Morgan; took gratuitously savage potshots at politicians, publishers and publishing, and foreigners of every type and description; and was rivaled by no one—not even Harry Stephen Keeler—in the formulation of eccentric character, place, and business names.

The Face of Stone, a nonseries "suspense" novel published two years before his death (and like the bulk of his fiction, never issued in this country), is Horler's *magnum opus* when it comes to names. Its plot, too, ranks right down there with such other of his Hall of Fame novels as *The Curse of Doone* and *Dark Danger*. Following is a brief synopsis of what happens, and to whom, in *The Face of Stone*. Remember, now, what you're about to read was not intended as satire or farce, but as dead-serious melodrama.

Susan Farraday is a professional "first reader" of manuscripts for Richard Twellingford Ltd., Publishers, of Largesse Square, London. She is also a typical Horler heroine: thirtyish, still a virgin, possessor of an attitude toward sex and marriage that is "positively antimacassar." Figuring that she really ought to get married, though, because "there's no real substitute for marriage for a woman, only the liars and freaks say otherwise," she has gotten herself engaged to Lamington Carpe, a drunken critic who writes vicious reviews for *The Scorpion*, "a waspish weekly" published by Obadiah Milk "in a scruffy building in a scruffy street" called Scurf Alley. Carpe, in addition to being one of what John Steinbeck once eloquently referred to as the "pale and emaciated critical priesthood singing their litanies in empty churches," is a notorious womanizer whose only real interest in Susan is deflowering her.

Susan, of course, being as chaste as she is, continues to spurn Carpe's advances, which only succeeds in honing Carpe's lust to a fine edge. So fine, in fact, that after dropping off his latest diatribe at Scurf Alley, he goes up to Susan's apartment with the intention of mounting an all-out assault on his intended's virginity. Susan isn't home, so Carpe lies down on the couch to wait for her. Enter, then, Cecil Whimbam, a female sex-novelist and nymphomaniac, who recently left that stodgy old publishing firm of Pimpley and Shortass Ltd. in order to go with Twellingford, even though Dick Twellingford (a highly moral man) at first didn't want to publish her sort of crap, considering it in the class of such scurrilous best-sellers as *Flaming Ginger* by Matilda Plumb and *See, Here is My Love!* by Duranda Drain. But Twellingford finally succumbed when he realized that by publishing Cecil Whimbam he could get back at O. Horatio Farthingale, who so offensively told him (Twellingford) at the Annual Dinner of the Associated Booksellers Benevolent Fund that he (Twellingford) never published anything that sells—this being the *only* reason Dick decided to publish Cecil Whimbam's crap, of course, the money factor never once entering into it.

Where were we? Ah, yes, Cecil Whimbam's arrival at Susan's apartment. Well, in she walks, because she wants to know why Susan hasn't yet read the manuscript of her latest piece of crap, and there's Lamington Carpe lying on Susan's couch looking very horny indeed. So Cecil, being a sex-novelist and a nymphomaniac, takes the bull by the horn, so to speak, and begins to merrily cohabit with Carpe. In the middle of this revolting act, who should walk in unexpectedly but—you guessed it—fair and innocent Susan. Shocked to the depths of her soul, she rushes over to Twitt Street to have lunch with her friend Martita Beatley, who advises her to leave London for a while, get over the trauma of her experience in more restful surroundings.

So Susan rents a cottage in Wrexeshire, a "remote part of England" loosely patterned on Cornwall—Creeper Cottage, to be exact, in the village of Creep. Little known to naive Susan, however, is the fact that Wrexians are mostly pagans whose characteristics include "treachery, deep-seated (if clumsy) cunning, double-dealing, and religious hypocrisy," one of the reasons for this "legacy of evil" being the mixed and foreign blood of their forebears. And what she also doesn't know is that Creep is a hotbed of sex-crazed Satan worshippers, containing as it does the Face of Stone, a half-human, half-devil face carved out of a cliff nearby which "has an evil reputation, and is of ill-repute" because the old Wrexian shipwreckers considered it a heathen god and once sacrificed virgins to it.

Among the individuals Susan encounters, both directly and indirectly, during her stay in Creep are Honoria Golightly, former occupant of Creeper Cottage, a nymphomaniac like Cecil Whimbam and a drunkard besides; Rebecca Bogging, the cleaning lady, and also a witch who may or may not ride broomsticks outside Susan's window in the middle of the night; Tom Rendick, one of the local physicians, a non-Wrexian who longs for an office in Harley Street like the famous diagnostician, Sir Barrington Broke; Luther Drange, the "local Casanova" and leader of the Satan worshippers; elderly historian Adrian Quoit; a corrupt minister, Reverend Jeremiah Panpoolardy, who has the best collection of smutty stories in all of Wrexeshire; Hezekiah Blunt, the barman at the Goat Inn, Creep, who isn't such a bad guy for a low-life Wrexian; an unidentified member of the devil cult who lives on Barfe Farm, in the nearby hamlet of Barfe; and last but certainly not least, Mother Dose, the diseased, cave-dwelling old head witch of Wrexeshire, one of whose witchly ancestors was convicted of "worshipping Satan in the form of a goat, and paying homage to him by means of the posterior kiss."

Now then. Tom and Susan fall in love. Luther Drange tries twice to murder Tom so he can seduce Susan (he's a sort of Wrexian Lamington Carpe, you see), and is thwarted in both instances when Tom uses a never-explained trick taught to him by a commando parachutist during the war to render him (Drange) unconscious. Drange, along with Mother Dose and Rebecca Bogging, decide to revive the "Festival of the Sea," the ancient ceremony in which a virgin is deflowered and then sacrificed to the Face of Stone, it being the middle of May and the festival day of May 16 or May 17 (Horler can't seem to make up his mind which) close at hand. Meanwhile, Honoria Golightly accidently meets and then tries to seduce Dick Twellingford, who is on his way to Creep to see Susan and relax for a few days with his old friend Tom Rendick (that scream of pain you hear is old man coincidence having his arm frightfully twisted). But Dick, being an honorable man and a secret

reader of hard-boiled American detective novels, especially those
featuring private eye Slim Stetson, and having a burning desire to *be*
a hard-boiled private eye, refuses to succumb to Honoria's jaded
charms and therefore arrives in Creep unsullied and eager, once he
learns what is going on, to help Tom and Susan out of their terrible
predicament with Luther Drange and Mother Dose and Rebecca
Bogging and the Reverend Jeremiah Panpoolardy and the rest of the
wicked devil cultists.

Unfortunately for Dick, he never gets to follow through on his
dream of being a British Slim Stetson and saving a beautiful woman
from the clutches of evildoers. Neither do Tom Rendick and his
commando parachutist trick come to the rescue when Susan is
abducted by Luther Drange and his band, all of whom are naked at
the time, and carted off to the Face of Stone on the night of May 16
or May 17 so the Festival of the Sea can be reenacted for the first
time in two hundred years. Who *does* save Susan and her
maidenhead? Why, the bobbies, naturally, they having been summoned by the only other good guy in Creep, Reverend Timothy
Pearn, the "comical cleric."

In an exciting scene in which the suspense is allowed to build to
unbearable heights over a third of a page, there is "an alarming
shout" just as Susan is about to be set upon by Luther Drange, "a
shout that drove the rampant lust out of the hearts of those naked
men and women" who were "dancing in a frenzy of eroticism."
What happens next, as a journalist puts it in a wrap-up article
published the following day (complete with misplaced comma):
"Panic-stricken, the worshippers who in a state of frenzy had
stripped themselves naked in order to avoid arrest, rushed headlong
over the steep cliffs, and were killed."

Susan and Tom get married, of course, and go off on a
Scandinavian honeymoon, where presumably she at last gives her
all to the man she loves. Horler does not say what, if anything,
happened to Dick Twellingford, Lamington Carpe, Obadiah Milk,
Cecil Whimbam, O. Horatio Farthingale, Honoria Golightly, Slim
Stetson, Martita Headley, the comical cleric, the stodgy old firm of
Pimpley and Shortass Ltd., or the remaining inhabitants of either
Creep or Barfe.

And there you have *The Face of Stone*, crime fiction's version of Ripley's Believe It Or Not. In the tongue of that European race Sydney loved so well: *C'est magnifique!*
Didn't I tell you he was a caution?

The Deadly Pick-Up, MILTON K. OZAKI (1952)

A Chicago newspaperman, artist, tax accountant, and one-time owner and operator of the Monsieur Meltone beauty salon, Milton K. Ozaki began writing mysteries just after the end of World War II. Between 1946 and 1959, he published twenty-four crime novels—a dozen under his own name and a dozen under his pseudonym of Robert O. Saber. The first two Ozaki titles, *The Cuckoo Clock* and *A Fiend in Need*, are hardcovers starring the oddball sleuthing team of Professor Caldwell, head of the psychology department of a large university, and his brash young Watson, Bendy Brinks. The other twenty-two are paperback originals, nearly all of the sex-and-violence sort popular in the early fifties; several under the Saber name feature private eyes Max Keene and Carl Good (who became Carl Guard in one Ozaki title, *Maid for Murder*).

The Deadly Pick-Up, one of Ozaki's early softcover mysteries, is narrated not by a PI but by Gordon Banner, a Fond du Lac, Wisconsin, salesman for the Tacoma Flour Company. It has plenty of violence but not much sex (unless you count three pairs of naked breasts gazed upon but never touched) and involves dope dealers and addicts, crooked cops, a not very believable female private investigator, counterfeit money that turns out to be real, and no more improbabilities than your average pb original of the period. In fact, it would *be* just another average fifties pb original—and Ozaki just another average fifties pb writer—if it weren't for one outstanding feature.

That feature was his uncanny ability to manufacture similes and metaphors of rare exuberance and ingenuity. The Ozaki/Saber canon is strewn with these nuggets (you will no doubt remember some from other of his books in Chapters 3 and 7), but in no other title will you find more sparklers than *The Deadly Pick-Up*. This embarrassment of riches is what elevates it to Hall of Fame status.

Feast your eyes on these shining lumps of alternative gold:

> She bent her head over [the package of money] and studied it intently. "No wonder!" she exclaimed softly. "It's as phony as a yellow pousse-cafe!"

> Her voice sounded as though it had been dipped in sleigh bells.

> The back of my head jumped spastically like a caterpillar on a hot stove and my cranial cavity seethed with thick volatile chili juice.

> I felt as gay and feverish and as desperate and inadequate as a lover in a t.b. ward.

> I felt as though a stone block had been lifted from my lungs.

> Thoughts came and went in my mind like guests arriving by mistake at the wrong funeral.

> He threw the words at me like a preacher getting ready to sweat out a tough congregation.

> An idea had been pawing at my mind like a nagging mendicant.

> She stood motionless, indecisive, with her hands clasping and unclasping in front of her like separate automatic things.

> Ponzio . . . kept watching me as though my nose were an independent organism likely to do tricks.

> The minutes crayfished along.

> Her shoulders trembled as though a breeze were playing beneath her blouse.

> Feeling as out of place as an uplift on a six-year-old, I sipped the Scotch.

Slowly, as though experiencing an exquisite pleasure like the first bubble of a seminal spring, she closed her eyes.

While I waited, tired-footed and homeward bound employees straggled past me, one by one like roaches on their way to a newly leased apartment.

His face rippled colors like a child's kaleidoscope.

The floor around him was a slowly oozing pool of crimson, shaped somewhat like Australia.

The Murder Business, PETER C. HERRING (1976)

This mean-spirited paean to violence is one of two Hall of Fame classics published by Major Books, a short-lived (1975–1981, *requiescat in pace*) paperback house operating out of the Los Angeles suburb of Chatsworth. (The other classic is William L. Rivera's *Panic Walks Alone*, about which see *Gun in Cheek*.) Major was a bottom-line house throughout its six years of existence, meaning that in the main it published what others had already rejected. Occasionally, as with other bottom-line houses, it lucked into a pretty fair manuscript: the first novels of Loren D. Estlemen and Western writer James Powell, for instance. More often, what appeared under its imprint were novels by the likes of Peter C. Herring.

The Murder Business, Herring's only published fiction, tells of the activities of a professional British assassin named Michael, a fun-loving lad who likes to cut people's throats with his trusty knife because the sight of blood gives him a jolly orgasm. Michael works for an ultra-secret outfit called the Board, comprised of ten men who, we are told, control politics, finance, and the value of life itself in every major country in the world. When rotten old left-wingers who prefer to think for themselves oppose the Board, Michael or someone like him is brought in to dispose of them. It was the Board, in fact, according to Red (for blood) Herring, that arranged the assassinations of both Kennedys.

We follow Michael all over London, Los Angeles, and Las Vegas as he fulfills his bloody contracts, then join him en route to the

South of France on a richly deserved vacation with his lady love, Jenny, who at first knows nothing about what he does for a living. But then guys start trying to kill the Englishman (as he is known) and he—with Jenny—is forced to commit more mayhem in return in order to save his hide. Seems what few good guys are left in the world have found out about the Board and about Michael and are trying to eliminate them/him. Or something like that; Herring never does make the motives of the counterassassins very clear. Bodies pile up and there is more copious bloodletting on the way to a predictable conclusion, in which both Michael and poor Jenny are themselves slaughtered.

All of which would make *The Murder Business* an unappetizing throwaway if it weren't for Red Herring's prose. Herring was a stylist of singular abilities—a man who could do really bizarre things with, and to, the English language. Red Herring may never drag himself across our trail again, but if he hadn't done so this once he would have not have left such spoor as:

> It was raining again. . . . Michael glanced up at the dark sky and as he expected, the moon was hidden behind the thick waterlogged clouds.

> The black tarmac shot streaks of light from the hordes of vehicles that, like Michael, were crawling through the busy evening streets.

> The butterflies in Michael's stomach became more unsettled until they felt like huge canaries as he remembered the importance of his success tonight.

> The side street where he was parked shouted back at him in utter silence and desertion.

> Typically sturdy for this type of house, Michael flexed his body upward and he sprang over the gate with ease.

> Cigarettes were lit and they stayed silent in the warm darkness smoking.

> He swallowed as his heart pounded the blood through his body at three times its normal speed. He could hear the blood whipping past his ears.

Like a bolt of lightning, a needle stabbed into his solar plexus as he realized that Jenny had been in his [overnight] bag.

For one second, nothing happened; then the hairs on Michael's neck screamed at him and he turned.

Walking down the plane steps, the intense dry heat of the desert hit him in the face like a blast from a powerful hair dryer.

The Winning Streak, ARNOLD GRISMAN (1985)

What first drew my attention to this recent novel was the unique quality of its dust jacket quotes. Usually such encomiums are provided by well-known writers in the mystery field; not so in Grisman's case. Famous (and not so famous) people from other walks of life have done the lavishing here. No less a personage than Lee Iacocca says that *The Winning Streak* "is a good read" and further deposes that "Goldberg's sharp insights and his penchant for gambling add pizzazz to the story." Mr. Iacocca is nothing if not astute; not many *writers* would have thought to mention that a professional gambler's penchant for gambling in a book about gamblers and gambling add pizzazz to the story. Then we have somebody named Sidney Olson, who says, "If the Raymond Chandler seat is still open, Arnold Grisman is an authentic candidate. This book is a jackpot." And finally we have this comment from Fred Gwynne: "High humor and devastating reality are strange (but wonderful) bedfellows in a novel. In *The Winning Streak*, Arnold Grisman serves them up in spades!" Fred Gwynne, in case you don't recognize the name, is the author of such books as *Chocolate Moose for Dinner* and *The King Who Rained*; he is also an actor whose most famous role was as Herman Munster in the TV series "The Munsters."

Could a novel with such distinguished advance praise live up to its billing? I wondered. The answer is yes, though not in the way its publishers, some reviewers, and the Messrs. Iacocca, Olson, and Gwynne would have us believe. *The Winning Streak* concerns the wild and woolly adventures (in Las Vegas, San Francisco, Atlantic City, and other locales) of this professional gambler, Goldberg, who has not only a penchant for gambling but a penchant for trouble. In these pages, the trouble comes in the form of fast dames, hot dice, tough crooks, and twenty million dollars in "funny money" which Goldberg happens to stumble on. The action is fast and furious. And so is Grisman's prose.

Kirkus Reviews, that great alternative reviewing service, says that "his language [is] bright and cocky," not to mention "rich" and "alluring." No argument from this corner; his language is all of that, and much more—every bit of it alternative. One of the pithier examples serves as an epigraph at the beginning of this chapter. Here are some of the others that earned *The Winning Streak* the honor of being the newest inductee into the Alternative Hall of Fame.

Goldberg was well acquainted with the feeling that started somewhere near his heart and blew down his arm like a trumpet call; it had betrayed him regularly for the past twenty-four months. Maybe, thought Goldberg tentatively, big and bent, only halfway out of his crouch, wearing a safari jacket, white pants, torn Adidas sneakers, still a man people noticed.

There was a cop on Goldberg's side now, tap-tapping with the barrel of his gun. He was a very fat cop with a belly the shape and just about the size of a keg of beer. His navel protruded from the too-tight shirt like a very large doorbell.

"You wouldn't believe how strong that broad is. She decked me with a lamp and I was out like a light."

She towered and swayed on platform heels like a figure out of the Macy's Thanksgiving Day Parade, a great swollen bosom and mammoth hips, encased in a loose tweed sack designed for some monster maternity. Black hair streaked with gray, which she patted and pushed and shoved into place. When she finished with the hair, she went to work on the bosom, swatting it peremptorily into fresh arrangements.

There's nothing unusual about shooting craps one-handed, but when the other hand is busy with a hundred-seventy-pound woman whose greatest ambition is to disappear, you lose the easy movements that tickle and excite the dice. Nasty little plastic cubes the color of cheap candy, the dice snapped back at him like discarded mistresses, deadly snake eyes peering at him evilly, threes rolling into sight, snickering, only to be replaced by the crunch of twelves; he crapped out in every way available, and then started all over again. Every time the dice arrived at his position they stayed for a single pass and then flirted on, whoring after more exciting palms.

"Who's this friend of mine?" he asked after a giant swallow [of Scotch] that sent the Adam's apple bobbing in his throat like an escaped balloon.

She walked into the room ahead of him and the hips were going like a grandfather clock, ticktock, ticktock, ticktock. Apple-ass, Goldberg thought automatically, and apple-ass, apple-ass, apple-ass, the hips echoed back.

Yes sir and yes ma'am, that's *language*!

Post-Mortem

What you have just read is not only a funny book about bad writing; it is also the second part of a crash course in alternative crime fiction. Taken in conjunction with *Gun in Cheek*, it provides all the essentials for the fledgling prospector—a sort of literary grubstake, if you will. Whether you take that grubstake and head into them thar fictional hills on your own hunt for alternative gold is of course up to you. But the fact remains, you can if you want to—and if you do, you'll almost certainly strike paydirt.

Let's assume you do decide to go prospecting. The first thing you should do is to head for your nearest library or secondhand bookshop specializing in, or with a large stock of, mystery and detective fiction. You can also write away for catalogues put out by mail-order dealers in used and rare mysteries, of which there are dozens these days; their ads can be found in such publications as *The Armchair Detective* and *Ellery Queen's Mystery Magazine*. Lay in a large supply of hardcovers and paperbacks both—titles by authors discussed here or in *Gun in Cheek*, or published by such houses as Macaulay and Phoenix Press, if you want to make things easy for yourself; titles by obscure authors published by better houses, if you want to make your search more challenging; titles by major authors of the past fifty to seventy-five years, if you prefer the most difficult excavation. Then start digging with the tools in your grubstake. Sooner or later, you'll unearth nuggets large and small, rich veins and startling bonanzas. And the first laugh, the first guffaw, will be yours and yours alone—a reward unlike any other in the enjoyment of criminous literature.

If you don't explore the rest of those dusty hills of mysterydom, then the rewards will be mine. For I surely will continue to prowl among them, and I surely will make many more strikes—some that might have belonged to you. Why, if I find enough new nuggets, enough new veins, I may even stake claims on them—just as I've staked claims on those in these pages and in *Gun in Cheek*—by gathering them together into a *third* volume. And you wouldn't want that to happen, would you?

Well, *would* you?

Bibliography

Alternative Hall of Fame Novels

Auslander, Joseph. *Hell in Harness*. New York: Doubleday Crime Club, 1929.

Avallone, Michael. *The Bedroom Bolero*. New York: Belmont, 1963.

———. *The Crazy Mixed-Up Corpse*. Greenwich, Conn.: Fawcett Gold Medal, 1957.

———. *The Fat Death*. New York: Curtis, 1972.

———. *The Hot Body*. New York: Curtis, 1973.

———. *Meanwhile, Back at the Morgue*. Greenwich, Conn.: Fawcett Gold Medal, 1960.

———. *Missing!* New York: New American Library (Signet), 1969.

———. *There IS Something About a Dame*. New York: Belmont, 1963.

Corbett, James. *The Merrivale Mystery*. New York: Mystery League, 1931.

Eberhard, Frederick G. *The Skeleton Talks*. New York: Macaulay, 1933.

———. *Super-Gangster*. New York: Macaulay, 1932.

Eby, Lois, and John C. Fleming. *The Velvet Fleece*. New York: Dutton, 1947.

Freeman, Martin J. *The Scarf on the Scarecrow*. New York: Dutton, 1938.

Gates, H. L. *Death Counts Five*. New York: G. H. Watt, 1934.

———. *The Laughing Peril*. New York: Macaulay, 1933.

———. *The Scarlet Fan*. New York: Macaulay, 1932.

Gaunt, Mary. *The Mummy Moves*. New York: Clode, 1925.

Gibbons, Cromwell. *The Bat Woman*. New York: World Press, 1938.

Grisman, Arnold. *The Winning Streak*. New York: St. Martin's, 1985.

Herring, Peter C. *The Murder Business*. Chatsworth, Calif.: Major Books, 1976.

Horler, Sydney. *The Face of Stone*. London: Arthur Barker, 1952.

Keeler, Harry Stephen. *The Case of the 16 Beans*. New York: Phoenix Press, 1944.

———. *The Green Jade Hand*. New York: Dutton, 1930.

———. *The Man with the Magic Eardrums*. New York: Dutton, 1939.

———. *The Marceau Case*. New York: Dutton, 1936.

———. *The Vanishing Gold Truck*. New York: Dutton, 1941.

———. *The Wonderful Scheme of Mr. Christopher Thorne*. New York: Dutton, 1937.

———. *X. Jones of Scotland Yard*. New York: Dutton, 1936.

Leinster, Murray. *Murder Will Out*. London: John Hamilton, 1932.

Morgan, Michael. *Nine More Lives*. New York: Random House, 1947.

Ozaki, Milton K. *The Deadly Pick-Up*. Hasbrouck Heights, N.J.: Graphic, 1952.

Pettee, F. M. *The Palgrave Mummy*. New York: Payson & Clarke, 1929.

Rud, Anthony M. *House of the Damned*. New York: Macaulay, 1934.

———. *The Rose Bath Riddle*. New York: Macaulay, 1934.

———. *The Stuffed Men*. New York: Macaulay, 1935.

Scott, Mary Semple. *Crime Hound*. New York: Scribner's, 1940.

Starr, Jimmy. *Three Short Biers*. Hollywood, Calif.: Murray & Gee, 1945.

Other Novels Cited

Allen, Leslie. *Murder in the Rough*. New York: Five-Star, 1946.

Allison, Clyde. *The Lost Bomb*. San Diego, Calif.: Ember Library, 1966.

———. *0008 Meets Modesta Blaze*. San Diego, Calif.: Ember Library, 1966.

———. *The Sex-Ray*. San Diego, Calif.: Ember Library, 1966.

Anthony, Bill. *Animals*. Chicago: Novel Books, 1963.

Arnold, Quint. *Erotic Awakening*. Chicago: Novel Books, 1964.

Baxter, Gregory. *Calamity Comes of Age*. New York: Macaulay, 1935.

———. *Murder Could Not Kill*. New York: Macaulay, 1934.

Beck, Henry C. *Death by Clue*. New York: Dutton, 1933.

Benet, James. *The Knife Behind You*. New York: Harper, 1950.

Bentley, John. *Mr. Marlow Takes to Rye*. Boston: Houghton, 1942.

Biggers, Earl Derr. *Seven Keys to Baldpate*. Indianapolis: Bobbs Merrill, 1913.

Block, Lawrence. *Eight Million Ways To Die*. New York: Arbor House, 1982.

Bowen, Joseph. *The Man Without a Head*. New York: Covici-Friede, 1936.

Brussell, James A. *Just a Murder, Darling*. New York: Scribner's, 1959.

Burke, Richard. *Barbary Freight*. New York: Putnam's, 1942.

Byrd, Max. *Fly Away, Jill*. New York: Bantam, 1983.

Chandler, Raymond. *The Lady in the Lake*. New York: Knopf, 1943.

Charteris, Leslie. *Vendetta for the Saint*. New York: Doubleday Crime Club, 1964.

Chase, Arthur M. *Peril at the Spy Nest*. New York: Dodd, Mead, 1943.

Chesbro, George C. *City of Whispering Stone*. New York: Simon & Schuster, 1978.

Clark, Dale. *Focus on Murder*. Philadelphia: Lippincott, 1943.

———. *Mambo to Murder*. New York: Ace, 1955.

———. *A Run for the Money*. New York: Ace, 1956.

Clouston, J. Storer. *Carrington's Cases*. London: Blackwood, 1920.

Collins, Max Allan. *The Baby Blue Rip-Off*. New York: Walker, 1983.

———. *A Shroud for Aquarius*. New York: Walker, 1985.

Collins, Michael. *Freak*. New York: Dodd, Mead, 1983.

Daly, Carroll John, and C. H. Waddell. *Two-Gun Gerta*. New York: Chelsea House, 1926.

Daly, Hamlin. *Case of the Cancelled Redhead!* New York: Falcon Books, 1952.

Davis, Frederick C. *Let the Skeletons Rattle*. New York: Doubleday Crime Club, 1944.

Davis, Kenn. *Melting Point*. New York: Fawcett, 1986.

Dean, Amber. *August Incident*. New York: Doubleday Crime Club, 1951.

———. *Chanticleer's Muffled Crow*. New York: Doubleday Crime Club, 1945.

Eby, Lois, and John C. Fleming. *Death Begs the Question*. New York: Abelard Press, 1952.

Ellroy, James. *Blood on the Moon*. New York: Mysterious Press, 1984.

Evans, Gwyn. *Mr. Hercules*. New York: Dial, 1931.

Fickling, G. G. *Naughty but Dead*. New York: Belmont, 1962.

Fisher, Louis, *Wild Party*. Chicago: Novel Books, 1960.

Fleischman, A. S. *Murder's No Accident*. New York: Phoenix Press, 1949.

Forbes, Stanton. *The Will and Last Testament of Constance Cobble*. New York: Doubleday Crime Club, 1980.

Ford, Leslie. *Siren in the Night*. New York: Scribner's, 1943.

Fredrics, George. *Consider Yourself Dead*. Reseda, Calif.: Powell, 1969.

Gardner, John. *Icebreaker*. London: Cape-Hodder, 1983.
Gerard, Francis. *Fatal Friday*. New York: Holt, 1937.
Gifford, Thomas. *The Cavanaugh Quest*. New York: Putnam's, 1976.
Gillmore, Rufus. *The Ebony Bed Murder*. New York: Mystery League, 1932.
Goff, Jerry M., Jr. *Rocco's Babe*. Chicago: Merit Books, 1961.
Goodchild, George. *Jack O'Lantern*. New York: Mystery League, 1930.
Haggard, Paul. *Death Talks Shop*. New York: Hillman-Curl, 1938.
Jacobs, T.C.H. *Silent Terror*. New York: Macaulay, 1937.
———. *Sinister Quest*. New York: Macaulay, 1934.
Jones, Charles Reed. *The Rum Row Murders*. New York: Macaulay, 1931.
Joseph, George. *Leave It to Me*. New York: Popular Library, 1955.
Kane, Frank. *The Living End*. New York: Dell, 1957.
Keeler, Harry Stephen. *The Box from Japan*. New York: Dutton, 1932.
———. *The Case of the Barking Clock*. New York: Phoenix Press, 1947.
———. *The Case of the Mysterious Moll*. New York: Phoenix Press, 1945.
———. *The Face of the Man from Saturn*. New York: Dutton, 1933.
———. *Finger, Finger!* New York: Dutton, 1938.
Kennealy, G. P. *Nobody Wins*. New York: Manor Books, 1977.
King, Rufus. *Valcour Meets Murder*. New York: Doubleday Crime Club, 1937.
Lane, Jeremy. *Death to Drumbeat*. New York: Phoenix Press, 1944.
Lariar, Lawrence. *He Died Laughing*. New York: Phoenix Press, 1943.
Lee, Steve. *Uninhibited Females*. Chicago: Merit Books, 1964.
Lenehan. J. C. *The Tunnel Mystery*. New York: Mystery League, 1931.
Low, Glenn. *Honey Blood*. Chicago: Novel Books, 1961.
Lucas, Jay. *Boss of the Rafter C*. New York: Green Circle, 1937.
Lynn, Jack. *Broad Bait!* Chicago: Novel Books, 1960.
MacNalty, A. Salusbury. *The Mystery of Captain Burnaby*. London: Pawling & Ness, 1934.
MacVeigh, Sue. *The Corpse and the Three Ex-Husbands*. Boston: Houghton, 1941.
Makagon, Thomas. *All Killers Aren't Ugly*. San Diego, Calif.: Vega Books, 1961.
Marshall, Raymond. *Make the Corpse Walk*. London: Jarrolds, 1946.
Marshall, William. *Perfect End*. New York: Holt, 1981.
Mason, Van Wyck. *The Cairo Garter Murders*. New York: Doubleday Crime Club, 1938.
———. *The Rio Casino Intrigue*. New York: Reynal & Hitchcock, 1941.
McBain, Ed. *Ghosts*. New York: Viking, 1980.

Meik, Vivian. *The Curse of Red Shiva*. New York: Hillman-Curl, 1938.

Myers, Isabel Briggs. *Murder Yet to Come*. New York: Stokes, 1930.

Nelson, Hugh Lawrence. *The Season for Murder*. New York: Rinehart, 1952.

Norman, Earl. *Kill Me in Shinjuku*. New York: Berkley, 1961.

————. *Kill Me in Tokyo*. New York: Berkley, 1958.

Ozaki, Milton K. *Dressed To Kill*. Hasbrouck Heights, N.J.: Graphic, 1954.

————. *Maid for Murder*. New York: Ace, 1955.

Packard, Frank L. *The Gold Skull Murders*. New York: Doubleday Crime Club, 1931.

Parker, Robert B. *Taming a Seahorse*. New York: Delacorte/Seymour Lawrence, 1986.

Pentecost, Hugh. *Sow Death, Reap Death*. New York: Dodd, Mead, 1981.

————. *The Steel Palace*. New York: Dodd, Mead, 1977.

Piper, Anson. *Black Creek Buckaroo*. New York: Morrow, 1941.

Pleasants, W. Shepard. *The Stingaree Murders*. New York: Mystery League, 1932.

Porcelain, Sidney A. *The Crimson Cat Murders*. New York: Phoenix Press, 1946.

Puccetti, Roland. *The Death of the Führer*. New York: St. Martin's, 1977.

Queen, Ellery. *The French Powder Mystery*. New York: Stokes, 1930.

Raison, Milton M. *The Gay Mortician*. Hollywood, Calif.: Murray & Gee, 1946.

Reed, Wallace. *No Sign of Murder*. New York: Phoenix Press, 1940.

Rider, Sarah. *The Misplaced Corpse*. Boston: Houghton, 1940.

Robeson, Kenneth. *Quest of the Spider*. New York: Bantam, 1968. (Originally published in *Doc Savage Magazine* in 1935.)

Rooth, Anne Reed, and James P. White. *The Ninth Car*. New York: Putnam's, 1978.

Rosen, Dorothy and Sidney. *Death and Blintzes*. New York: Walker, 1985.

Runyon, Charles. *The Prettiest Girl I Ever Killed*. Greenwich, Conn.: Fawcett Gold Medal, 1965.

Saber, Robert O. *Sucker Bait*. Hasbrouck Heights, N.J.: Graphic, 1955.

————. *Too Young To Die*. Hasbrouck Heights, N.J.: Graphic, 1954.

Scherf, Margaret. *The Green Plaid Pants*. New York: Doubleday Crime Club, 1951.

Shallit, Joseph. *Lady, Don't Die on My Doorstep*. Philadelphia: Lippincott, 1951.

Singer, Shelley. *Free Draw*. New York: St. Martin's, 1984.

Streib, Dan. *Hawk #6: The Seeds of Evil*. New York: Jove, 1981.

Taylor, Sam S. *No Head for Her Pillow*. New York: Dutton, 1952.
Thomey, Tedd. *I Want Out*. New York: Ace, 1959.
Towne, Stuart. *Death Out of Thin Air*. New York: Coward-McCann, 1941.
Traubel, Helen (Harold Q. Masur). *The Metropolitan Opera Murders*. New York: Simon & Schuster, 1951.
Wallace, Arthur. *Passion Pulls the Trigger*. New York: Valhalla Press, 1936.
Wambaugh, Joseph. *The Glitter Dome*. New York: Morrow, 1981.
Waugh, Hillary. *Parrish for the Defense*. New York: Doubleday Crime Club, 1974.
Wayne, Rich. *Play Rough!* New York: Rainbow Books, 1952.
Wood, Ed., Jr. *Security Risk*. Agoura, Calif.: Pad Library, 1967.
Yates, George Worthing. *If a Body*. New York: Morrow, 1941.

Short Stories

Bellem, Robert Leslie. "Death Dance." *Spicy Detective*, January 1942.
Graham, Donald. "Where Beauty Dwelt with Terror." *Uncanny Tales*, March 1940.
Morgan, Michael. "Charity Begins at Homicide." *Dime Detective*, September 1950.
Pettee, Florence M. "The Clue from the Tempest." *Black Mask*, June 1921.
————. "Death Laughs at Walls." *Detective Classics*, January 1930.
————. "Exploits of Beau Quicksilver: #1, A Tooth for a Tooth." *Argosy All-Story Weekly*, February 24, 1923.
Rud, Anthony M. "The Feast of the Skeletons." *Detective Fiction Weekly*, August 25, 1934.
Wallace, Arthur. "Passion Before Death." *Spicy Mystery*, September 1935.

Nonfiction References

Albert, Walter. *Detective and Mystery Fiction: An International Bibliography of Secondary Sources*. Madison, Ind.: Brownstone Books, 1985.
Boucher, Anthony. *Multiplying Villainies: Selected Mystery Criticism, 1942–1968*. Privately printed, 1973.
Cleaton, Irene and Allen. *Books and Battles: American Literature, 1920–1930*. Boston: Houghton, 1937.

Collins, Max Allan, and James L. Traylor. *One Lonely Knight: Mickey Spillane's Mike Hammer*. Bowling Green, O.: Bowling Green University Popular Press, 1984.

Cuthbert, Jack. "Another Side of Harry Stephen Keeler." *The Armchair Detective* 7, no. 2, February 1974.

Drew, Bernard A. "Anthony M. Rud's Weird Tales." West Barrington, Mass.: Attic Revivals #6, 1983.

Goulart, Ron. *Cheap Thrills*. New Rochelle, N.Y.: Arlington House, 1972.

Hagemann, E. R. *A Comprehensive Index to Black Mask, 1920–1951*. Bowling Green, O.: Bowling Green University Popular Press, 1982.

Harrison, Harry. *Great Balls of Fire!: An Illustrated History of Sex in Science Fiction*. New York: Grosset & Dunlap, 1977.

Horler, Sydney. *Now Let Us Hate*. London: Quality Press, 1942.

Hubin, Allen J. *Crime Fiction, 1749–1980: A Comprehensive Bibliography*. New York: Garland, 1984.

Johnson, Diane. *Dashiell Hammett: A Life*. New York: Random House, 1983.

Jones, Robert Kenneth. *The Shudder Pulps*. West Linn, Ore.: FAX Collector's Editions, 1975.

Morgan, Michael (Dean M. Dorn and C. E. "Teet" Carle). "Let's Call It Gun in Girdle." *The Armchair Detective* 16, no. 3, Fall 1983.

Nevins, Francis M., Jr. "Harry Stephen Keeler's Screwball Circus." *The Armchair Detective* 5, no. 4, July 1972.

———. "Murder Like Crazy: Harry Stephen Keeler." *The New Republic*, July 30, 1977.

———. "The Wild and Wooly World of Harry Stephen Keeler." *The Journal of Popular Culture*, nos. 3, 4, 5, 7, 1970–1973.

———. "The Worst Legal Mystery in the World." *The Armchair Detective* 1, no. 3, April 1968.

Nicholls, Peter, ed. *The Science Fiction Encyclopedia*. New York: Doubleday/Dolphin, 1979.

O'Brien, Geoffrey. *Hardboiled America*. New York: Van Nostrand, 1981.

Pronzini, Bill. *Gun in Cheek*. New York: Coward, McCann, 1982.

———. "The *Worst* Mystery Novel of All Time." *The Armchair Detective* 13, no. 1, Spring 1980.

Reilly, John M., ed. *Twentieth Century Crime and Mystery Writers, Second Edition*. New York: St. Martin's, 1985.

Rodell, Marie F. *Mystery Fiction, Theory and Technique*. New York: Duell, 1943.

Schreuders, Piet. *Paperbacks, U.S.A.: A Graphic History, 1939–1959.* San Diego, Calif.: Blue Dolphin, 1981.

Scott, Art. "Dumbfounded in Keelerland." *The Mystery Fancier* 1, no. 1, January 1977.

Scott, Sutherland. *Blood in Their Ink.* London: Stanley Paul, 1953.

Starrett, Vincent. "The Life and Death of Harry Stephen Keeler." Chicago *Tribune*, February 12, 1967.

Zinman, David. *Saturday Afternoon at the Bijou.* New York: Arlington House, 1973.

Index

61